Also by Adela Crandell Durkee:

The Fable of Little Tzurie

A Ship of Pearl
(A Novel)

Adela Crandell Durkee

This book is a work of fiction. Names, characters, businesses, organizations, places, events, and incidents either are the product of the author's imagination or are used fictitiously. Any resemblance to actual persons, living or dead, events, or locales is entirely coincidental.

Copyright © 2016 by Adela Crandell Durkee

Cover design by Chad Green

ISBN 978-0-9979124-4-9 (eBook)

ISBN 978-0-9979124-1-8 (Paperback)

All rights reserved. Published by Black Tortoise Press.
www.blacktortoisepress.com. **Black Tortoise Press**

The author donates 10% of her profits to help America's homeless and hungry.

DEDICATION

For Dad, whose "Life is abundant" philosophy
lives on through the stories he told.

Table of Contents

CHAPTER 1 REMEMBERING THE BEGINNING 1
CHAPTER 2 REMEMBERING WHEN I MET EPHRAIM 12
CHAPTER 3 CRONK SCHOOL.. 20
CHAPTER 4 REMEMBERING PEARL: MY VERY FIRST DAY OF SCHOOL.. 27
CHAPTER 5 DIBBLE'S FIVE AND DIME..................................... 37
CHAPTER 6 REVEREND ZOLLAR 44
CHAPTER 7 REMEMBERING PEARL.. 52
CHAPTER 8 REMEMBERING THE VERMILLIA STREET FIRE 64
CHAPTER 9 TORREY RAIL YARD 78
CHAPTER 10 REMEMBERING HOW I GOT TOOTHLESS .. 87
CHAPTER 11 DOWN BY THE RIVER 101
CHAPTER 12 REMEMBERING BUTCH.. 109
CHAPTER 13 WASHED IN THE BLOOD OF THE LAMB... 121
CHAPTER 14 REMEMBERING FORBIDDEN FRUIT 129
CHAPTER 15 THE PROMISED LAND... 140
CHAPTER 16 CHICAGO BOUND 149
CHAPTER 17 FATHER PEROTTA 157
CHAPTER 18 REMEMBERING VERMILLIA STREET 165
CHAPTER 19 DIBBLE'S FIVE AND DIME................................. 173
CHAPTER 20 KERSCHKE FARMHOUSE 180
CHAPTER 21 4TH OF JULY PICNIC 188

CHAPTER 22 ANOTHER KIND OF FIRE	197
CHAPTER 23 A LAND OF MILK AND HONEY	206
CHAPTER 24 EXODUS	217
CHAPTER 25 A NEW BEGINNING	226
CHAPTER 26 LABOR DAY	237
ACKNOWLEDGEMENTS	II
ABOUT THE AUTHOR	IV

Chapter 1
Remembering the Beginning

I have the best memory for things I want to remember. 'Course I gotta take the good with the bad. I have the best memory for things I wish I could forget, too. Come to think of it, after some time goes by, I end up wanting to remember the very things I wished I could forget. So, I guess a good memory is all for the best.

Dallas says it must be a burden to remember as well as I do. I even remember things from before I was born. He says that with his eyes rolled back in his head, 'cause, 'course, nobody remembers before he got born. Mama says my imagination is better than my memory. I heard some stories so many times it's hard to figure which parts are my own memory and which parts are somebody else's.

I heard the story of how I came to our house in Pearl, Michigan more times than the number of years old I am. I might have filled in some parts with other people's memories, mostly Daddie's and Auntie Laura's, some Mama's. Daddie's the best storyteller I ever heard, and Auntie Laura likes the facts. Mama says sometimes my imagination fills the spaces between what I hear and what I remember. Anyways, this story is one of the best I ever told, and that's the God's honest-truth. That's because it's about how I got here.

I knew Mama back then, and I heard Daddie's voice, strong as ever. Mama said I got here in Doctor Reeve's black bag. Maybe he visited a lot back then. I never knew about Dallas; he was a surprise. I probably heard his voice; maybe just a squeak or a squall. I had no idea Dallas would be the most important person in the world to me. And I bet it stands true for me my whole entire life. 'Least it has for the first twelve years of it.

Back then, I knew next to nothing about Dallas. Well, maybe I just ignored what I knew about Dallas. I did hear Mama say his name and talk to him, but I never paid attention to that. Mostly I thought about how crowded I was, and warm. Too warm. Bordering on hot. Even then, I didn't like heat.

On that particular day, Mama stepped back from cleaning the breakfast table. She suspected what I never guessed, 'cause I was clueless as all get out. She guessed I was about to come into the world. Still, it seemed different to her this time. I gotta admit, this part of the story sorta confuses me, 'cause if Dr. Reeves brought me in his bag, how did Mama suspect this was the day I was coming? I asked that question before, but Mama and Daddie just laugh in that secret laugh grownups have.

Mama was glad Thanksgiving was behind her with plenty of leftovers in the icebox for Daddie. No need to cook anything from scratch right away. Mama, for once, thanked God for the early and hard freeze that year. The icebox was chock full of ice. She hates the cold as much as I hate the heat.

Mama glanced over at Dallas, playing next to the wood stove. He chewed at the sock monkey she made for his first birthday just last month. The monkey smelled of wood smoke soaked in baby drool. For some reason, Mama was partial to the way it smelled; said it smelled of a happy baby. She still has that same sock monkey, even though it's tattered and sorta smells more like a scorched bird's nest. It's one of the few things left from our house in Pearl.

I'd heard Mama say that it took most of the whole day for Doctor Reeves to get Dallas into the world, but that second babies come faster.

She prayed that Daddie would get back from church before too long. I knew all this on account of I looked at, and heard and felt things from the inside out. Most times Daddie liked to stay long after the service was over to visit with everyone. A great storyteller's gotta have somebody to tell his stories to.

Mama fretted with finishing the table cleaning, then set out the linens and towels. I kept getting squeezed tight as all get out. A black bag is no place for a baby. Mama stopped her work and breathed in and out slow. She buried her face in the towels so she could breathe in the smell of bleach and fresh air left over from the clothesline.

"Nothing to get excited about yet," Mama whispered to me. Leastwise, I'm pretty sure it was me she was talking to.

She got down on all fours, her belly about touching the floor, pulled her big tapestry bag out from under the bed and packed it with some of Dallas's things.

"Six diapers ought to do. No, maybe it will be quite a while, could be just like last time, and Dallas is quite the wetter. He can pee straight through the mattress if you don't keep him changed."

She might have just thought that part. Sometimes I got her thoughts and words mixed up. Plus, Mama's and Daddie's and Auntie Laura's stories are all mixed up in there with mine. So, maybe I just heard that part later.

She added four more diapers, four woolen soakers, and three clean gowns. Well, he won't need three; she put one back, then got it out again.

"Gowns don't take up much space; better safe than sorry. Lew can wrap Dallas in his quilt for the trip to Laura's house."

I could tell she thought those things, and didn't say them right to me because she said Lew instead of Daddie, and she left off Auntie when she talked about her sister. I got a little confused about that at first, but I got it straightened out the more I listened.

Mama looked out the window. The snow sparkled in the sun like those little flecks of glitter pasted on a Christmas card; the only footprints from a lone sparrow: crisscross, splink, splink, splink across the yard. The wind came from the West. A bad sign this time of year, but, so far, so good: the sun shone still bright in the sky.

At about lunchtime, Auntie Laura stopped by, as she did near every day now. No one ever guesses that Auntie Laura is Mama's sister; they're so darned different. Auntie Laura is five years older, tall and spider thin. She has dark eyes that peer deep into a soul and straight black hair, like a crow's, every hair obedient, stretched back and staying right where its put, in a neat bun, as if each hair is afraid to stray. Mama is short and soft and rounded, even without her big belly. And she's got bright red hair, like a new penny. Mama's hair refuses to behave, in spite of her constant taming. Sometimes strands get away from her, curling out in every direction, some tight to her head, some waving in the air. Mama's eyes are the color of honey and sparkly when she's happy, just like the snow on a bright December day. No one ever claims Mama and Auntie Laura are two peas in a pod; more like different as night and day.

"Do you think I have enough packed up for Lew?" Mama looked at her sister and pressed her lips together into a line. Still and all, blue eyes never lie and Auntie Laura knew what's going on.

"Oh, Ida, when did your labor start?"

"Right after breakfast. It seems the baby's a long way off. Only about twice an hour."

That seemed like a strange thing to say, on account of me being right there. Still, it got me thinking, how come Dr. Reeve's bag was there and he was somewhere else.

"Sit down and rest. I'll make you some tea. And I'll make Dallas his lunch."

Auntie Laura took control of the kitchen; her smile stretched the skin around her lips. Her mouth's usually more on the dry side, like a blade of October grass. With all that stretching, her cheeks looked as if they might split, the way a tomato does at the end of summer and a hard rain makes it so's the tomato can't stretch to make room for all the moisture comin' up from the roots. 'Course, that's the way I imagine it, from what I know of Auntie Laura now.

Mama sat at the table and let Dallas climb up next to her. 'Course Dallas was just a voice and a force back then. I was already feeling crowded and I shivered from the inside out, even though I was hot as all get out. The last thing I needed was something or someone horning in on my space, kicking and squirming and crowding up against me.

Auntie Laura busied herself taking the Thanksgiving leftovers out of the icebox. She cut ham into tiny pieces and made some milk gravy with the ham juices, then added in cold mashed potatoes. Dallas's lunch smelled like Thanksgiving all over again. Auntie Laura sliced off two big wedges of wheat bread and melted a piece of cheese on each. She sat one down in front of Mama and the other in front of the vacant chair.

The tea kettle whistling on the stove gave a last gaspy scream, like it wished Auntie Laura would leave it be. She poured hot water over the tealeaves and put a cinnamon stick in each cup and the teensiest sprinkle of sugar.

"Laura, that's the teapot Mother brought from Wales," Mama said. "I only use it for special occasions."

I could tell, even back then, that Mama got a little peeved at Auntie Laura sometimes.

"I know, Birdie. Wouldn't you say this is special?"

Auntie Laura called Mama by the same pet name Daddie called her. Now most everybody calls Mama Birdie, because her legs are like little bird legs, and maybe because her body is little and round, too, like a bird's. It's not a mean name like you might think, but a cheery kind of name for a cheery kind of person. Come to think of it, Mama does move around like a chickadee sometimes, lighting here, then there, always seeming busy at something, and happy; almost always she seems happy. Except when she's praying. Then she's just quiet. You might not know she's listening to God, 'cept for she's really, really still.

Auntie Laura sat down in the chair next to Mama and took hold of her hand. The cinnamon drifted up in a warm cloud and seemed to sink right down into Mama's heart. I think she felt like her own Mama just whispered in her ear. I swear, I remember how the cinnamon and tea tasted that day, even though Dallas tells me that must be my imagination.

Auntie Laura placed one hand on Dallas's forehead and looked into his eyes until he stopped his fidgeting. Mama put her free hand where I was getting ready to meet the world. I got quiet and still. That's the way it is for me, to this very day. When Mama prays, it makes me still inside and out.

Mama and Auntie Laura bowed their heads for a few moments, their breath getting steady and even slower yet. When they raised their heads, Dallas reached for his bowl. For sure, I could smell that ham and milk gravy, and I wanted some. That's why I decided to get the show on the road. Maybe I just want to remember things that way, 'cause I sure do love ham and milk gravy.

By the time Daddie got home, Dr. Reeves was there. Auntie Laura started pulling on Dallas's woolen bonnet and booties as soon as she saw Daddie with one foot on the running board, getting out of his Model A. He still has that car; back then it was next to brand new.

Auntie Laura pressed her lips into a tight line, which come to think of it, might be the one thing that Auntie Laura and Mama do that's the same. Dr. Reeves picked up the tea kettle to quiet its screaming, only he never made tea. The boiling water was for something else, but I never did figure out that part. Every doctor visit comes with him sending someone for a teakettle of boiled water. I think it's something a doctor asks for, to get people out of his hair so's he can concentrate on the sick person.

Daddie took one look at Mama's face: her red hair, usually pinned back with combs, was tied at the back of her neck. It looked wild as all get out; like she forgot she even had hair. 'Course, just because you forget about something, doesn't make it go away. Her hair frizzed out in every direction, with beads of sweat standing out like dew against curly grass fern. To be honest, this part I'm guessing is part of Daddie's storytelling. Mama's skin is soft and smooth as one of those china faced dolls. I never saw her sweat.

Daddie wrapped the quilt around Dallas, tucked him snug under his arm, almost like a runt pig. His eyes darted around the room, as if it might be the last time, and he wanted to see everything, but fast 'cause he's in a hurry, and then he grabbed the satchel Mama left out for him. He left, banging the door hard against the outside wall. He never even said anything to Mama. The door just hung loose, complaining every time the wind caught it. Auntie Laura huffed on over there and pulled it shut with a loud clack.

I suppose Daddie was busy thinking about last time. He never said it, but Daddie's afraid of being kept in the dark. Later, Mama said his heart clenched up in the center of his chest with feelings, rather than actual thoughts with words attached to them. I learned about that later on when I heard Mama talking to her lady friends. She said 'that's the way of men,' and everybody nodded or shook their heads and clicked her tongue in the back of their throats. With ladies, a head nod or a shake can both mean they agree. Sometimes it's tough to decipher.

Daddie walked away in long, deliberate strides. Auntie Laura reached out and shut the door up, erasing Daddie from Mama's view, and then she wiped her hands against each other like a school marm getting rid of chalk. Mama never in her life saw Daddie run. Me either. He always, always looks relaxed. Mama can read Daddie's insides by how much his shortish legs stretch out when he walks.

After dark, Daddie came back with Dallas. Auntie Laura had everything quiet and tidy. Daddie stomped the snow off his boots and slapped his thigh with his hat. Dr. Reeves washed his hands in the kitchen as Daddie lowered a sleeping Dallas to his mattress beside the stove. That's the same bed the two of us slept on until the fire burned it to nothing at all.

Daddie looked at the puddle of melted snow by the door all mixed up with guilt and befuddlement, like he never saw snow melting or like he was trying to figure out how it got there. He knew how mad Mama gets when her floor gets mussed up.

"You've got yourself another son, Lewis," said Dr. Reeves.

"And Ida?" Daddie's easy smile drifted up one side of his face. He lowered his head slightly and rubbed at the few fine lines he had on his forehead.

"She's fine. Go on. She's ready for you." Dr. Reeves motioned with his head toward the bedroom.

Daddie had on his full grin. He pumped Dr. Reeves's hand in both of his.

"Thank you, Doctor. Thank you."

Daddie's blue eyes twinked as he headed for the one bedroom our house in Pearl had; Mama and Daddie's bedroom. The hair in his nose pulled his nostrils in tight against the smell of iodine mixed with blood.

Mama lay on her side of the bed, half-hidden in all the covers piled on top of her. Daddie said she was as pretty as their wedding night: all relaxed with her hair brushed neat and tied with a blue band of cotton over her one shoulder. Her face was still flushed, more excited than as if she'd just been pulled through the ringer. For the second time that day, Daddie's mind whirly-gigged around.

"Lew, I want to name the baby after you." Mama held me out for him to take.

"Where'd this boy come from?" Daddie said.

"Why Dr. Reeves brought him in his satchel," Mama laughed.

Daddie never did get used to holding a baby. He never much liked it either, but he did it for Mama, 'cause she liked it. He tried to hold my hand, but the first crink of his forefinger covered up the whole thing. His forearm was longer than the whole of me. He said I was hairless as a newborn piglet and had ears tiny and tender as mushroom caps, the kind he and Mama hunt for in the spring and bring home to fry up with bacon. He studied me and I studied him.

I pinched my lips together in a tight pucker. I was so used to being warm and in the dark. Plus, I was tired of being so stretched out. I had a hard time sleeping with all that empty space around me. I had just about enough of the coldness that was all over Daddie from him being outside.

"He looks like you when you're angry, Birdie." Daddie smiled at me. When he looked at Mama, a tear sneaked out of one eye. My whole insides changed with that tear. I felt as warm as mother's milk from the inside out, seeing that tear sneaking out of my Daddie's eyes; all his coldness seemed to melt right off of him.

"Now Ida, you know how I feel about naming a child after someone that's still alive."

Daddie's eyes hardened. Daddie always uses Mama's real name, when he means business. "I don't want my son named after me. You know that."

Daddie settled me back into Mama's arms and tucked the covers up under her chin.

"Please, Lewis. I want one of my sons to have his father's name."

"No. Now that's the end of it." Daddie's voice was almost always gentle, but Mama knew not to push any further. She'd already been through this with Dallas and a hundred other things, and she knew this was his final word.

"I'd like to name him after your father then."

Daddie sighed deep. He sat down on the edge of the bed. Once more, half of his mouth smiled as he rubbed his forehead with his open palm. He combed his fingers through his hair, and gave a big huffing sigh.

"All right, Birdie. You win this time. Eldridge it will be. I'm only givin' in 'cause my Daddie's already gone."

Daddie ran the tip of his thumb across Mama's forehead, tracing her hairline down behind her ear and across her jaw, to her chin, then gently down her neck. He let his finger stop at the small hollow between her collarbones. Mama squeezed his elbow.

Daddie took the Bible from the top of the dresser and turned to the third page. Under Dallas Michael, he wrote Eldridge Dean, December 1, 1922. He put his pen down, studied the page, and sighed. After a bit, Daddie picked the pen back up again and added (Eldie.)

"Eldridge is an old man's name," he said to no one in particular. Daddie ticked the cover closed over the pen nib, and he blew on his new entry.

That day was a good day to be born, 'cause sometimes my birthday comes right after Thanksgiving, and then I get to stay home from school for the holiday.

Daddie took a quilt out of the cedar chest and lay down on the mattress by the woodstove with Dallas. He traced Dallas's curly coppery hairline with his thumb.

"Your workmanship is marvelous, Lord, and how well I know it," he whispered.

Daddie likes quoting scripture. Mama just likes praying. After that, I fell asleep with Mama's breath coming slow and steady on the top of my head.

Daddie woke up to the smell Mama's coffee tickling his nose hairs and the sound of bacon sizzling around basted eggs. Mama fried up pieces of her home baked bread in the bacon grease. She pinned her hair up in the normal way, not flying all over and loose. Daddie watched from the mattress beside the wood stove. Her hands worked fast, setting the table, as if she forgot all about the miracle of the previous night. She wiped her hands absently across the front of her cotton apron before she stopped to give her belly a little push with both palms.

Daddie's sorta on the small side for a man, but he seems big next to Mama on account of her being so fine featured. He gave her a little squeeze when he got to the table, before he sat down to eat his pile of breakfast. Mama disappeared outside with a bucket and a handful of clean rags hidden in her apron pocket. That made me scared, so I started crying, which set Dallas off crying for no good reason at all. We kept on a-crying even after Mama came back. Daddie gave her a quick peck on the cheek and headed out the door. This time, the door opened smoothly without a bang, and he remembered to close it behind him.

Mama tied a diaper around Dallas's neck for a bib, and grabbed the remaining pieces of the fried bread from the plate on the table. I whimpered and rutted around in the bedclothes. I worked myself up to a full-blown howl 'cause of hunger turning me inside out. Mama shuffled Dallas to the bedroom so she could feed me. Dallas sucked on the bread beside her. He touched my head with his greasy fingers and smiled before his brown eyes clouded over from the stillness in the room, and pretty soon he fell full asleep.

Drunk on mother's milk, my eyes rolled back in my head and my lids fluttered shut. Mama threw back the quilt on the bed I was born in just last night and lay Dallas and me down next to each other on the clean sheets. She pulled the quilt to our chins, like Daddie did to her just the night before, but she tucked it in at the sides to keep us from rolling out of the bed. Mama gazed down at us, closed her eyes and put her open palm on each of our foreheads and paused. That was the first time I knew about Mama's way of prayer from the outside.

Tucking a stray copper curl behind her ear, Mama went back to the kitchen and poured herself a cup of coffee from the green porcelain coffee pot on the stove. She sat down at the table to finish off the last of the now cold fried bread.

That was twelve years ago. A whole lifetime. Me and Dallas have been best friends ever since that first day. Nate came along two years after me, but somehow he seems way younger than me. And 'course Itsy-Bets. Nobody can forget Itsy-Bets. It's me and Dallas that are thick as thieves, as Auntie Laura likes to say. We get bumpy sometimes, but we always clonk back together again. Nothing's ever gonna change that. Least nothin' in my imagination.

Chapter 2
Remembering when I Met Ephraim

I never knew Ephraim Moore before the fire. I never met him until this year, seventh grade at Cronk School. Even so, he's always lived just a couple miles from our house on Vermillia Street. I walked straight past his house sometimes when me and Dallas went to Torrey Rail Yard, which is on the other side of the downtown. Whenever we went to town with Mama, we always, always walked straight down Vermillia Street to Church Street, then past the Second Baptist Church to Main. When it's just me and Dallas we take different ways. We short-cut through some folks' yards, which we know's wrong. Sometimes we get in too much of a hurry to stick straight on the sidewalk. That way we got some extra time to hike over to Torrey Yard to explore. 'Course we gotta cut through folks' yards again on our way back, so Mama's none the wiser. We coulda cut right through the Moores' back yard for all I know. Like I said, I never knew Ephraim back then.

Ephraim's house looks like every other house on his block: a square box with a peaked roof and a cement front porch tacked on in front. His house has a window box full of Nastursiums in the summertime, falling almost down to the ground by the time August gets here. Ephriam's house is bigger than ours was, on account of him having a room upstairs under the eaves for a bedroom. We just had a downstairs with one bedroom, a bathroom, and a one big room for everything else. Daddie said that kept us a lot warmer than a whole bunch of separate rooms.

Besides all that, Ephraim's Popi and my Daddie work at the Shop together. That's how Daddie knew Mr. Moore. Daddie says Mr. Moore was a cracker-jack horseshoe player. I probably saw him, and Ephraim and his Ma, too, at the picnics and all, but never paid him no mind, or gave him a second thought. Even though sometimes I wonder about that. Mr. Moore is taller than most, with skin the color of chestnuts. He holds his head proud and looks down without bending his neck, so a fella is always looking straight up at his nose and past that into half-closed eyes. He makes me think of that Blacksmith fella in the poem Mrs. Bidrall made us memorize: "a mighty man is he, with large and sinewy hands.." Yep, that's Mr. Moore, alright.

I always hung close to Dallas, being he's my best friend. And Nate hung close to me, like rubber glue, that's what Nate was like. That was enough for us three brothers back then, before the fire. Before I knew Ephraim.

After the fire, me and Dallas stayed together at the Pedersons' house 'til I begged Daddie to let me stay with the Moores. I was crazy about Ephraim the day I met him at Cronk School. He was the best thing since sliced bread; all smiles, and puffed up, and full of vinegar. Mama said I was attracted to him like moth to a fire. I never knew back then what she meant. Maybe I do now.

Anyways, that very same day I met Mrs. Bidrall. Funny how those two got linked together in my memory. Me hating one and loving the other one. Then time flip-flopping everything, and then back again.

That first day at Cronk School seems like a century ago. I remember thinking my and Dallas's and Nate's new teacher, Mrs. Bidrall, had all the kids trained like cows going into stanchions. Nothing like our old school where Teacher just rang the bell and everyone came a-running, happy to be called into school, still talking and laughing as we all hung our coats in the cloak room.

At Cronk School, everyone lines up in straight as arrow lines and buttons their lips down tight when Mrs. Bidrall appears on the schoolhouse porch. Grades one through eight, first the girls, then the boys. I never saw anything like it before in my life. It's like if Dallas and Nate and I woulda turned left and went to our old school, things were happy and breezy and light as air. And when we turned right we walked straight into some sorta prison. 'Course I was clueless on that first day, just thinking the line-up was a bit peculiar.

The girls' dresses spilled out from under their woolen coats and rippled out of the front with each step they took, splashes of color, prints, stripes, and plaids. Next, marching along like little soldiers in one of those movie house newsreels, plain old grey wool short pants on all the littller boys, scratching their legs through their long woolen stockings with their shoes, sticking out from under mid-thigh woolen coats. Nate was one of those kids. How'd he know to get in that part of the line instead of sticking by my side? Maybe he spotted somebody he knew from the Tabernacle.

Last came me and Dallas and the rest of the older boys, all dressed in plain gray woolen coats. 'Cept for me and Dallas. We had on hand-me-downs from Mr. Pederson's son, George: wool flannel school pants, and his outgrown navy wool peacoats from a couple years back. Our own stuff was gone on account of the fire. Dallas already stuck out like a sore thumb with all his freckles practically blending into one big freckle and his copper hair standing in paths where he ran his fingers through.

Tiny Mrs. Bidrall was stiff as a broomstick sitting on the schoolhouse step. Her dark brown hair brushed at her face in little wisps from under her black helmet-shaped hat. Her long, black woolen coat covered all but the hem of her black pin-striped dress. The only color she seemed to allow herself was the scarlet knitted muffler around her neck. Right then I thought she looked just like one of the women in *LIFE*, Mama's favorite magazine, 'cept Mrs. Bidrall had one of them long map pointers in her hand, instead of a new toaster or a box of Post Toasties. *What's LIFE? A Magazine. How much does it cost? A dime. I only gota nickel. Well, that's life.* I remember that running straight through my mind as lunch pails scritched onto the shelf and coats slipped on to the hooks straight below. Girls to the right and boys to the left, the line slipped all quiet into the schoolhouse and everyone stood up straight and tall beside the rows of desks, still in line, still quiet as death.

"You're in for it now, new kid." The boy next me to cupped his hand over my ear and hissed into it. That was Eprhaim, only I still had to find out that part. Holy Makerel, this kid's whisper buzzed my ears until my whole neck twitched and I practically sunk down to my knees.

"Dyn-o-mite's gonna git you. Fix your clock. She will, I'm telling you, it's the God's honest truth."

This kid talked like his tongue got stuck in the bottom of his mouth and he made "God" sound like *Gawd*. I had to concentrate to get the gist of what he was telling me. Now I'm so used to listening to Ephraim, I never even notice he's got a funny accent, on account of him moving here from Pittsburgh.

"Fix my clock?"

"Dyn-o-mite's not afraid to clobber a kid."

I looked straight into the darkest eyes, dark as any one could have, like the center of a black-eyed Susan. He was shorter than me, but thicker. His skin dark like a hickory nut, different than anybody I knew. But it was his hair that really got my attention: dark as his eyes and the deepest curls I ever saw. Dallas has wavy hair, and Mama had hair that sometimes looked like corkscrews. Ephraim's hair curled so thick, the first thing I wanted to do was touch it. 'Course, I never would just touch some other fella's head out of the blue, no matter how amazing it looked.

"I'm Ephraim Moore."

Something about Ephraim. He just lights up when he talks. And even when he's still, it's like he's ready to move; like a spring or like one of those wind up toys that hold still until you let 'em go only he never moves around all jerky and unpredictable. Ephraim's got a proud rich-man look about him; he moves like his bones are made of licorice, all fluid and straight at the same time.

"Eldie. Eldie Craine."

"Don't have to tell me. Your house burnt to the ground. Everybody knows that."

I just stared at him. There was nothing I could say to that.

"Look out," Ephraim hissed. "Dynomite."

He rolled his eyes over at Mrs. Bidrall before he pulled his face all serious and glued his eyes straight ahead of him, like he never even saw me.

I might have been new to Cronk School, but I recognized a practical joke when I heard it. Mrs. Bidrall was more like a red-winged blackbird than a stick of dynamite. She flitted down the center aisle of Cronk where her neat line of kids stood at the end of rows of desks, her red muffler winging out on either side of her. She picked at the hair of what looked to me like a first-grade girl, getting it off her shoulder, and smoothing it in a straight line down the girl's back, like a bird arranging a piece of grass in her nest. Mrs. Bidrall fluttered around a third grade boy until he got the message and stood on both legs, straightening his back.

I sidled up to Ephraim so I could whisper in his ear. I had my mouth open ready to lay one on him, but before I could get one word out, my head hurtled out of control and caused me to bend over at the waist. I about fell over, 'cept I stuck my foot out to steady myself. I have some balance, if nothing else. That I can say without sounding too prideful. Spit trickled down the front of my pea coat; the back of my head felt like somebody clobbered me with a rock. I turned to see what hit me.

"Your hat, young man." Mrs. Bidrall chirped, her face red and puffy.

I got pretty used to that sort of thing from her, but back on that first day, she looked sorta like one of those Banshee creatures. Little beads of sweat seeped out of her forehead and wetted the wisps of hair into tiny spears coming out of that helmet sort of hat. Her map pointer was aimed at the top of my head and whistled down to the floor. All I could think of was, *so that's what hit me*. No wonder my head hurt so bad.

My hat lay on the ground where she pointed. Must've fallen off when I stumbled. 'Course I bent down to pick it up and get it back on my head. That's when she dive-bombed me, like a bird going after a cat near her nest. Just like a red-wing. I heard the pointer whistle over my head, but she didn't land it this time. I raked my fingers through my hair and set my hat straight. Yup, there was a big welt swelling up under my hat. I looked at my hand. No blood.

I heard a whoosh of air like wings beating the air around my head and the sting of the pointer landed on my legs. Before I got a chance to turn, she flogged at my behind, my back and again at my legs. God Almighty what the heck was ailing this lady?

I grabbed at each part of me as she hit, which got my hands stung, too. I shoulda stopped grabbing, but it was like my hands had a mind of their own. Ephraim pulled his face poker straight, all the while his eyes danced like fireflies in summertime. He mouthed *Dy-no-mite* at me. I shoulda been mad but all at once I started to see things from his eyes. I bit down on the inside of my cheek to stop myself from laughing.

"Take. Your. Hat. Off. In a. Public. Building."

Mrs. Bidrall pressed her face so close to mine, I smelled her cottage cheese breakfast and saw bubbles of old coffee spit trying to wash a toast crumb out from between her teeth.

With each word came a blow somewhere on my backside. I got afraid to turn around for fear of where the stick might land. I caught Dallas out of the corner of my eye. His brown cow-eyes locked down on mine. I'm telling you, he can have the saddest eyes in the world. His eyes knocked every silly notion straight out of my head. If he was a teacher, he'd never need to use a map pointer on a kid. All he'd have to do is look at him with those eyes of his.

My hat was on the floor again, two feet in front of me. So that's what she was getting at. She coulda just told me. I reached over, picked up my hat and raked my hand back through my hair, checking in what I thought was a keen way, so anyone watching me, which was probably everyone, figured I was collecting myself. Still no blood, but that goose egg was a doozie. I gripped my hat with both hands, like it just might hop up on my head on its own.

Mrs. Bidrall for sure was just like a red-winged blackbird. No getting away from her once you step into her territory. I half expected a 'chip-chip-cher-reeee,' to come out of her and a bunch of other helmeted, school marms to come in through the door to come to her aid.

"Told ya," Ephraim hissed between his teeth, without even moving his lips. Ephraim's eyes got as wet as mine felt. Dallas studied his shoes.

That's when I first saw Cecilea in the line of girls. 'Course, I had to learn her name yet, same as every other kid in the school. She turned to shush us; finger to her lips. I saw Mama do it a hundred times, and Teacher, too. I mean my old teacher, not this new red-winged Mrs. Bidrall.

Cecilea's eyes pierced straight into me. Blue-green, like the lake in late summer. Her hair was the same color as chestnuts and new straw all mixed together; loose around her face. She turned and followed the younger girls to her desk. Her skirt kissed against her calves and her hair brushed across her back as the line of students moved like clockwork, and everybody took their assigned places. I still had to be assigned mine. Dallas and Nate and I just stood there out in the aisle, waiting for instructions.

Jeez-o-Pete's. School was gonna be something else, here at Cronk.

At recess, I sidled up to Ephraim to get the lowdown on Mrs. Bidrall and Cronk School. Dallas stayed right there beside me like a hungry puppy. Nate was over playing marbles with some new friends. There was something about Ephraim that just made a fellow feel like adventure was just around the corner. By the time we put away our lunch buckets after noon hour, I felt like I knew Ephraim forever.

After that, I went right over to the Taylor's house and begged Mama and Daddie to let me stay with the Moores. Daddie needed no convincing at all, since he knew Mr. Moore from the Shop, and besides a being a hard worker, which was next to godliness in Daddie's book, Mr. Moore was a born-again Christian, which was the frosting on top of the cake for Daddie. Mama got half-way convinced when Daddie pointed out it would be easier on the Pedersons' to have just one hungry boy to feed, instead of both Dallas and me and the Moores were used to feeding two boys on account of them having an older son, Thomas still back in Pittsburgh.

That was half the battle won. The tough part was Mama had to work up the courage to ask the Moores. Mrs. Moore's just as proud looking as her husband. That's where the similarity stops. Ephaim's Ma's short like Mama, and round, too, but round in a way different way than Mama. Mrs. Moore's got roundness around the hips, with tree-truck legs, where Mama's all around the belly, and nothing but stick legs for her. Mrs. Moore's got straight black hair, she keeps in a braid down her back, and a straight sharp thin nose that comes down almost to her top lip. I bet she can touch her tongue to the tip of her nose if she wanted too. Ephraim's Ma has dancing eyes like Daddie's, only coal black.

Anyways, Ephraim hatched a plan to get his Ma and Popi to think up the idea on their own. That's something I was going to love and hate about Ephraim. He had the charm, that's sure as shooting. He could drop an idea and let it lay there until some hapless fella or gal picked it up and made it his own, and that was fine and dandy with Ephraim. Lots of fellas gotta get some boasting in on their idea. Ephriam just smiled his pearly whites and let all the boasting go on in the inside.

'Course, Dallas was sore as all get out, on account of him having to do all the chores around the Pedersons' on his own. 'Least that's what he said bugged him about me going over to the Moores. Everytime he talked about it his skin pinked up under his freckles, so I turned the subject to something else as soon as I could.

Chapter 3
Cronk School

Sometimes I wish I never met Ephraim. Then it would just be me and Dallas and once in a while, Nate, like it was before we got split up. When we lived together on Vermillia Street, before the fire, maybe even before Daddie got a job at the Shop and we moved away from Pearl. Dallas is my big brother; he'll always be my first and best friend. Well anyways, that was true until I met Ephraim. I wish I never met Ephraim.

It's not only Ephraim that gets me all irked: it's Mrs. Bidrall, and Cecilea too, and Mama and Daddie and just about everyone and their brother, 'cept maybe Itsy-Bets; she's too little to be anything but cute as the dickens, but you're not gonna catch me saying that out loud to anybody that matters. Even if I've got no beef with Itsy-Bets, she's a girl, and girls are no good at playing fun things like mumblety-peg and kick-the-can. Plus, she's practically a baby.

"Pssst."

It's Ephraim trying to get my attention. It's hard enough keeping my mind on school without him pssting at me. I just ignore him, 'cause I don't want any trouble with Mrs. Bidrall today.

"Psssst, Eldie. Eldie."

Ephraim thinks he's whispering, but he seems loud enough to wake the dead to me. He might be louder in my mind's ear, on account of me wanting to avoid Mrs. Bidrall and any other trouble coming my way.

Ephraim keeps at it, and finally he gives me the look that always makes me laugh. The one with one eyebrow up, and the other one down, and his face all cock-eyed. Dallas tries to make that face now, but he never can pull it off. First of all, Ephraim has those black, black Charlie Chaplin eyebrows, and Dallas's eyebrows are pretty near invisible sitting on a ridge that makes his eyes look deep. Besides, Dallas's face moves all over tarnation, his eyebrows going way up, or scowling way down. He looks like a darned boob.

I mouth shut up to Ephraim, and real quick I stare straight at the blackboard, pretending to study what Mrs. Bidrall wrote up there, which has nothing at all to do with what we're studying right now. I wipe my hand over my mouth, so I can stay out of trouble.

Today's poetry reciting day at school. I have no use for poetry, especially some poem about a giant snail lying down there on the ocean floor. What's that got to do with me, anyways? I never saw the ocean. Probably never will. I got a good memory but there's no sense wasting it, crowding up my brain on stuff of no use to me today or ever.

Mrs. Bidrall never calls on me first anyhow; mostly she calls on the girls first. I just go over the poem while the smart kids recite. By the time Mrs. Bidrall gets to me, I've got it down good enough. But, today my mind is all over the place. I keep going back to last night. To get my mind off that, I stretch my fingers where I scraped 'em, and curl them into a fist, so the pain comes back, and that gets my mind off Cecilea. My little finger hangs limp against the heel of my palm, I can't curl that finger ever since I injured it when our house on Vermillia Street burned down. Anyhow, the skin splits open where I scraped it last night and first clear fluid, then blood seeps out. It feels like a pincushion full of Mama's quilting needles poking into my hand, so I suck at the saltiness, and for some reason that makes me think of Cecilea all over again. It's like those quilting needles are poking right into my soul and I can feel the blood creeping hot up my neck and into my scalp and I know my face is all red and flushed.

Sometimes I just want to bust right out of my skin and be somebody else, or somehow go back in time and be my old self. The clueless self. Instead, I'm sitting in the classroom that's cold as all get out: frost all over the windows, and the stove getting low. I wish I could at least go back to yesterday and undo what I did.

I feel like everything about me is wrong. My hands are all rough and clumsy, somehow too big now, and my knuckles hurt from where I scraped them. Look at these joints, will ya? Like field corn infected with smut, all gnarly-white and stained black with coal dust. Last night I scraped my knuckles on account of my own sheer stupidity. I overloaded the coal scuttle I was filling up for Mrs. Moore, because I was in a hurry so I could join Dallas and Ephraim at the Torrey Yard. I gotta earn my keep now that I'm living with the Moores. It's not that I'm a weakling or anything. I'm strong enough. The trouble came when I went to shut to the coal-cellar door. The scuttle got all unbalanced and a few pieces of coal started to get away from me. I tried to balance the scuttle with my knee and catch the renegades with my free hand. The loosed cellar door banged down and scraped across my knuckles. I felt like such a dope; nobody even saw me, but still I felt like a dope. How much dopier can a guy get, anyhow? What if Cecilea had been there?

I had my mittens off, so's Mama wouldn't get all sore about me getting them dirty. Besides, mittens are for babies. My hand was too cold to feel the skin all peeled back and bleeding, until I had the coal all collected and put in the kitchen behind the stove and I was leaving the house again. That's when I saw the smear of blood by the back door and saw the streaks of blood on my knuckles. I tried to rub the blood off the door with my handkerchief, 'cause for sure that was gonna make Mrs. Moore mad. She even hates having fingerprints on the molding that no one but she can see, so she was gonna be real mad to see blood left there, plain as daylight.

Mrs. Moore lets every feeling out, even before she knows she's feeling it, and all those feelings come out loud as a church revival. She's gonna be shouting, "What in the love of God!" I can hear it already.

Mama calls that kind of talk wooden swearing. She never yells. Still, I hate it when Mama's mad: she just stands there with her lips pressed together tight, straight as a ruler's edge, like she's holding back something; her throat working away swallowing her words. She turns away from me, waiting until the time is right to talk about the matter, as she says. That kind of angry is harder to take. It just sits there, like a weight on my chest, and reminds me I could be so much better. Mrs. Moore's mad could get a guy jittery and jumpy on the outside, but that's about it.

Anyways, I was just gonna let sleeping dogs lie, so I made a bandage with my handkerchief, tying it with my free hand and my teeth. Dallas showed me how to do that once when we played Robin Hood on Vermillia Street and he scraped his hand against the sidewalk catching himself when he fell down. That was before we met Ephraim, before I moved into the Moores' house with Ephraim and his Ma and Popi. Me filling up what extra space they had saved up for Thomas. Thomas is Ephraim's big brother. He stayed in Pittsburgh by himself. Mrs. Moore says he's coming soon. I just gotta be patient.

I wish I could go back and convince Dallas and Ephraim to change their minds. I wish I just went over to the Taylors' last night and listened to the Lone Ranger or The Shadow on the radio with Mama and Daddie and Nate and Itsy-Bets instead.

I think of Cecilea all over again and the blood rushes out of my face. I move my book of poems into my lap and concentrate on *The Chambered Nautilus*.

I wipe my hot palms on the legs of my overalls and notice a hunk of dried cuticle hanging off my middle finger where my pencil rests when I'm writing, so I pick at it and pretty soon I'm biting at it again like I'm always doing whenever I'm trying to get my mind where it belongs.

Next thing I know, there's Cecilea up there right beside Mrs. Bidrall's desk, reciting *The Chambered Nautilus*. My heart starts to pound so hard I can feel it in my ears.

> *The Chambered Nautilus* by Oliver Wendell Holmes:
> This is the ship of pearl, which, poets feign,
> Sails the unshadowed main, —
> The venturous bark that flings
> On the sweet summer wind its purpled wings
> In gulfs enchanted, where the Siren sings,
> And Coral reef lie bare,
> Where the cold sea-maids rise to sun their streaming hair…"

Cecilea pushes a loose strand of hair behind her ear. I grind at my cuticle like a cow chewing grass, until the little nub of horny stuff comes off in my mouth. Now I'm just sitting there staring at the base of my nail 'cause there's a bead of blood where the ugly cuticle was hanging, so I put my finger in my mouth and suck hard. That does no good and another drop oozes out, so I squeeze the nail bed between my thumb and forefinger and try to say the poem along with Cecilea. *Jeez-o-Pete's, what's wrong with me?* That's wooden swearing, too, if I say it out loud.

Cecilea's so smart, and her voice is soft. She practically sings that entire poem out without one single slip, and somehow she makes that stupid poem sound almost like something worth remembering. Her sisters, Theresa, Margaret, and Analie, sit with their backs straight and hands folded in front of them. Those Tamarack girls look like they never even thought of doing anything wrong. They must be praying every single minute that they're not studying or playing the piano, or taking a bath, or some other girl thing. Besides being girls, the Tamaracks' are Cat-lickers. Cat-lickers are always praying.

That gets me to praying that Mrs. Bidrall will pass over me today.

"Very good, Cecilea," she says.

"Thank you." Cecilea sounds almost like she's talking to herself.

Mrs. Bidrall beams at Cecilea. Ole Dynomite looks at me and her expression changes: her eyes go all dull, the corners of her mouth twitch. I can feel her eyes boring into my brain and I know she knows I don't know that poem for squat. My mouth tastes like I chewed a penny.

Cecilea smiles and lowers her head as if to apologize for how proud she is, that she got that whole stupid poem out with not one mistake. She's gotta go past me to get to her desk, and when she does, she raises her eyes and looks right in my eyes and at the very same time her dress brushes against my desk. I coulda touched her if I wanted to. One of her Sunday-china hands clutches her lace-trimmed handkerchief, and the other flutters up to the hollow of her neck and I imagine delicate collar-bones down there below her hand.

I look away real quick and just stare at the back of my hands, like some sorta dope. I can feel the blood rise up my neck again and over my cheeks. My ears are burning. I'm moving before I even think about it. I gotta get out of here.

Mrs. Bidrall grips the map pointer in one hand and slides it back and forth through her other curled palm. She always seems to have that pointer in her hand, just in case someone needs a swift rap to get his attention back on his schoolwork. I look up at the clock over her head. The long hand wipes out the 'e' in Seth Thomas. Ten minutes before school is out. I'm gonna escape recitin' today. I'm positive.

"Eldie? Eldie? El-die Craine."

Mrs. Bidrall's voice finally registers.

"Where are you going?"

She's rapping her pointer against her open palm now.

"The stove's low," I say. "Gonna get some more wood, so we can all be warm." Mrs. Bidrall's lips turn up a little and she lets the pointer slide down by her leg.

I'm home free, I can see it. I just gotta smile at that, and Mrs. Bidrall's mouth turns up a little more. I'm pretty sure she's not gonna let me put any wood in that stove this late in the day.

"That's kind of you, Eldie."

She lets me go.

The cold air mixed in with all the outside smells, makes my nostril widen up a little. In spite of it being cold in school, the air is dead and my head is clouded with the smell of burning Applewood, which I never notice sitting at my desk, but I do once I'm back outside. By the time I head back in, kids are hightailing it out of there. I see Ephraim shove his shoulder up against Dallas. Dallas laughs and shoves back.

"You can go home now. Be ready tomorrow. Last chance to recite," says Mrs. Bidrall, turning to erase the blackboard.

"Yes, Ma'am."

I used to like school when we lived back in Pearl, back when I was littler, and didn't know anything; back before we moved from Pearl, and before our house on Vermillia burned down. Heck, I even liked school when we lived on Vermillia Street.

I take my time strapping my books together and getting my lunchpail, like it's the most important thing in the world, 'cause I really don't want any company right now and for sure Dallas and Ephraim are waiting outside. Besides that, I'm still daydreaming about Pearl. I'm back when I first started school and Middie took me and Dallas to Kindergarten Hill sledding in the winter time and down that same hill in a wagon come summertime. She let me steer the wagon. That's how I almost knocked my front tooth out of my head and why it still hurts when I suck in cold air.

Chapter 4
Remembering Pearl: My Very First Day of School

I remember when Dallas woke me up, crying away like a baby in Mama's bedroom. The day after the Labor Day Picnic. Sun streamed in through the kitchen window and made a yellow rectangle with a dark cross through it on the linoleum. Dallas was my big brother, a whole five years old and almost six, but sometimes he was kinda a crybaby and a chicken-liver. Daddie says big boys never cry.

"No Mama. Don't make me." Dallas's voice shivered.

Dallas pulled on brown corduroy knickers over his high socks and tucked his shirttail in. I thought I was dreaming at first, 'cause Sunday was just the day before yesterday, so why the heck did Dallas have on his Sunday clothes? Daddie must've left for work already, 'cause the sun was shining full on the kitchen table. That's the best thing about where Nate and Dallas and me slept in our Pearl house. We could see everything as soon as we opened our eyes, 'cause we slept right beside the woodstove, and our Pearl house only had two rooms, plus the bathroom.

Nate was practically a baby back then, not all Goody-Two-Shoes, like he is now. He sat up in his highchair, stuffing corn meal mush into his mouth with his fists. I closed my eyes and pretended to be asleep, 'cause for one thing, I was about to laugh at Nate's hair sticking out, full of corn meal mush, like Pogo in the comics. For another thing, I could find out a whole lot more if Mama thought I was sleeping. Dallas always said I woke him up with my awake breathing. So, I forced my nose to suck in and out slow and steady, so no one would get wise to me. Breakfast smells came in and tickled at my nose hairs.

Mama looked like she always did, with her apron around her waist, cheeks all red and rashy-looking from the heat of the stove, copper curls breaking free from her tight bun. Itsy-Bets wasn't even born yet. She was only a baby when we left Pearl.

When Daddie talks about Pearl and before Itsy-Bets was born, he says Itsy-Bets was just a twinkle in his eye. I think I know what that means, 'cause Daddie lights up whenever Itsy-Bet is around; like she's an angel that just touched down on his front porch and decided to stay. He never in his life looks at me or Dallas or Nate like that.

"Come now Dallas. You must get ready for school," said Mama.

Dallas stuck out his lip. Tears and spit and snot pooled there.

I could hardly wait to go to school, 'cause Middie went to school. Why in blue blazes was Dallas putting up such a fuss about it? Middie lived around the block from us. She was still a kid; a big kid, almost as tall as Mama and older than any of us Craines. Middie loved school; she was all the time pretending to be a schoolteacher.

Mama turned her back on Dallas, wiped her hands straight down her legs, and turned toward me. Her lips all but disappeared on her face, leaving only a straight line where a mouth should be. I was only four; still I knew she was in her 'no-nonsense' mood.

Dallas acted like he was getting punished by going to school. That got the gears in my head turning. All the same, with Mama's face looking like that, it was way better to stay still and pretend to be sleeping, so that's just what I did. I closed my eyes again.

From our mattress, I could see Dallas wipe his face with the palms of his hands and follow Mama to the table. His freckles stood out against fraidy-cat skin. The kind of skin that goes all white when a fella is getting ready to hide or tell a lie. Mama flipped pieces of fried johnnycake onto his plate. My mouth started to get all wet inside and I felt my tongue want to reach right over to the table.

I can feel my tongue like that now, just thinking about Mama's johnnycake. Before I could think the situation over again I got up off the mattress and made a beeline to the table.

"You go to the toilet first," Mama said. "Your breakfast will be ready when you get back."

'Course she was right as rain which I never even knew until she said something. I grabbed hold of myself and headed for the toilet, 'cause now I needed to go bad.

She coulda just put that spatula down, and relaxed her jaw. I was four, almost five; I didn't need to be reminded to go to the toilet. I kept that thought to myself. Besides, I was a whole lot more interested in what Dallas was crying about.

A daddy-long-legs skitched across the floor in the bathroom right in front of the toilet and stopped for a moment where the floor met the wall, as if considering which way to go. I was always studying bugs when I was littler. Now that I'm at Cronk school, I hate studying just about anything. Probably 'cause I gotta do it now. Forcing a fella to learn things is for the birds. Besides, I got better things to fill up my brain than poetry, like Mrs. Bidrall's always making us memorize.

That morning, back when I was a little kid, and Dallas was blubbering me awake, and I was on my way back from the toilet, I remember that I stopped to watch a daddy-long-legs stretch its legs out in lop-sided old-man strides across the wooden planks with two of its eight legs on the plaster wall. Wonder where he's is goin'? I crouched down to watch closer.

"No need to be afraid, little fella," I said out loud, 'cause everybody knows if you kill a daddy-long-legs, it'll rain and I sure never wanted it to rain. Rain meant I'd be stuck inside all day. Besides, I never even thought twice about talking to bugs when I was that little.

"What took you so long?" Mama said as she slid johnnycakes onto my plate.

That made me forget all about Dallas and how he was blubbering about something. I just started eating those johnnycakes with one elbow on the table holding up my head and the other one cranking my fork into my mouth.

"Get your elbow off the table, and eat proper," Mama said. She was always watching out for bad manners when we all lived together. I straightened up and put one hand in my lap like she taught me.

Next thing you know, Mama was pushing Nate's buggy out the door, tugging me with her free hand. Dallas clutched a fistful of Mama's skirt, dragging along behind, with one knickers-leg up over his knee. I remember wanting to laugh 'cause Dallas looked like a pirate. He stopped his blubbering, but his face was blotchy and his eyes were half swollen shut from the crying. He sorta looked like all the water ran out of his eyes and nose, and he would cry more, but nothing was left.

Dallas had a pair of new boots on, with a little pocket at the ankle and a real pocketknife tucked inside. That's how those shoes came: with a real pocketknife. I wanted to ask Dallas if he got the shoes special for school, 'cause up until that very moment I thought Mama just bought him a new pair of Sunday church shoes. But I kept it to myself, on account of I didn't want him to start up crying again. If I went to school, maybe I'd have a pair of boots like that.

When we got to the schoolyard, Mama loosed Dallas's grip from her skirt and pulled her handkerchief out of her dress pocket. She wiped Dallas's face and told him to blow his nose. She put her hands on top of his head and we got quiet 'cause Mama was praying. Dallas took a slow, deep breath, almost like a yawn, and let it out again.

"Hey there, Mrs. Craine."

It was Middie Sterling, smoothing down her skirt and smiling pretty at Mama. She held a reader close up to her chest like she was holding a baby. She liked reading that much.

"I'll make sure he gets along okay," said Middie.

Dallas's breath came out all jerky, like a shiver. He grabbed Middie's hand, and the two of them walked up the three stairs into the schoolhouse. Dallas looked back the whole time, until the door shut behind them. I sure wished I was Dallas.

Mama and me just stood there all quiet looking at the door, while a few more of the big kids went inside, opening and shutting the door. Nate whined a bit, so Mama jiggled the buggy and we turned to go home. It sure was a quiet walk back home without Dallas.

I kept looking up for Dallas all that morning. I remember that clear as yesterday. My chest had a heavy feeling, like when Dallas sat on me. He did that all the time for fun, like if we pretended to be mountain lions fighting each other, 'cause he was bigger than me. Mama kept asking me to fetch things for her and do little jobs; the kinda things she probably would have asked Dallas, and that made me clench my teeth together hard. I was kinda proud that Mama thought I was big like Dallas, but mostly it made me mad at Dallas, 'cause he should be there, too.

Just before lunchtime, out of the blue, Mama told me to go to the toilet again. We walked the same path to the school and there was Dallas, looking just the way we left him—tear-stained and all out of sorts. He stayed that way the rest of the day.

Dallas tried to tell me what school was like. The big kids, the books, the desks with the inkwells. I kept thinking it sounded exciting and fun. I thought about Middie and tried to imagine where she sat and where her big brother, Tom sat. I tried to imagine the games the boys played at recess, and what other kids I never even met might look like, what they talked about, and how far away they lived. Maybe there were other boys on this very block that I never even saw before.

Even though Dallas told his story between sobs and tears, I wished I could go to school, too. I'd trade with Dallas anytime, and then I felt a little bit bad, 'cause Dallas just hated it so much. I guess Dallas got wise to school way before I did, 'cause it took me until this year, in seventh grade and Mrs. Bidrall, to figure out school was just about the same as torture.

Back when we lived in Pearl, or before the fire, when we all lived together on Vermillia Street, Mama always stroked my forehead before bed, while she prayed over me. She always looks so serious when she prays, but her face is soft and her eyes look like she's gazing at something pretty and far away, or like when Daddie tells stories about the Old Days, not tight and puckered like she looks when she's in her 'no-nonsense mood,' or about to give me a scoldin', like when I got mud on the floor, 'cause I forgot to scrape my boots off.

Mama's face when she prayed made me feel safe and sleepy and like nothing in the world could go wrong. That was true back in Pearl, and is still true. Except now we're all split up, living apart from each other, so when I see Mama's prayer face, it seems like something special's going on.

The next three mornings, Dallas kept on a-crying and a-begging to stay home, blubbering away like a baby. At the same time, I got eager to get up and get dressed for the walk to school. Dallas walked home all by himself after the first day. If I was real good, Mama let me walk to the corner and meet Dallas coming home.

"Did you get called up to the blackboard today?" I begged Dallas to tell me everything at lunchtime.

"Yes." Dallas looked at his hands resting on the table.

"Then what happened?"

Sometimes crumbs flew out of my mouth when I tried to get Dallas to talk, and Mama stood there with one hand on her hip looking at me, saying nothing, but I knew what she was thinking and I started picking crumbs up off the tablecloth.

On Friday, when we walked Dallas to school, the schoolhouse door stayed open extra-long, while a bunch of the big kids went in all at once. I saw the cloakroom and the shelf for the big kids' lunch pails. The desks stood all in a row, with the big black slate behind the teacher's desk. The cloakroom blocked all that, but I knew what was beyond, 'cause Dallas told me all about it and how he hated to get called up to the blackboard in front of everybody.

Every day, Middie met us outside the schoolhouse.

"I could come by and walk Dallas to school," Middie offered, smiling at Mama.

"That's kind of you," Mama said. "Let's see how he does after the weekend."

Dallas kept up the crying even on the next Monday.

On that next Monday, when we all got to the school, Mama hoisted Nate on her hip and stretched out her other arm around Dallas and me, like she was a hen and we were her baby chicks. She got us right into the school and right up to the teacher, Miss Riece. Ink and chalk dust filled up my nose and went straight up into my head. Kid noises buzzed behind me. I kept my eyes going back and forth between Miss Riece's face and Mama's.

"Dallas can't take being away from us like this. We've got to do something." Mama's voice was in that quiet voice.

I bet that's the way the angel talked to Joseph in that dream he had before Jesus got born and then after when the angel told Joseph to hightail it out of Bethlehem. Mama's voice, all quiet and steady, and the way her eyes looked at Miss Riece meant listen up, because what I'm about to say is important. It's sorta like her no nonsense voice, but for grown-ups.

"Well, what do you suggest?" said Miss Riece. "Dallas must go to school."

Mama's bottom eyelid twitched just a teensy bit. I bet she wasn't expecting any backtalk from Miss Riece. I looked at Mama, then at Miss Riece. No one said anything. I moved in halfway around behind Mama's skirt, 'cause now I was getting kinda scared. Still, I only went halfway back there, 'cause most of me wanted to know what was gonna happen next.

"Eldie's going, too," Mama said.

Mama voice was just as soft as always, but she looked right into Miss Riece's eyes, like she dared her to look away first. I saw her jaw ripple just a little, so I wanted to warn Miss Riece not to disobey Mama, but I was a still a bit afraid, so I just kept my thoughts to myself.

"Well, the boy's got to have shoes," was all the argument Miss Riece had to offer.

I guess Miss Riece was a little scared of Mama, too. Mama looked down at my feet, which made her look humble 'cept for her Irish was up; first her neck got red and rashy, before it spread to her cheeks.

"Tomorrow he will have shoes, but keep him here with Dallas today," she said.

For the first time I can remember, I felt heat climb up my neck and into my cheeks. I looked at Mama's face and kinda knew that's just what mine looked like, only I thought my ears were red as a hot coal.

Miss Riece's open palm was on my back and my whole body got hot, like every bit of me was turning red under my clothes and my knickers started to itch behind my knees. I didn't scratch because Daddie said it's rude and because right that very second, I noticed that Miss Riece smelled just like lilacs and vanilla all mixed together. Maybe all that ink and chalk dust cleared the way for her good smells. Plus, I saw Middie sitting over with the big kids, smiling and nodding at me.

Dallas never minded going to school after that. I was happy as a pig in mud. I was crazy about all the new people and friends I had at school, and I filled Mama in on everything when I got home. Sometimes nothing much interesting happened, so I made up a story just to have something to say. Best of all, after me and Dallas started going to school together, Mama let us walk to school with Middie or her big brother, Tom, or sometimes all by ourselves. For some reason, Middie almost always walked over after school, even though we were already long home by the time the big kids got out. Sometimes she stayed around and talked to Mama.

I sat right behind a girl named Phyllis in school. She was way bigger than me and she had long brown hair in two neat braids that hung down her back and brushed the front of my desk, which about made me crackers. Those braids of hers brushed right up against my inkwell and the little tips of hair at the end of each braid looked just like the end of a paintbrush. All I had to do was just flip with two fingers and a braid would dip right into the ink. Good thing I had a lurchy stomach. That's the only thing that stopped me dead in my tracks. I imagined the inky tip of the braid brushing the top of my desk and the back of Phyllis's dress.

Sometimes I had to clamp my hand over my mouth and hold it there with the other hand, to keep from laughing just thinking about her reciting multiplication tables at the front of the classroom with ink stripes on her back. Phyllis had a way of lifting her nose and jutting her chin out with each correct answer, and that ink on the end of her braid would be painting some strange design on her back while her front side was looking all proud and happy.

Reading and writing was hard, but 'rithmetic was fun. After school, when I finished chores, Dallas and me practiced numbers with Mama. After, Daddie read the Bible. I had to take a turn reading for practice, which I hated 'cause my reading made the whole business go slower than molasses in January. Daddie was better and faster at reading. With Daddie reading, the stories came to life. It was like he was there and just remembering what happened.

Me and Dallas took way longer to read. I sorta lost track of the story in all that deciphering of words. Anyways, listening was so much better 'cause I could do other things while I listened. I watched a fly buzz around Daddie's shoulder, land and crawl in a zigzag patch onto his shirt collar. I tried to guess how many verses before Daddie's hand slapped at the fly. The fly buzzed way off toward the ceiling, made a lazy circle in the air, and came back to land on Daddie's shoulder.

If me and Dallas sat really still, we got a special treat.

"Want a magazine story?" Daddie said.

'Course he already knew the answer. Both of us ran to the smoking stand to get the *LIFE* Magazine. Once, Daddie read a story about the Detroit Auto Shop. The story that went with the picture on the front cover, the one with so many smoke stacks that the factory looked big enough to be a whole town, a lot bigger than the screw factory where Daddie worked in Pearl.

"That's where our car was made, boys," Daddie said.

His eyes lit up like Christmas morning, and they opened so wide it looked like they could fall out. Daddie slapped the back of his hand against the picture.

"That's where most every screw we make at the factory gets sent these days."

I wanted to grab *LIFE* right out of Daddie's hands and start reading for myself. I betcha Detroit was one fine place. *LIFE* was something worth deciphering. Still, I knew better than to do any grabbing. Mama never allowed me to look at magazines all by myself.

Every night, back then, Mama snugged us down under the covers on our mattress with the stove still toasty warm. She put her hand first on Dallas's forehead, then mine and last Nate's, to say a silent prayer.

After Itsy-Bets was born, she got to sleep in the bedroom with Mama and Daddie, 'cause she's a girl.

Mama said, "It's just improper for girls to sleep with boys."

I asked why Daddie got to sleep in the bedroom. Mama just laughed. It was that secret laugh that grown-ups have when something's funny, but only adults know why.

Mama and Daddie say lots of things are 'just not right.' Most of the time, no one tells me the reason, but I know what will happen if I do those things, and that's the important part.

"Why won't you let me read *LIFE* by myself?" I asked Mama one night after her praying was done. "It's mostly pictures, and I can read pretty good now."

"There's some unwholesome things in that magazine," she said. "Some is not fit for little boys."

"I'm big now. I go to school."

"I know," she said. "You're not ready yet."

I suppose Mama was old enough to skip over the unwholesome parts.

Chapter 5
Dibble's Five and Dime

"Whoa, Eldie," says Ephraim.

I keep walkin' 'cause I'm in a hurry to get to Dibble's Five and Dime.

"Eldie, Dallas, wait."

Ephraim's the last person I want to see; I'm fed up with him.

"Wait for me. Eldie."

Ephraim slaps me on the back so hard I stumble forward. Dallas catches my arm, just with his hand, he keeps his arm real stiff so's it just jerks a little, and I'm pretty sure Ephraim doesn't see.

"What'd ya want?" I ask Ephraim.

"Hey, slow down. Where're you going?"

"I guess I hafta wait now."

I brush at my overalls, keepin' myself busy so's I don't have to look Ephraim in the eye, and so he forgets I never answered his question.

"We're goin' to Dibble's, for our Mama," I say. I already know what he's gonna say.

"I'm coming with you." Ephraim says 'widja' instead of 'with you' cause that's the way fellas talk from Pittsburgh. Sometimes I gotta stop a second and figure out what he's saying. 'Specially with stuff like gum bands, instead of rubber bands. Most of the time, I get the gist of what he's saying right off. People from Pittsburgh sure have some funny ways of talking.

"Suit yourself, but I'm just running an errand for her. It's gonna be dull as watching paint dry."

I know he will come anyway, and I know it will be more fun if he thinks he has to weasel his way in. I sorta wish he was somewhere else, so I can just be with Dallas for a change. At the same time, I kinda do want him around, 'cause when Ephraim is along, I never know what's gonna happen, and that gets my nerves jumping. I like that feeling.

"What are you buying for her?" says Ephraim. He says wahdya, 'cause that's the way people talk from Pittsburgh.

"Just her *LIFE* magazine. That's all. I gotta get it back to her with no wrinkles, so you can't even look at it."

"Yeah," says Dallas, just 'cause he wants to say something.

I see Dallas is getting his Irish up, for no reason at all. Dallas is like that. He gets all up in a knot real easy. I can tell it's coming on account of his neck gets all blotchy red first, then the tips of his ears, and the skin under all his freckles gets blushed. Mostly, nobody sees that first sign, the one where his neck gets blotchy. I do, 'cause I've been seeing it my whole life. First with Mama, then Dallas.

"How much money did she give you?" Ephraim says.

"You're just full of questions."

I try to look all mad and such, but my lip starts to twitch a little on the left side, so I pull my hand down over it, like I'm thinking hard, but Ephraim catches on and slaps me hard on the back again. Only this time it's different. For one thing, I see his face and he's grinning, his pearly white teeth all showing in two straight lines, like he flew outta the booby hatch. Second of all, I see it coming, so I'm braced and I stand firm, I don't even flinch forward.

"Mama gave us a dime and a nickel, just like she always does on Saturday, so's she can get LIFE," pipes in Dallas. "We get to buy Lemon Drops with the nickel, some for us and some for Nate and Itsy-Bets."

Heck, Nate gets Lemon Drops anytime he wants on account of him living at Dibble's since the fire. 'Least that's what he tells us fellas. Mama makes us share with him anyways, 'cause he's our brother.

Dallas's got his Irish back down. That's the way it is with Dallas: Irish up, Irish down, just like that. Mama's more like a slow simmer; Dallas is a match lighting.

"Aw, ain't that sweet," says Ephraim.

He's feeling a little left out.

I say to Dallas, "Too bad Itsy-Bets isn't here, Mrs. Dibble has a soft spot for her and for sure would give us an extra somethin' or other," which is my way of letting Dallas know he shoulda kept quiet about the Lemon Drops.

"Mr. Dibble's pretty good to Nate, too. On account of him living there and doing all his fetch and carry for him." I'm blabbering to fill up the dead space.

Dallas looks all down-in-the-mouth, and I'm sorry all over again, and for some reason, Cecilea and her sisters flash behind my eyes, and I'm even sorrier. I'm that way ever since that day Ephraim dared me and Dallas to sneak over to the Tamaracks' with him after chores and supper and spy on them. It's already been a couple of weeks, but every time I think about it, I still get mad at Ephraim all over again. I'm starting to think I know why Dallas is all red in the face and agitated.

"Well, what're we hangin' 'round here in the slush for?" I say.

I start back out toward Dibble's. Ephraim is grinning like a Looney-Tune all over again and I can't stay mad with all that happiness just oozing out of him for no reason at all.

Of course when we get to Dibble's, we gotta look around and see what they have. Mostly just the same old stuff that you can get in any five and dime. Right up close to the door is yarn and embroidery floss and stuff for tatting doilies. Women's stuff. I supposed that's on account of women turn up their noses at tungs oil and mustache wax. Mrs. Dibbles still keeps some shoe hooks that nobody wants, 'cause nobody 'cept old grannies wears those kinda shoes anymore. She dusts it off every week, even when no dust is settled there. That's the way women are; always cleaning stuff that's not even dirty. The whole place smells like lemons and Murphy's Oil Soap, plus some fruity sugar smells laying underneath it all, drifting over from the candy counter.

The next aisle over is men's stuff: pocket knives and tobacco, and mustache wax, and shaving soap. Lots of stuff that smells real good and makes me remember when we first moved to Vermillia Street. But, nothin' new. Like usual.

We head on over to the magazines and newspapers. Dallas takes the look-out first, so I can peak under the cover of *LOOK* and see if those crazy guys in the city are still sitting on the flagpole, which they'd been doing for more than a week.

Ephraim picks up the January 14 Time, which is more than a month old, and just like always, looking for stuff about Benny Goodman and Al Jolson, and other bands that he's crazy about. Instead, he finds a peculiar story comparing our government to oysters. I guess, on account of oysters make a lot of little oysters, and Representatives make a lot of bills, that never get talked about. Anyways, Ephraim thought it was funny enough to crack a grin. I did, too, but now for the life of me, the reason flits away from me.

Ephraim is hell-bent on going to Chicago and getting in one of those bands, or just playing at a saloon. I never told Mama or Daddie about that 'cause knowing them, Daddie would be bringing the Bible over to the Moores' house, and trying to set Ephraim straight. He's got enough of that from his own Ma and Popi, he doesn't need my Daddie piping in.

"Hey," says Dallas from down at the end of the aisle, where he's standing look-out. Dallas doesn't exactly say it; he more like coughs it out, so's we hear, and so's Mr. Dibble is none the wiser.

That's our signal to snap the magazines shut. I grab *LIFE* for Mama and walk toward Dallas, like nothing is unusual. I know I'm only supposed to open magazines after I buy 'em, but as long as I don't wrinkle any pages, I'm not hurting anybody. It's like stealing whiffs of fresh bread from the bakery. Anyways, that's what Ephraim says.

"Jeez," says Dallas. "Will ya look at that?"

Right there in the middle of the next aisle is a big pile of boxes of ready-strike matches, all stacked up higher than my head, like bricks, one layer overlapping another. Dallas is already heading that way, hitching up his left leg, looking more like Daddie than he even knows.

"Man-o-man," says Ephraim. His dark eyes are full of stars.

Ephraim tugs one box out, right from the middle, and the whole thing just stays there, steady as ever; that's how sturdy Mr. Dibble built that match-box fort.

"Watch this."

Ephraim holds up a match by the stick and flits off the white tip.

Phphphttttt. Sulfur fills up my nose and I see the flame turns yellow then red, then yellow again, with blue in the center. Time seems almost to turn backwards; it goes that slow. Ephraim gives the match a shake, and all that's left is the black ash end of the match, which he spits on and puts in his pocket.

I look around quick for Mr. Dibble. I can feel my heart pounding and my legs are ready to hightail it outta there, 'cause for sure Mr. Dibble can smell that sulfur still hanging heavy in the air, but I don't wanna be the first to dash, 'cause then Dallas and Ephraim will call me chicken.

Dallas pulls a face I'm trying to understand: he looks like he's going to bust out laughing. At the same time, the tips of his ears are redder than red and his neck is peppered with red blotches. He pulls one of them boxes of matches so it's halfway out of the tower before he slides open the little drawer-like part of the box. He takes one match out of there. I'm just watching like I'm in a dream. Still, 'til now I can hardly believe what Dallas does next.

Dallas takes that match and sticks it back in the box, red and white tip sticking up. He closes the drawer up tight, so the match sticks out straight. Dallas quick flicks off the end with his fingernail, same way he saw Ephraim do it.

Phphphttttt. Hot sulfur fills up the air again, only this time, I swear, I can taste it. I don't even think, I just turn-tail and run. I can hear feet beating on the plank floor behind me, then I see Mr. Dibble at the cash register, looking all bug-eyed surprised and holding one hand up like he's gonna say something, but I just get outta there with LIFE still in my hand.

I'm half-way 'round the block before I think to look back for Dallas. He's slower running than a third-grader, and sure enough he's nowhere.

I have to go back around the corner, and there he is, holding his side, looking like he just run a mile instead of half a block. Ephraim is gone. Good. Dallas would've never done something so stupid without Ephraim there, and now here I am, with a stolen magazine in my hand, and probably just committed another crime too, even though I didn't start the fire, I was there. But I got no intentions of going back. I wait for Dallas, just hoping Mr. Dibble stays in the store, 'cause as long as we're on the same block he can see us and we'll stand no chance of escaping his clutches. I breathe a little easier, when we round the corner again.

"Hey."

Ephraim's comin' around the corner ahead of us running and waving. He folds at the hips and grabs his knees for a couple seconds before he laughs and slaps me on the back.

"I went around the block the other way, so Mr. Dibble would chase me instead of you guys. For sure he woulda caught up with you two."

Ephraim laughs that big wide laugh again, like nothin' in the world worries him, and I just have to laugh, too. Dallas kicks a stone down the sidewalk and runs after it to kick it again. He knows Ephraim's talking about his slow running. Still, before long, Dallas loses his hang-dog look. Nothing keeps him down for long.

"Hey, let's go to Torrey Rail Yard," says Ephraim.

"Hot dog," chimes in Dallas.

"Naw. I gotta get *LIFE* to Mama," I say. "For sure it'll get wrinkled and smudged, if I go to Torrey Yard."

"The words'll all be there, won't they?"

Ephraim pushes his shoulder against Dallas, and Dallas pushes back and grins at him. Shucks, I know they're going without me, which sorta makes me sore at them.

"I'll catch up with you later," I say.

They shake the dust off their shoes, soon as the words leave my mouth. I start to feel the cold seeping in through the bottoms of my feet. Funny how I never feel that when I'm having fun, running around, but soon as I'm all by myself, the weather creeps into my bones.

I turn down Church Street, just in case Mr. Dibble comes walking down Locust, which runs smack in back of the five and dime. He's probably back in the store, but you never know. I play it safe. All the churches and the Tabernacle are on Church Street, plus the houses of all the pastors. Shopkeepers and pastors all live right where they work.

Father Perotta is letting somebody into the front door of his house, which I heard is called a rectory. A girl or a woman, it's sorta hard to tell, on account of his big porch, and it getting late in the afternoon, and because women and girls got on the same wool coats and scarves this time of year. Still, the scarf looks sorta like the one Cecilea's sister, Theresa wears. The Tamarack girls all wear those things called babushkas, which are sort of the same as a scarf and a shawl all combined into one. I look a little closer and I'm pretty sure I see there's two girls. Maybe that's Cecilea's other sister, Margaret.

'Course that gets me thinking again about what Dallas and Ephraim and I did. Ephraim says nobody got hurt, so nothing to worry about. Nobody even knows 'cept us. None of us are planning to blab. I still feel bad. Plus, the whole thing keeps popping back in my head, making me wonder, and making me feel bad at the same time.

Back at the Taylors', I hand Mama her magazine. She's in the kitchen, doing the ironing. I'm never getting content with her and Daddie and Itsy-Bets living there. I tell Mama I gotta get back over to the Moores' and get my chores done, so I have no time to stick around and look at *LIFE* with her.

Mama's nickel and dime clink together so loud in my pocket, I tie them into my handkerchief. I say silent prayers thanking God that Mama forgets all about the Lemon Drops or the change. I try to take it back, 'cause for some reason, it seems wrong to thank God for not getting found out about breaking one of his commandments. No use in trying, God already knows my every thought.

On my way back to the Moores' I figure none of it matters anyways, if God already knows what I did, and what I feel. I get to wondering why He never does anything to stop bad things from happening. Especially since he knows about everything and is all-powerful and all. Maybe He gets a kick out of us down here trying to figure everything out that He already knows.

I get thinking about Pearl and Daddie's itch to move over by Flint, so he can get a sure-fired job at the General Motors, and make cars, and how we'd be living on Easy Street before a year was out. I suppose somebody in heaven is getting a big laugh outta that one.

Chapter 6
Reverend Zollar

I start to hate Wednesday. It's hard enough going to church every Sunday and hearing about hell and damnation with all the stuff I did and the other stuff I just thought about doing, and figuring that even if nobody found out, God knew, 'cause God knows everything. That's not even counting about what Dallas did at the Five and Dime, and Mr. Dibble never saying a word about it.

On Wednesdays, Reverend Zollar is reminding me what a wretch I am; Reverend Zollar and his Church of the Air on the radio. Daddie said I should be proud that Reverend Zollar was right here in our hometown and we got to help him build his tabernacle. Now Wednesdays, me and Dallas and Nate go over to the Taylors' and sit around their Stromberg-Carlson radio with Mr. and Mrs. Taylor, Mama and Daddie. Jeez-o-Pete's. Least we play checkers beforehand at the Taylors' dining room table. Daddie loves checkers. So does Dallas.

The Taylors' house is huge compared to anyplace I ever lived. They have a front porch that goes across the whole front of the house, with a rail all the way around, to catch someone from falling off. That porch is as big as the Moores' kitchen. It's even got a swing hanging from the ceiling big enough for two grownups to sit on and keep cool all summer long. The Taylors' have a whole upstairs with rooms and regular ceilings, not like where I sleep with Ephraim, up under the attic rafters, so's a fella can bump his noggin if he forgets about the low areas. The Taylor's house has a kitchen and a dining room with a light hanging from the ceiling, all separate, and a frunchroom, too.

"You planning to help out at the Tabernacle tomorrow?" Daddie sounds like he's asking a question, but I already know there was only one good answer, so I just say, "sure," and Nate just sits there on the floor, Indian-style, looking at the radio like he's about to see Reverend Zollar climb up on the pulpit. Dallas gets all serious about putting the checkers away, looking like it takes a lot of concentration, so he has no time for small talk.

"Can Ephraim come?" I say.

"Isn't he a Second Baptist?" Daddie says.

I want to ask why that matters, but I keep my mouth shut about that.

"He says he got baptized down at Flint River last summer."

"I heard those Moore boys play that jazzy music on the piano?" Daddie says it *pie-anno*.

Mrs. Taylor busies herself pulling the King James out of the buffet drawer. She settles down on the davenport with Mr. Taylor. Daddie already has his Bible. His face is all scowly. I bet he's still thinking about the Moores. Sometimes he's like that; he gets a thought stuck in his head and it just latches on like a leech between his toes. He doesn't like the kind of music the Moores play on the piano. He says it's devil music. All Ephraim's family can play the kinda music that just makes me jump inside, and I want to dance, which I know is a sin, but I can't help it.

"He can play with no sheet music at all," is all I say.

I'm glad *Church of the Air* is announced on the radio. All this time, Nate just sits there still cross-legged on the floor, looking at the radio, quiet, like he hears nothin' but Reverend Zollar.

Reverend Zollar booms out of the radio. *If someone is given the gift of speaking in unknown tongues, he should pray also for the gift of knowing what he has said, so that he can tell people afterwards, plainly.* Daddie forgets about Ephraim and opens his King James to 1 Corinthian 14, just like

Reverend Zollar tells him to. Itsy-Bets is sitting down by Mama's feet playing with the sock monkey that Mama rescued from Vermillia Street. Even Itsy-Bets knows to get quiet when Reverend Zollar is on the radio. Mama's going heel-toe in the rocker while she embroiders, pulling the thread tight, then worrying it looser, not saying a word, same as Nate, 'cept Mama's lips are puckering and relaxing like she's having a silent conversation. Seems to me she's holding in some thoughts she wants to keep all to herself. Dallas sits down on the davenport with Mr. and Mrs. Taylor and crosses one leg over the other, making himself take up as little room as he can.

Daddie rubs his knee, which causes Mama to get up and tuck an afghan tight over his lap. She moves the lamp a little closer to him, real quiet-like, so he can keep his finger marking his place in Corinthians. Still, Daddie's breath comes out in a little puff and he pulls his eyebrows together all the while his finger underlines his place in the Bible. Mama lets out a long breath, before she clamps her lips together again and turns her head toward me. I look over at Dallas, 'cause I don't want Mama to see me watching her and when I peek back she's concentrating on the French knots that make up the center of her daisies in the dust cover she's embroidering.

As smooth as butter, a belly-vibrating voice calls out from the Stromberg: *Come to the Lincoln Park Free Methodist Church on Church Street on Thursday afternoon. Prayer service to feed the soul and food to feed the body*

Daddie doesn't work on Thursdays anymore, so for sure me and Dallas and probably Nate will be over there helping out with the soup kitchen. This gets me thinking about Cecilea, 'cause maybe she'll be there with her father. Lots of farmers come over to Reverend Zollar's Tabernacle, which is the same as the Lincoln Park Free Methodist Church, only faster to say. Even Cat-licker farmers like Cecilea's father help out. Maybe she'll bring over a bucket of buttermilk, like last time. That gets me thinking about Cecilea and her hair, just the same color as chestnuts, with wheat strands coming out of her bow all around her face which is so white, no freckles at all like me and Dallas have; her skin just as smooth as one of Itsy-Bets's china dolls.

"You seem flushed son. Are you feelin' alright?" Daddie says, which makes me jump, 'cause I'm thinkin' so hard about Cecilea and how I half want her to be at the Tabernacle and half hope she stays at home with her mother, so I can just think about talking to her and don't really have to.

"I'm okay. Just thinking about those hobos down at the Torrey Yard."

Partly that's true, on account of the Taylor house is filled up with the smell of bean soup they had for supper. At the Moores', we just had milk toast again tonight. Mrs. Moore sprinkles a little brown sugar on top, so I tell myself I am the luckiest guy in the world, eating nothing but pudding for supper. Now with that bean soup smell sticking up there to my nose-hairs, I get hungry all over again.

Dallas pipes right in then, 'cause now he has something to say.

"You shoulda seen them, Daddie. We was playing Robin Hood, in one of them rail cars on the side rail. Not the main rail, we don't play in those cars."

Dallas shoots me a sideways look, sending me a signal. I have to hand it to Dallas, he keeps pretty quiet, but when he does talk, he knows how to tell a straight story, so he stays outta any trouble. Maybe he is thinking on just how to tell his story all that time he is keeping quiet.

"Did those men have anything to eat with them?" Mama says.

"I didn't see anything," I say. "Most didn't even have a bundle with them. Just a whole lot of nothing."

"One guy asked if there was any work around here, and I told him the Shop was down to three days a week, just to keep people out of the bread line," Dallas says, uncrossing his legs and bending forward to face Daddie.

His eyes get all sparkly, like he's talking about a newsreel at the Palace theatre, not some real people.

"One of 'em told me his name. Quinn O'Brien, he's from Pittsburgh, like the Moores. Mr. O'Brien said he had to leave his two boys and wife with neighbors, 'cause of losing his job at the foundry and that reminded me of what it was like after the fire, and made me want to cry for that guy, 'cause at least after the fire no one had to leave town. We are all close by, even if we are all split up in other folks' homes, wearin' other people's hand-me-downs, and Daddie still has a job, even if it is just three days a week. So we all get to see each other almost any time we want."

Mrs. Taylor breaks in right then, "It's no trouble. Your mama helps out with the cleaning and the wash. You're not obliged to us. Not a bit."

Mama looks up from her embroidery and nods at Mrs. Taylor. "Still, and all, we thank God for your charity."

"No charity involved," says Mrs. Taylor. "You're helping us as much as we're helping you."

"You're a good woman."

"I think Mr. O'Brien mighta originally been from Saskatchewan, like you, Daddie," Nate says.

"What makes you think that?"

"He says his words different, kinda the way you do. Plus he calls a davenport a chesterfield. Ephraim talks different too, 'cause he's from Pittsburgh, but his is a different kind of different."

That makes everybody give a chuckle.

"Now, how do I talk different than you?" Daddie says 'yoose,' and never even notices.

"He says 'cleeerly' making the word sound like a bell ringing. That's same as you," Nate says.

Mama smiles.

"That's the way the word is supposed to sound," Daddie says, pronouncing both parts of 'supposed' instead of saying 's'posed' like everybody else. Everybody laughs at that, even Daddie, 'cause he gets the joke right off.

Dallas starts up his story again, like he never stopped.

"Mr. O'Brien last saw his family Easter, two years ago, but he's going to find work and send for them, he was sure of it. Most he could find was some odd jobs, painting fences and fixing shingles. That's why he was up north again, now that it was close to springtime and people would be needing a handyman."

"You boys go over there after school and bring whoever will come over to the soup kitchen," Mama says.

She looks up at Daddie just the same way she looks at me, saying with her eyes that she's not in the mood for discussions.

"And keep quiet about Reverend Zollar. They can find out about him soon enough," she says to me and Dallas, all the while keeping her eyes fixed straight on Daddie's.

Daddie stands up, takes a step out away from his chair, with his eyes still on Mama like he wants to say something and deciding whether it's worth it. He stoops over and picks up the afghan that's puddled down around his feet, 'cause he forgot all about it when he stood up.

"You boys want some apple pie?" Mrs. Taylor says.

I start to say yes, then I remember what Mama taught me about manners.

"I'm awful full from supper," I say.

"Maybe me and Eldie can share a piece" says Dallas.

"Not me," says Nate. "I'm stuffed to the gills from supper."

He must remember how that probably sounds like he's bragging about his good fortune over at the Dibbles 'cause right away he adds in how Mrs. Dibble can make beans into a meatloaf like nobody's business and says he can hardly tell the difference.

"The apples are getting old anyways, so I had to bake them up. You boy's be doing me a favor by eating some."

"Well, you boys better get to sleep," is all Daddie says. That ends it. No pie for any of us.

Dallas and me and Nate get our coats and hats on and get ready to head out. That thing about March coming in like a lion, never says how long March will stay like a lion. Sometimes it roars all month long. I start thinking about Daddie and why he keeps mum to what Mama says, even though I can practically see the words trying to slip out between his teeth.

Ephraim's Ma and Popi are all the time yelling and hollering at each other. That house is full of people arguing and bickering. It's full of music and singing, too, with Ephraim and Popi singing like Al Jolson, and one of them a-banging away at the upright piano. I never told Mama, but Popi smokes cigarettes, too, and taught me how to play Rummy. Those things will send a person right to hell according to Daddie, but Ephraim's father says they've been 'washed in the blood of the lamb.' They've been saved, and there's no undoing it.

Mama comes over to bless us before we get outside. She puts her open hand on Nate's forehead for a few minutes, then mine, then Dallas's. Mama never says anything out loud the way Daddie and Reverend Zollar do, or the way Popi or Ma do. She just keeps quiet and still. Pretty soon, I'm feeling quiet and still, too. I guess it's the same for Nate and Dallas, 'cause we stay quiet all the way to the Dibbles' and we say good-night to Nate.

"Remember the last time we helped at the soup kitchen?" Dallas says to me as we walk back to the Moores'.

"Yeah. Those kids were so hungry they gnawed on the bread soon as they got outside, before they even got home."

"Daddie says we gotta count our blessings."

"We'll be back together sooner than you can say Jack Sprat could eat no fat," Dallas says to me. I just shrug, 'cause even though it's been almost a year and a half since the fire, some day he'll be right.

Dallas heads on over to the Pedersons' and I walk up the sidewalk to the Moores' house. Warm yellow light spills out of the windows, and I see Ephraim and his folks moving around inside like black cutouts, no features or smiles or nothing. Still, the way they move is happy and full of life. I think about both of our houses, when we were all in one place, and how me and Dallas and Nate all slept together. I'd get curled up in a ball and try not to move, so as not to touch another cold section of sheet, and Dallas put his back up against mine, taking some of my heat. I swear he has cold blood in his veins. Nate just splayed out all over the place, like he never even knew he was sharing.

My mind starts racing about Reverend Zollar and the Tabernacle he's building and Mr. Dibble and how he never said a thing to me about *LIFE* or that fire Dallas started. I'm pretty sure he knows who did it, 'cause there was nobody in the store but us. I heard Daddie say that Mr. Dibble was lucky the whole place didn't burn down and so much for safety matches. Then I start thinking about our house fire on Vermillia Street, and how Itsy-Bets wandered off and I tried so hard to help Mama put it out, and maybe we'd still live there if Daddie hadn't been working third shift.

I start thinking about how if I still lived on Vermillia, I would never have met Ephraim or Cecilea, and that gets me thinking maybe it's a good thing our house burned. I feel bad all over again.

Chapter 7
Remembering Pearl

Dallas says I have a made-up memory. That's because I can remember things from when I was two years old. He says I never even knew how to talk back then. It's just 'cause his memory is so poor, 'cept for things like poems and stuff. I save my memory for important stuff. Lots of times I figure out why they're important later on. Other times, I guess I remember stuff for no good reason at all. Or maybe I'm just gonna figure out why they're important sometime in the future. 'Course, memory is a funny thing, the way other people's memories can mix in with my own until it's hard to tell which memory started in whose brain.

Anyways, two times I remember Daddie wanted to move away from Pearl. One time, Mama talked him out of it. I was two going on three. That's when we were all in the train station on our way to go live in Saskatchewan where Daddie's family lived. I remember that one because of all that slippery marble on the floor and the big clock in the middle of the benches and everybody dressed up like it was Sunday. Sunday clothes itch and make people sit straight and walk stiff.

Mama opened and closed the clasp on her pocketbook, 'ca-click, ca-click,' without even noticing, and her jawbone kept popping out below her ear. She still does those things when she's thinking hard about something. Daddie balanced his hat on one knee, looking straight ahead. We sat that way for a long time.

Daddie got up to study something on the wall. It was the train schedule, but I never knew that back then. Nobody told me where we were, but I knew from the guts out, we were somewhere other than church, even if everyone looked all serious and only talked in whispers. I pieced it all together later, after I got bigger and knew about train stations.

Mama jiggled the baby buggy where Nate was sleeping away.

Me and Dallas got off the bench and slid around on the cold floor. Man-o-man, that marble was slippery and cold as the Flint River. That's another thing that sticks in my memory. Even now that I'm bigger, whenever I'm in a train station, I want to sit right down on that cool sleekness and just enjoy it for a while. 'Course I never do. I'm not a moron.

Daddie came over and told me and Dallas to get up. He grabbed ahold of Dallas's hand.

"Let's go home," he said to Mama without even looking at her.

Mama's pocketbook went ca-click one more time, before she grabbed me by the hand. She handed Daddie her big tapestry bag and he helped her lug the buggy up the stairs to the entryway.

Daddie stuck his hat on his head, but it blew off when he stepped outside the train station and Dallas went running after it. Daddie and Mama laughed like that was the funniest thing in the world.

That's all I remember about that time. Sorta like the pictures Mama's Brownie camera takes. I never knew any of the particulars like was our house rented out or sold, and how'd Daddie get our little bit of furniture to the train station and back, or if he did. It's only now that I even think of those things. Anyways, I got the feeling that somewhere in all Mama's pocketbook ca-clicks was an argument to stay in Pearl, and her pocketbook won. That's the real reason we stayed put for a few more years. The whole rest of the hows and whys just got worked out between them with more eyes moving over eyes than words coming out of lips. That's the way those two seem to work. Anyways, that's the way it seems to me.

The other time, well, the other time, we ended up on Vermillia Street, over on the other side of the State. Pearl's nearer Chicago and has all the lake snow blowing over. Vermillia Streets got the same woodsy smell as Pearl, but no lake air swirling around overhead. Flint's further from Saskatchewan than Pearl. Still, most folks that lived in Flint all their lives have the same kind of slow tongue as Daddie: leaving long gaps of thinking before they say anything out loud, and making "no" sound more like "noo," and saying "sorry" like it's "sorey."

The day I first heard about Flint, me and Dallas were getting ready for a 4th of July picnic. Well, to be straight about it, I saw pictures of the factories in Flint, but the place itself was like something in my imagination, based on things I heard Daddie and Uncle Frank talk about. I was four and a half. That was the summer before me and Dallas started school, so before I could read a thing, only look at pictures and fill in the blanks with my mind's eye.

To tell the truth, I probably remember the day more because of Mama cutting my hair, and because of that darned Kiddie Kar. The one that pinched me like nobody's business, right in the taliwacker. That's probably the real reason the whole day is etched in my memory clear as daylight.

"There you go now. Let's get you dressed for the picnic," Mama said.

She blew on my bare back, soft as a whisper and the last of my hairs twirled to the ground like a dandelion gone to seed meeting up with Dallas's curls like rusty marigold petals. I never looked in the mirror back then, I just trusted Mama with her mixing bowl and scissors. Besides, between the hair and her breath blowing on my bare skin, I crumpled in a ball; tickling made me laugh like that.

Dallas already had his haircut and was pouting, like usual. He sure got down in the dumps easy. He leaned up against the stove, cold in the heat and damp of summer.

"Dallas, let's get outta here. Let's go play with Middie."

He started to say no, but I could see the wheels turning in his head, and I knew right off, he had an idea going. Just like now, Dallas got in the dumps fast, then watch out, some sorta fun pulled him right out.

"Okay," he said, then put one finger over his lips and looked sideways at Mama.

We got out the screen door before Mama even looked up from the pile of hair she was sweeping up. I knew enough to hold on tight to keep the door from slapping, and giving away our escape. Dallas grabbed his Kiddie Kar from the shed and rode it to the sidewalk. It was too small for him. His legs looked like a daddy-long-legs, which made me cover my laugh with my hand, on account of Mama maybe hearing and all.

"Let me ride." I said.

I grabbed ahold of the handle.

"Shhhh. Mama'll hear us."

Dallas scootched back, so's I could sit in front of him. We musta looked ridiculous; two of us on the Kiddie Kar. I was almost as big as Dallas, and he was too big. 'Course I was staying on, no matter what. We scootched along like that, kinda battling each other, Dallas pushing me up against the handle and me leaning back against him. We got to the corner and turned toward Middie's house, just around the block from us. That's when it happened.

"Owww. IIIeeeee, Ahhhheeeee."

I jumped off and held onto myself, 'cause the handle pinched me right in the taliwacker. Anyone woulda cried; even a grown man.

"What's wrong? Shhh. Mama'll hear ya."

"You pinched my taliwacker."

Laughing spit gurgled around in Dallas's throat and it would've flew out all over me, 'cept for Dallas clapped his hand over his mouth. His eyes twinked around 'til I expected tears to spill out on his face.

Middie sat on her porch swing, just behind her lilac bush. All I could see was her toes pushing off the planks, back and forth in a slow rock. The kind of swing-rocking girls and grownups do. That kinda swinging gives me the jitters. I just want to push off hard and get the whole thing pumping. Jeez-o-Pete's, what's the use of a swing going three inches to and fro.

Middie was probably about the same age as I am now, give or take a year or two. Lots of times she stopped over asking Mama if she needed any help. She came right before suppertime and left after Daddie got home. Young as I was, I thought it peculiar the way she looked at Daddie; sort of goofy, the way Ephraim would say it. I get a feeling in my guts she was thinking about Daddie, the way I think about Cecilea.

"You boys need any help?" she asked.

Middie stepped off the porch and skipped down her brick pathway to the sidewalk. She was already all dressed pretty for the picnic. She smoothed wrinkles nobody but she could see from the front of her dress and threw her curls, flicking her wrist back.

"No," I said.

"You said something different a second ago," piped in Dallas.

He gave me a shove in the shoulder.

"No," I said, and tried my best to land the stink-eye between Dallas's eyebrows.

Dallas swallowed hard, all the while his eyes danced like nobody's business. I saw his Irish creeping up. The color drained out of Middie's face and she kept her eyes on her shoes. She looked kinda sick.

Dallas threw his head back and laughed so hard that he was about to bust a gut, and there was me, all slack-jawed and wondering what was so funny. He grabbed ahold of me from behind in a big bear hug and shook me right off my feet. My hands snapped away from my pants. That's when I realized I was holding onto myself. Middie started to giggle as she knelt on the sidewalk and circled her arms around both of us.

Whenever I think of Middie, I think of sugar cookies. That's the way she smelled and her hugs were the warmest 'cept for Mama's. I bet Middie tasted like sugar cookies. Sometimes I just wanted to taste her neck just to see if I was right. 'Course I knew better than to do such a fool-headed thing as nibble a person. I was no baby.

"Does your Ma know you're here?" Middie asked.

"We want to play," Dallas said.

"Well, she'll be getting worried."

Middie smoothed down her dress again and with one finger pushed her hair behind her ear. "Let's get you home."

She jumped up and fluffed her dress out away from her legs. Her dress had two circles of dirt about knee high from where she had knelt and hugged us.

I climbed on the Kiddie Kar and headed back to our house. Dallas had to get on too, which started the trouble all over again. I pushed back at Dallas.

"Get off. There's not enough room."

"Worried about your taliwacker?" Dallas whispered in my ear.

I shoved my elbow hard into his stomach. He jumped off the Kiddie Kar, catching one leg in my armpit. We both tipped over on the sidewalk. He lay there, tears and dust mixing together on his face. Cry-baby.

"Dallas what are you doing to Eldie? I'm gonna tell your Ma." Middie's face went from sick-pale to redder than red.

"I didn't do nothin'."

Dallas pulled his face straight, but laughter boiled up out of him anyways.

"Eldie, come hold my hand," Middie said, helping me get up and putting the Kiddie Kar right again.

By the time we got back to my house, Mama was on the porch with Nate on her hip. He was just two years old. Mama's thin strawberry eyebrows were squinched together and her lips were puckered into her mad look.

"I was just comin' to find those boys," she said, looking at Middie.

Mamma's voice was soft. I knew she was mad 'cause she said every word clear when she was mad.

"What a mess the three of you are," she said. "Looks like you've been sucking on pigs." Mama pulled her handkerchief from some secret pocket in the folds of her dress. "Stick out your tongue."

I did. Mama wetted the handkerchief with my spit and scrubbed at my face. That one thing is probably why, to this very day, I keep my face clean all the time. I hated the smell of my own spit on Mama's handkerchief. Plus, Dallas's and Nate's spit most the time was mixed in there too, 'cause they were no good at keeping clean.

"Pull your face tight," Mama said. "You're like a lump of wet clay."

Mama started laughing with her head tipped back so I could see all her back teeth and that little hanging-down thing in the back of her throat. That kind of laughing made my chest feel all light inside. That's the same kinda laugh she and Daddie did when we left the train station and Dallas chased Daddie's hat down the sidewalk.

"What a sight we must be," she said. "Look at me, trying to get you clean like some sort of cat licking her kitten."

She put a hand on my back and pushed me toward the house. "Go on inside. We'll have to start all over. Dallas, get in there and take your clothes off. Don't touch me, I don't want to get dirty, too."

Everything felt back to normal.

"Do you want me to help?" Middie said.

"That'd be fine, but we have to make sure you get home in time to clean yourself up," said Mama. She put a hand on her round belly. "I hope this next one's a girl. I'm tired of these dirt digging' boys."

Middie looked down at her own dress. Her breath came out in a rush and her smile melted right off her face 'cause right then she caught her reflection in the glass of the front door. I remember that, 'cause up until then, I never even noticed she'd smudged dirt on her face and even on her neck when she was tucking her hair behind her ears. I guess I was busy thinking about her and sugar cookies. Besides her face, Middie had the kneeling-down dirt, and more spread around from all that smoothing and patting she did to neaten herself up, which made her messier. All on account of all the grime she picked up from me and Dallas.

By the time Daddie got home, all three of us boys were ready for the picnic. Middie was back, in a clean dress, sitting on the floor tying my shoes. I could do it myself if I wanted to. Everything was calm and quiet, just the way Daddie liked it after work. Mamma brushed a frizzy curl up toward the bun at the back of her head. She untied her apron and gave Daddie a hug, and the two of them looked right into each other's eyes for what seemed like a long time. Just watching them two like that always did make me feel about the same way I do having a cup of hot cocoa in the middle of winter.

Middie sat in Mama's chair fussing at her dress, primping at her hair, with her hands fluttering all over the place looking for a place to hide. At last, she locked them up together in her lap.

Daddie held out his hand to help her to her feet. I remember that 'cause it seemed so oddball. Middie was just sitting there on Mama's chair. Daddie never helped Mama get out of her chair. Anybody can get up from there with no trouble at all. Middie's face got all red again when she put her hand in Daddie's. Her hand looked like a piece of Mama's china next to Daddie's calluses. Come to think of it, Middie's hands were a lot like Cecilea's. So tiny and delicate looking.

"Why Middie, you're blushing," Daddie said.

He put his fingertips under her chin forcing her to look into his blue eyes. Daddie had his mischief eyes going. I suppose that's where Dallas got his mischief eyes; only Dallas's are brown, not true-blue like Daddie's. Middie lowered her eyes and moved away.

"Well, ma'am, I best be goin'," she said in the direction of Mama, but at the same time her eyes slid over at Daddie.

"Best be goin'," Daddie mocked and he stomped his foot in her direction.

Middie startled, caught her breath and laughed a short high-pitched tweet. She sidestepped around the table, pretending she had to get away from Daddie. He went after her, then switched directions and came from the other side of the table. Middie hooted, and reversed until Daddie did the same. Each time Daddie changed directions he stomped. Middie kept on a-hooting every time. They kept it up back and forth around the table until they both laughed so much they had to stop. Daddie stepped back, his blue eyes like stars, and Middie flew out the door, never stopping to make sure it latched behind her. I could hear her giggling all the way until she turned the corner to her house.

"You shouldn't tease the girl so," Mama scolded. "She's sweet on you."

Back then I had no clue what that meant. I just thought of how Middie smelled like sugar cookies. Still, that might be different than what really happened 'cause right about then me and Dallas started jabbing at each other, pretending to box, like we heard on the radio and saw pictures of in Mama's *LIFE* magazine. Nate grabbed onto Dallas's short pants and pulled, trying to get in on the game.

"Stop that, boys. Or we'll have to start over again."

This time the scolding was different, 'cause no neighbors were listening. At the same time Mama's honey-colored eyes danced away all happy. That's one thing I noticed about Mama's eyes. I can always see right through them into what's really going on. Her eyes can never hide a thing.

At the picnic, all the ladies laid the table out in one big potluck. Mama brought the deviled eggs and ham slices and of course the sourdough bread she baked that morning. Just thinking about Mama's bread made my nose flare out trying to sniff all that yeasty goodness. I swallowed a mouthful of nothing but spit, wishing I had a bite. 'Course I had to wait. Middie's mother laid out a bowl of apples and her chocolate cake. The apple skins puckered in places on account of them wintering over. The chocolate cake was a different story altogether. Mrs. Sterling's cake was everyone's favorite. They all pretended not to notice the finger track, which went all around the bottom edge in the frosting. Middie probably sneaked a taste. Auntie Laura brought the potato salad and some of her sweet breads. Auntie Laura is still in Pearl. Some other ladies laid out cherry pies made from preserves and a bucket of lemonade. I guess most of those ladies are still there with Auntie Laura and Uncle Frank and Middie.

Everybody made short work of all that good food. All 'cept Mrs. Sterling's bowl of apples. They just set there on the table looking like wrinkly old maids.

All the men gathered near Daddie's black Model A. Middie's father sat on the running board and smoked his pipe. Uncle Frank sat beside him and pulled his jackknife and a piece of pine out of his pocket and started whittling. He was always whittling, like he could only talk with a piece of wood and a knife in his hand. By evening, each of us boys would have a fine pine whistle to blow during the fireworks. Daddie stood beside Uncle Frank with one foot on the running board. Some other man, leaning against the back fender, crossed his arms. All those men worked at the screw factory, same as Daddie.

I could never remember every bit of this on my own, even with my good memory. Mama had just got a brand, spanking-new Brownie camera, and those men by Daddie's car were in one of the very first pictures she snapped. Daddie said it was a silly picture and a waste of good film. I like it on account of Mama caught all those men just being themselves with no one telling them to look this way or that. I remember Mama taking the picture, 'cause Daddie shooed her away after that, and that's when I sat down by Uncle Frank and watched him whittle. Curls of wood twirled down to the ground for a while. I was only four then; watching Uncle Frank made me sleepy.

"I'm thinking about moving the family to Flint," Daddie said to Uncle Frank.

"Gonna try to get a job at General Motors?"

"Well, ya know," Daddie paused getting his thoughts together, "all the screws and bolts we're making every day's going to Flint and Detroit to the auto makers. And I hear they're paying half again as much as we make."

"What's Ida say?"

"Haven't told her yet."

"Well with the baby coming, you might want to wait."

"What's that got to do with anything?"

"You know Birdie won't want to be away from Laura."

Right about then, Mama came over with Dallas and Nate and told me to come pose for a picture. She had Dallas's Kiddie Kar in one hand.

"Now, you sit up in front of Dallas. Dallas you get on behind."

"No, no, I won't sit there, Momma. It hurts my taliwacker," I said.

Mama's eyes got bigger than I ever saw. She clapped her hand over my mouth and stooped down to my eye level.

"What's the matter Eldie? Come on, sit on the Kar."

"No Mama, it hurts my taliwacker."

"Dallas, do you know anything about this?"

Mama looked Dallas straight in the eye, which was a relief for me.

Dallas grinned so hard his freckles squinched into brownish lines. He shrugged in a 'beats me' way. "I don't know Mama. He kept crying about it when we went to Middie's."

"Well, let's just take a look here."

Mama stooped beside the Kar and turned the handle back and forth. She put her finger up against the part where the front wheel joined the handle.

"Come here, Eldie. I see the problem."

She put my finger up against the space.

"I know how to fix it," she said to me.

This time when she looked straight in my eyes, it felt good.

She took her Sunday handkerchief, the one with all the embroidery, from the secret fold in her dress and tied it around the shaft of the Kiddie Kar, close to the washer. She knotted little bunny hears and faced them toward the seat.

"Here now. Don't get too close to the bunny ears. That bunny will bite. If you don't get too close, you can ride just fine."

Mama is pretty smart for a lady. I trust her, she's never lied to me before or since. Plus, she put Nate on first and me right behind him. Dallas stood behind me 'cause there was no room for him on the Kiddie Kar with me and Nate taking up all the space. Come to think of it, that might be another reason I felt a lot better about sitting there.

Mama snapped a picture of us three brothers with her Brownie. That's the one picture she saved from the fire. I wish she would have saved the one of Daddie's car and Uncle Frank, and all those men instead, on account of I hate the picture of me and Dallas and Nate. Of course it reminds me of getting my taliwacker pinched, but there's another thing I hate even more. Mama's haircuts made the three of us look like the Three Stooges, only no one was bald like Curly. Me, I look just like Moe, only my hair is lighter. Dallas's Larry, only his copper hair is just wavy, not going every-which-a-way and big. Nate's chubby cheeks could be a baby Curly, before he got old and lost all his hair.

Mama had another baby boy, but he got sick before I got to know him much. Mama got real sad for a while after that, so Daddie changed his plans, and never even brought it up. 'Least from what I remember.

Maybe Daddie was right. Mama did get happy again, that's for sure. Especially after Itsy-Bets came along. But that's not what really made Mama happy again. That came slow, like springtime: a little at a time, plunging back into darkness and cold, then into warm days again, until a fella thinks Mother Nature is just messing with him. Then one day, all of a sudden, he notices it's full-on green and blooming again, like the sunshine and warmth never left at all.

Itsy-Bets was just a baby when Daddie decided a change would do us all good. Getting busy at moving into a brand-new house, with the insides still smelling like sawdust, can make anybody excited as all get-out. Anyways, we moved away from Pearl and everything I knew, to a place called Flint, and a street name that sounded like we moved to another country: Vermillia.

CHAPTER 8
REMEMBERING THE VERMILLIA STREET FIRE

I s'pose nobody that was there can ever forget about our house burning down. Even Itsy-Bets remembers it, and she was still new to walking, and not even out of diapers yet. Still and all, we never talk about it. I remember everything about that day, like it happened yesterday. It's like a movie I watch over and over. Only it's real.

I was ten years old, and in the 5th grade at Hope school. Roosevelt was our new President and he had a New Deal. Mostly, Presidents mean next to nothing to me. But that year Mrs. Tedeman–me and Dallas called her Teeter Totter, and so did Nate, 'cause back then he did everything me and Dallas did–made us have a mock election and I voted for Roosevelt on account of his "chicken in every pot" idea. We had plenty of chickens, because we had room in the back yard for a little coop. Still, mostly we ate eggs, not chicken.

"Why kill the chicken and lose the eggs?" is what Mama said.

She had a point, that's for sure. I gotta hand it to her. She keeps pretty quiet most times, but when she has something to say, it's something worth remembering.

"Mr. Roosevelt has a hard row to hoe," Daddie said.

"We've been lucky," said Mama. "That's for sure."

Daddie just laughed one of his big whooping laughs. He got out his handkerchief and wiped tears off his face.

"We've been lucky all right," he looked right at Mama. "We never had much of anything, so we never noticed a Depression hit us."

"Lew," Mama said his name like it was two syllables, instead of just one. She put on her angry-lips-together look, but I knew better on account of how she said Daddie's name. Plus, even if I lost track of that clue, the gold flecks in her amber eyes told it all. They sparkle and gleam like real gold whenever Mama's tickled.

Still and all, I was thinking there was something to this talk of Depression and the lack of chickens, because the number of cars on the train going by at 3:30 seemed to be getting less and less. Even back then, I liked to keep track of the train cars on the stiff grey cardboard back cover of my Big Red tablet. I did that so as to save all the writing paper. I knew long division since 4th grade and could do the averages in my head. Same as I still do now: average number of cars for the weeks in December 187; January 107, February 86. This month, March 142 in all, so far. Each week I add up the train cars that go by. Last month, February the weeks averaged out to 94, 87, 83, 78. Here's how I figure the average for the month: First, I do some rounding. 3+7=10 and 4+8 is 12, take 2 away so everything ends in naught. That leaves me with 80+80 and 90+70, so now I have 160+160, which is the same as 160 X 2, plus 2 X 10, plus the 2 that I dropped to make everything round: 342. Next divide that by the four weeks by going half, and half again. There you have it; the average is 86 'cause, there's no such thing as half a car. I gotta do that for each week first, and sometimes I loan or borrow a partial week, 'cause no month has an exact number of weeks. Anyways, that's the way I do it all in my head. It's simple as eating pie. Maybe I should say easy as eating milk toast, seeing as I get a lot more of that.

"Eldie. What is the capitol?" I remember Mrs. Tedeman rapped her ruler on her desk and I snapped to full attention. I hated Citizenship class back then. Still do.

"Lansing, Ma'am."

By 5th grade pretty near everyone knew how to listen with one ear. Besides, I knew Mrs. Teeter Totter was getting us ready for Michigan Week, so I memorized the capitol, state flower, state bird, and Governor Wilber Brucker's name on the way to school. Mrs. Tedeman sure did like government.

"Whatcha wanna do tomorrow?" Dallas came up behind me and slapped me on the back while I buckled up by books.

"How about going to see *The Invisible Man*?" Nate said, his eyes all dancing and happy as all get out; tomorrow was Saturday. The three of us could stay all day at the movie house for a dime a piece.

That seems like a lot now, but back then we were living high. Nobody needed to sneak into the movie house. We had our own Crosley radio, and a Victrola and Mama had a real automatic wringer washing machine. Daddie gave Mama a brand new Singer sewing machine for Christmas that year, along with a bunch of fabric for new dresses for her and Itsy-Bets. Daddie never noticed the way Mama's lower eyelids pulsed up just a little right before she pulled her face in a big smile and clapped her hands together under her chin, like that sewing machine was the best Christmas present in the world.

"So how's the train numbers going?" Dallas asked, making his voice go all serious and pulling his eyebrows together, so they touch each other. He tried to get my tablet loose, but I already had it pulled tight.

"Roosevelt's gonna give his inauguration speech tomorrow," Nate said.

Dallas's voice went to soprano. He curled his little finger as he twiddled a piece of hair at the back of his ear. "You are an astute citizen, Mr. Craine. I suppose you voted for Roosevelt in the recent election?"

Dallas mocked Teeter Totter by swishing his hips back and forth as he walked.

"It's a private ballot. No one knows how anyone voted," I said. "Leave him alone about it."

"Hey, let's go on over to the Kerschke farm," said Nate. "They've got new piglets already. I heard they will stay still as a kitten if you pick them up by the hind legs."

Nate was right. Anyone can calm a piglet down and make it cuddly, if he knows just what to do. I suppose a piglet could make a great pet: all pink and smelling like straw and milk, their beady eyes looking as intelligent as any dog I ever saw. Their hair's stiff and bristly. I can see why someone thought up tying boar's hair into tight tufts and fastening them onto a hairbrush. Pigs' hair, even on a tiny two-day-old pig, is stiff as wire and soft at the same time on account of all the oil in it is what Mama said.

Anyways, the piglets slipped around on their sharp little hooves, until one of us boys grabbed hold of a hind leg, and, hee-yup, pulled the baby right out from under the sow, with never a whimper. The sow nuzzled each of her piglets, counting them up and noticing some gone. She started grunting and pushing the straw around, looking for her young'uns. People that never been to a farm are clueless about how good a sow and her litter can smell. Pigs are far from dirty like a lot of folks think. I tried to cradle my piglet and pet its back, but as soon as he went horizontal he started squealing for his Mama. After all the counting and rustling about, looking for her baby, the poor mama sow practically went mad when she heard her baby squeal bloody murder. I thought for sure she would come right over the rail fence after me. I quick pulled the piglet up by its hind legs and that was the end of the squealing, which made the sow start rutting around in the straw again and just glancing up at me with her beady eyes. Maybe pigs can't see all that well.

"Sue-sue-suey," I said in a soft voice, 'cause I had heard Mr. Kerschke say that when I was out there with Daddie. Daddie was trying to get the Kerschkes to come to the Tabernacle on account of them being Cat-lickers and never asking Jesus to come into their hearts like real Christians and worshiping idols and all. 'Course Cecilea sets me right about the idol-worship part. Anyways she tries. I think I just about got it, then it all slips away from me.

I looked at Dallas and Nate, they looked at me; back and forth like three frozen idiots with piglets hanging from our hands.

"We better get home," I said.

"The sun's sinking, and we got chores to do," Nate said.

"I dare you to kiss your pig first," Dallas challenged Nate and me.

"I double-dog-dare you," I said.

I never passed on a dare, and Nate went right along too. Still, if we were getting stuck kissing a pig, Dallas was getting in just as deep.

Later, when we got in eye-shot of our house, there was Mama, on the porch wiping her hands on her apron.

"Supper!" she shouted.

For such a tiny woman, she sure could get loud when she wanted to. Mostly, she was quiet, though. In fifth grade, I was already almost as tall as Mama, but she was rounder in the middle. Anyway, that's probably why everybody calls her Birdie instead of her real name, Ida. I have her bird legs. I never thought about it then, but once I started living with the Moores, Ephraim started always calling me 'lady-legs.'

"Eldie, get in here for supper!" Mama called out again.

Mama tamed a free wisp of her copper hair. Same hair as Dallas only brighter. I admit it, I straggled behind playing with a stick, pretending it was a gun and I was on an elephant hunt like the white hunters, and Dallas was Johnny Weismuller's Tarzan. We tried to get Nate to be a chimpanzee, but he got mad and ran on ahead, which was probably half the reason Mama looked so peeved.

Daddie was home when we got home from the Kerschkes' on account of him working 3rd shift at the Shop. Daddie being home when she was preparing supper took some of the fun out of Mama; she looked pretty darn serious. So many pots were on the stove, you'd think it was Sunday. She bent over and pulled a pie out of the oven.

"It's a mock apple pie," she said all pleased as punch and red in the face. She picked up Isty-Bets and threw her on her hip. Nate was already at the table. He sure knew how to be a good boy. Me and Dallas got in the bathroom and washed up without saying a thing to each other.

"Don't forget your face. You boys look like you've been sucking pigs," Mama called after us.

Dallas and I had to stuff our fist to our mouth to keep the laughing in. Spit gurgled around in the back of our throats, 'cause laughter always tries to get out somehow once it starts bubbling around inside. I thought about Dallas kissing his pig and how me and Nate never had to, because we heard Mr. Kerschke coming through the barnyard from his house.

Dallas held his squirming piglet tightly under his arms and tried to hold its mouth shut. He closed his eyes so tight, about three hundred of his freckles disappear. Just as he was about to plant the kiss, the piglet gave a squeal like a maniac and wiggled free, smearing Dallas's face with pig snot.

"Yecht!" Dallas wiped the back of his hand across his face. That only spread the snot around on his face and onto his hand. He bent over and wiped his face on the knee of his bib overalls.

"Your turn."

"Uhn-uh. you didn't kiss it. It just slobbered on you," I said.

"Well, the darned thing sure seemed to kiss me!"

"I don't think her heart was in it though," said Nate and he about doubled over laughing.

Dallas took out after me. Dallas coulda whipped me 'til I cried uncle, I woulda still been laughing. It was that funny. Maybe all the squealing and us tussling around is what got Mr. Kerschke coming to the barn. Maybe it was just chore time. We never stuck around to find out. We hightailed it out of there. Anyways, Dallas never could run as fast as me, so he tuckered out and started to see the funny side of things.

"Boys. Get to the table. Supper's getting cold."

Mama's voice broke my thoughts and sobered me up a bit, but I never did wipe the smile from my face. I thought I'd be smiling for a week or more.

"Remember now, it's Daddie's birthday."

Mama said the blessing and we all ate bean soup and corn bread, staying as close to silence as we could get. No talking at the table; that was Daddie's rule. If we fooled around, we got sent from the table with nothing more to eat. We finished up with Daddie's birthday pie. I was stuffed like a Christmas goose.

"You take care of the stove while I'm gone," Daddie said to me, putting on his hat and gloves. "Get some wood in now, the nights are still cold as stone."

"Yes, Daddie. Happy Birthday."

"Dallas," Daddie said, "you are in charge of the Bible reading tonight."

"Yes, Daddie."

"Ecclesiastes, Chapter 1."

Daddie gave Mama a hug. He always did that when he left for work.

"Birdie, make sure he remembers," he said to Mama. "Don't let it slip this time." Daddie closed the door heavy behind him.

When I went to fetch the wood, the dampness seeped right in through my coat, and I wished I woulda put on a hat. Already, I could feel frost crunching under my feet. I brought in as much wood as I could carry and stuffed the stove full up. Not one more log coulda fit in there. Then I got another load, to be ready for morning. I hate going straight out in the cold from my warm covers in the morning.

Dallas got lucky. Mama did the reading and asked us to think about it. Mama never told us what the Bible meant. She said it was up to us to open up our hearts to it. I tried, but most the time my mind wandered off on something entirely different. I'm pretty sure that was the case that night too, but lots of times I think about that Chapter of Ecclesiastes and about things being for naught and man's vanity. 'Cause of what happened after that. Right there, while I was supposed to have my heart open. Right there, in all our silence.

BOOM. It sounded like Daddie's Model A backfired on top our roof. We all looked at each other.

"Holy smokes. What was that?" I said.

Dallas laughed and pointed at Nate, who had his ears covered up. Itsy-Bets immediately began to bawl. Mama picked her up and started singing to her, telling her everything was all right and shifting her weight from one leg to the other.

"I smell smoke," Mama said. "Dallas, check the damper on the stove. Is it open all the way?"

"It is Mama. I checked it when I put the logs in," I said, before Dallas even got up. "Besides, there's not an ounce of smoke in here."

I knew better than to close the damper. For Pete's sake, Mama didn't need to get Dallas to check up on me.

"It's open all the way, just like Eldie said."

"There's a fire somewhere," she said all matter-of-fact.

Mama sniffed at the air like a bloodhound and the rest of us did the same. Even Itsy-Bets tried sniffing, but she kept her mouth open and sucked through her baby teeth instead. Mama set Itsy-Bets down in her highchair and walked outside.

"Maybe there's a barn fire," she said.

She stepped out on the porch and looked out over the field behind the house. Dallas and Nate crowded around the door and peered up at the sky, as if they could see what Mama missed. No signs of smoke. I was in the doorway watching her run her hands down the sides of her apron like she does when she's trying to figure out something that's puzzling her. She turned to come back inside, hugging her shoulders like she just realized it was icy cold out there.

"Shut the door, you're going to give Itsy-Bets a chill," she said.

She said low down to herself, "I wish Lew could get a day job and be home nights."

Mama looked up at the sky like she was looking for God to grant her wish. Her eyebrows pulled together to make two straight lines between 'em right before her face pulled into something I never saw before. Her eyes got wide and darted back and forth in her head. Mama sucked in air like a kid does when the Reverend plunges him down in the icy river at baptism day. She covered her open mouth with both her hands holding everything back that might escape. When she looked at me and Dallas and Nate, her eyes stopped darting around, but looked sorta dead. It all happened faster than a blink, but my brain seemed to slow everything down, so I saw it like it happened one thing at a time.

"Oh, Lord! Boys, the house is on fire! Get out here. Get Itsy-Bets out here. Get some water. Get out of the house."

As soon as she spoke, the dartiness came back in her eyes.

I just stood there, for what seemed like an hour watching Mama run a few steps in one direction, then back toward the house, and then a few steps toward one neighbor, then toward another. She looked like one of our chickens after it's stopped laying and it's no good for nothing but soup and Mama chopped the head off, and its body doesn't seem to know it, so its legs just churn around, running blind and hopeless.

"Get out. Get out. Eldie. Move."

Dallas pushed me from behind with Itsy-Bets in his arms. I remember thinking how odd she looked being carried by someone other than Mama; her blue eyes big and bright, and laughing out loud, her hand-me-down sock monkey flopping in the breeze. Maybe it was the loony way the monkey bounced or Dallas's jostling her around sorta tickled her or something or just that she was way too little to know something bad was going on.

"Get the neighbors. Fast."

Mama ran back into the house, not stopping to find out whether we understood her or even if we heard her. Nate ran out with Daddie's King James hugged close to his chest.

I ran from house to house, my legs churning, my chest pounding, excitement and fear mixed together. "Our roof's on fire," I shouted as I pounded on doors. I pointed at our house as if no one knew where we lived. The street came alive with neighbors scurrying like ants in a ruffed up anthill, black against the flames licking at our roof and Mama's lace curtains curling out of the windows and blowing away in bits and pieces toward the heavens.

Every neighbor knew just what to do, like they did it before. Quicker than lightning, we had a bucket brigade going. Even though we had indoor plumbing and all, we still had a pump in the front yard. Mama grabbed blankets and bowls and dishpans and that one photograph of me and Dallas and Nate on the Kiddie Kar.

I never in my life will forget the heat of that fire and how hard me and Dallas worked right alongside of every neighbor that we roused, men and women and boys, all helping us; hoping they could save us. My face and arms got so hot, it seemed like my skin was gonna split wide open and my lips got all dry and they did crack. I licked at my crusty lips and the spit boiled right there on my face. My eyebrows and eyelashes singed off in an instant. My back got oily wet with sweat that the March air never touched.

Someone brought a ladder, but it was too late; a piece of the roof broke through and Mama's rose patterned linoleum bubbled and curled on the floor. There's nothing ranker than the smell of charred linoleum mixed in with burnt paint and scorched metal. Mama grabbed a blanket and started beating at the fire, but it was no use, the fire kept growing.

"Ida, stop." It was Mr. Taylor.

Mama looked like that Medusa person Mrs. Tedeman told us about. Red eyes stuck out of a charcoal face with her china white skin bubbling out in blisters underneath. Her tight hair bun was all but gone. Instead her hair ran in wild waves in every direction, her eyebrows and eyelashes scorched completely off and her face and arms blistered red with heat. Mama struggled to continue, but even that was useless against Mr. Taylor's big body. She stood there sobbing, tears making trails in the soot on her face. I saw Mama sad before, but I never saw Mama full-out sob like that before or since. It seemed like she would cry her insides out.

Mr. Taylor stepped in front of Mama, wrapped her in a blanket and set her down by the sidewalk. He signaled to us boys to stop and we walked over to Mama. A good thing he did. The kitchen windows exploded and what was left of Mama's curtains waved a goodbye with black ashy fingers.

I looked at the flames licking the cross beams. All that was left of the place where I slept and ate, and played. Mama's dress clung to her legs in ragged filth. She looked like Job's wife, from the Bible, covered in ashes and sackcloth. I looked at Dallas and Nate. Their hair was stiff with soot and their faces greasy black. Job's sons.

A scream like I heard once when I saw a hawk tearing apart a chicken ripped through my guts. My mind screeched to a halt and emptied out of all thoughts. I never ever had that happen before or since. It was like someone got in and wiped it clean with one of those erasers for the blackboard. That's why it took me forever to register it was Mama screaming, up on her feet, blanket in a puddle around her ankles. She stood there screaming like that 'til she ran out of breath, then she took off running toward the house. She would have run right inside, if Mr. Taylor hadn't grabbed a-hold of her.

"Elizabeth," she called out, her arms reaching toward the house. "Where's Elizabeth?"

Dallas and I got on our feet and started looking around like we got hit with a hot poker. My mind reeled trying to come up with who Mama was looking for. I'm telling you, the gears were pretty near frozen by her scream, but after what seemed like forever, the wheels started to turn. Itsy-Bets. God Almighty. Where was Itsy-Bets? I felt like somebody reached down my throat and tried to pull my stomach out. I hope to high heavens I never have that feeling again.

"Mama," said Dallas. "Mama. Simmer down, Mama. She's not in the house. I took her out myself."

Dallas put his hand on Mama's arm, calm as a cucumber like Daddie liked to say. I gotta hand it to Dallas; it worked. Mama's wild eyes settled in on Dallas. I heard her suck in a slow breath and hold it before she let it back out even slower. I could almost see calm wash over her. Her eyes steadied in on me.

"Find her," she said.

"We will."

Of course we did. Me and Dallas and Nate set out to find her. Panic kept creeping up out of my stomach and into my throat. I pushed it down by remembering Mama's face.

"Where could she be?" Dallas's throat cracked out the words.

"How should I know. Last time I saw her, you had her."

"I sat her down with you on the Taylors steps." Dallas pushed Nate on the shoulder.

"She squirmed out, and that's when the windows shattered and I don't know where she went off to," Nate started to bawl and tripped on a piece of gravel on account of all the snot and tears covering up his face.

I picked him up by both elbows and gave Dallas the stink-eye.

"We just gotta find her," he said.

'Course we did. That part's history. It took us a while, but we found her. She was way over at Dibble's Five and Dime, sitting on the counter, sucking on a Valmik, face all smeared in chocolate, happy as can be.

"I figured someone'd be by to pick her up," said Mrs. Dibble.

She wiped at Itsy-Bets's face with her handkerchief. "Mr. Dibble's at the fire."

I felt my heart lift up out of my stomach.

"How'd she get here?" Dallas said.

"Walked, I guess."

"Holy Mackerel."

"Mr. Dibble was on his way to the fire. We didn't know whose house it was, just saw the sky all red, and we knew right away someone was losing their home, or maybe their barn. It's a pity. Seen it more than I'd like. Itsy-Bets was standing there right at the door. Looked like she was waiting for us to open up and let her in."

"I'll run tell Mama," said Nate.

I turned to look at Nate behind me. Cripe almighty. I forgot Nate came along with me and Dallas.

Back at the house, Mr. Taylor stood there watching Mama still beating uselessly at the fire, which was everywhere. He had to get people organized to save the houses on either side of ours.

I heard Mr. Taylor talk about the fire later. The neighbor women went from door to door, fetching the men, some with their boots already on and coming off their own front steps. I heard Mr. Taylor tell some fellas later that our house came from Sears, just like everybody else's. That's the first I heard of such a thing. I thought we practically lived on Easy Street compared to Pearl. A whole 850 hundred square feet divided into a bunch of rooms: a frunchroom, an eating room, separate from the kitchen by the wood stove, and Mama's and Daddie's bedroom. Plus, a tiny room for a toilet. All us boys still slept by the stove like always. Itsy-Bets stayed in Mama's and Daddie's room, like she was still a little baby.

Daddie never even knew the fire happened until he came home from the Shop the next morning. What a sight that musta been for him; thinkin' he'd get some breakfast and rest up for the next night, and seeing nothing left but char and chimney. I heard Mama was standing right there waiting for him all tidied up with a clean apron on she borrowed from Mrs. Taylor. That's just what I heard. We got shuffled off to sleep on bedrolls in the Dibble's Five and Dime back room until things got sorted out. As far as I know, Daddie never breathed a word about how he felt that day. Least-wise, I never heard anyone say so. He just got busy trying to set things right.

Mr. Taylor sold some fire insurance to Daddie back when we first moved in, so at least we could re-build. Mr. Taylor said that Daddie was a smart man to take out $1000 in coverage.

When the check came, Daddie went straight to the bank and deposited the money. Someday we were gonna build out by the Kerschkes' farm. Daddie already had the property paid for, he was just saving up to build us a big house, at least three bedrooms, maybe four, so Itsy-Bets would have a room of her own, and stop sleeping in Mama's and Daddie's room, and us boys could spread out upstairs. Daddie had the whole house up in his head, not one out of a catalog.

So many bedrooms we'd get lonely from the distance from us and we'd have to shout to hear each other. Mama had a big kitchen planned out, with one of those new gas stoves.

That was two years ago. We've been living apart from each other ever since. The Taylors, the Pedersons, the Moores, and the Dibbles all giving us room and board in exchange for chores and odd jobs. Lots of other neighbors offered to help, too, 'cause that's the way neighbors do.

Right after Daddie put the money in, the bank closed down. The very next day. The insurance money and all Daddie's savings, gone. Like it was never there. The banking crisis of 1933, some folks called it. A Run is what Mr. Dibble said. Daddie said it was just life, that's all. Nothing new under the sun and all is vanity. That sounded like Bible talk to me, but I never looked it up to check or anything.

Anyways, all of our belongings gone like that. Just the few things Mama grabbed up and carried out and Mama's sewing machine, which someone pulled off the porch right before it collapsed.

Chapter 9
Torrey Rail Yard

"Have you decided yet?" Dallas pokes his fingers through the slots in my desk chair and digs them between my back ribs.

I give him a sideways look that should be telling him 'Shush,' on account of I already got in trouble with Mrs. Bidrall once today. Besides that, I'm paying attention to Cecilea play the piano, while I'm daydreaming about a bunch of stuff I remember from Vermillia Street.

I went by our old place yesterday. Mama's crocuses are popping up all over. That makes me sad and happy at the same time. All that emptiness over on Vermillia Street where we lived. Almost two years on now and nothing left but the water pump out front and the chimney standing straight up, like it's accusing me of something, or at the very least reminding me of that night. All the neighbors there are coming and going, like nothing ever happened. Of course, they all know about the fire. No way of escaping that. Heck, most tried to help any way they could. But that's old news and these days everybody has their own business and troubles on their mind.

Mama's crocuses stick their yellow and purple noses up out of the ground, some of them straight through the snow that's left, all crunchy and fun to step on because it's been thawed and frozen again. I never will tell anyone out loud, but crocuses are about the most hopeful thing in the world. Faithful bits of happiness reaching out of the snow; they act like the sun's gonna shine down warm and welcoming. Pretty soon it will happen.

Those happy buds make me feel like there's something left of us there on Vermillia Street. That makes me think of summer and how much I wish school was over. Seems like everybody thinks that way, 'cause even Mrs. Bidrall let us take extra time at recess, and today, because it's raining, she lets Ephraim and Cecilea play on the piano. Last time she gave extra recess was Christmastime.

Mrs. Bidrall's face even looks less dried out and pruney since the weather warmed up a little and the sun's in the sky a little longer; even though some days it's winter all over again.

"Psst." It's Ephraim, bringing me back to the here and now. "What's it gonna be, Moron?"

"Yeah, I'll come," I say, quiet as I can. "Get off my back."

I look straight at Cecilea's fingers on the keys, even though my ear feels like it has a string on it, pulling my head right over toward Dallas and Ephraim.

Cecilea loves the piano. She puts her music up on the holder, sits up straight as a board, and places her fingers over the keys, waiting for some secret signal. Her fingers glide over the ivory and black as she strokes the music out of the piano. I can tell when things are getting tough for her, 'cause her eyebrows pull together so that one fine line points straight in the middle and down to her nose, and she bites her bottom lip.

Ephraim never uses sheet music. He just sits down and plays. His hands start pounding those keys and his whole body starts moving 'til his hind-end leaves the piano bench and his smile's so big his mouth opens up and all his teeth and the insides of his bottom lip shows. He looks like he's in a dream or something, but then he looks up and around at us and nods his head. It's like his music is talkin' for him and talkin' to each one of us in the language we understand. Pretty soon everybody's bobbing and clapping and smiling just like Ephraim, only nobody has teeth as straight and pearly as Ephraim, or fingers that move so smooth.

Cecilea's playing is more like a prayer, everything about her gets still and it's like there's nothin' but her and the music.

I feel sorta bad for Cecilea, 'cause she's mostly alone with her music. Maybe my pity's misplaced and she likes it just fine like that. Still, it seems to me like the other kids are just waiting her out 'til Ephraim plays. I can tell Dallas is, 'cause of him getting the jimmy-leg, like he does when he wants to hightail it outta there. His eyebrows pull down over his eyes, until I can tell his brain is way far away. To tell the truth, I suppose that's exactly what I've been doing with my mind over at Vermillia Street. That's the sorta thoughts that Cecilea's music coaxes outta me. I wonder if Cecilea notices. When she gets up from the piano bench, she smiles that sorta shy smile of hers, and touches her fingertips to her collarbone.

"Nice," I say, on account of the only thing I know how to play is the radio, and I'm not even that good at that.

Beside, when Cecilea touches herself near her throat like that and her lips pull up at one corner, like a smile apologizing for being so beautiful, my mind empties out of thought, so's 'nice' is the only thing I can pull out of my head, which I know sounds pretty darned dopey.

Cecilea just looks up at me, her blue-green eyes looking bigger than usual. The hollow of her neck gets all splotchy-red, and I feel my ears start to heat up. Mama calls that getting my Irish up, but Cecilea is Polish, and she's a Cat-licker, so it must be something else. I look away really quick, with my eyes the last thing to turn away. That's why I see her doing the same thing, like she has something to be ashamed of, same as me, which I know can't be true. That's just my own conscience working at me. I'm hoping Dallas is clueless, which I guess he is because his eyes are on Ephraim sliding his hind-end across the piano bench, getting ready to put his fingers on the piano keys and make them jump.

Most day, we high-tail it over to Torrey Rail Yard after school. I do like goofing around there. Especially now that so many cars are just sitting there, empty with the doors splayed open, sometimes off the track and dangling by one roller like a loose tooth. Lots of times we see a hobo or two, which is kinda spooky and gets my insides jumping. 'Cause right in the middle of a good game of Kick the Can, a low voice might speak softly asking if I know of any odd jobs around town. It's sorta like a mouse jumping out from under dead grass. Nothing to be scared about, but still the surprise makes me jump. After a while, I get jumpy just thinking about who might be there just hangin' out.

It all feels less spooky and more sad, since me and Dallas started inviting the hobos to Reverend Zollar's on Thursdays. Those hobos sort of remind me of the woman I saw back before the fire. The one who gave me my old dog, Butch. Someday, I'm gonna find Butch and get him back from the farmer Daddie gave him to; or I'll get another dog and the next one will be healthy and stick around and do tricks and protect the house and maybe I'll teach it to sniff out fires and bark warnings like those real police dogs do. My dog will be smart as Rin Tin Tin, and I'll know enough to give him a grand name, like Butch or Colonel or even Prince. I'd never name a dog Rin Tin Tin. Rin Tin Tin sounds like a bell with a bad clapper.

"I'm still keeping a tally of the trains going by, just for the heck of it," I tell Dallas. It's sorta funny how I can still see the train going by, even though it's a different school that when I started keeping track.

"Shhhsht. Ephraim's getting ready to play," says Dallas.

I get sorta riled at Dallas, but I can't hold on to it, 'cause Ephraim's piano playing just clobbers any bad feeling right out of a guy. I figure I can grab Dallas's attention better when school gets out anyways; besides, Dallas's head is all on Ephraim and the piano music fills up the whole school room.

After school, I dawdle around, taking my good old time, 'cause it's just about time for the 3:30 o'clock train, and I want to count the number of cars.

"Let's get over to the Torrey," Ephraim says, giving me a slug on the shoulder. He sure likes to do that.

"Hold on. I'm keeping track of the cars on the trains."

"Yeah?" says Ephraim and Dallas almost at exactly the same time.

All of a sudden, Dallas is interested. He acts like he never heard of my car-counting and he knows all about it. Man, Dallas sure as heck is getting close to Ephraim. Sometimes he even walks all loose-legged, like Ephraim does, instead of his usual hitch walk, so now he looks less like Daddie.

"Yeah, I got it all down on the back of my Big Red Tablet."

I'm watching out the window and counting and getting ready to calculate, right on schedule for the next train.

"See, look at these numbers," says Dallas.

The two of them put their heads together over the back of my Big Red. Dallas's hair is all pathed where he ran his fingers through during History and Ephraim's black, tight curls so dense it's impossible to even see his scalp one bit. Ephraim's father's hair is just like that only half white mixed in with the black, just like Jesus will be when he returns on Judgment Day. I mean the white part. Jesus's hair will be all white. Well, almost. Jesus's hair will be all white and like lamb's wool. Mr. Moore's hair is only headed that way.

"How'd you do all this figuring?" says Ephraim.

"In my head," I say. "It's easy."

I start to explain, how I keep it all straight in my head, but nobody's listening. Ephraim and Dallas are just poking and slapping at each other and laughing.

When we get outside, the air is cold enough that I have to keep my lips pulled down, 'cause breathing in cold air sends a sharp pain up between my front teeth, straight up to my brain. The one pretend tooth of mine, the one with the gold trim, looks pretty snazzy, but it sure is a bother in cold air. It sends ice-headache through my brain every time I let cold air in over it. Early springtime is the worse, 'cause sometimes I forget to close my mouth and I don't have a muffler on anymore to keep the cold air out. Same thing happens with lemonade or ice cream, only I got a habit of keeping my tongue up tight behind my teeth when I eat.

"Let's get outta here," I shout over my shoulder.

I start to run, staying careful to just breathe through my nose. Ephraim and Dallas get left in my dust just like I knew they would. Dallas can't run for beans, he's slow as Nate, who's faster than any other third-grader, but still, Dallas is the oldest; he should be able to outrun me. He's thin as a string bean to boot, but clod-footed, I guess. I can run faster than anybody, and I like to run. I can clear my head when I run. Besides, I know Ephraim and Dallas are gonna ride me about getting put under Mrs. Bidrall's desk today.

I wasn't doing nothin' wrong, just staring at the backs of Cecilea and those sisters of hers, Theresa and Margaret, sitting all straight up and holy looking. Ephraim told me Theresa and Margaret are going away to be Cat-licker sisters. They're gonna get all their hair shaved off and a starched white cap stretched tight all around, so they can hardly think at all, and they'll do nothing but pray all day, and only be allowed to talk one hour each month. I hope Cecilea will never do something so lame-brained, 'cause I'd never see any of what makes her so beautiful 'cept for her eyes and mouth, and never get to talk to her, 'cause one thing's for sure, if Cecilea could only talk one hour each month, she sure as shootin' will spend that time with someone other than a boy who can only think to say one word at a time, like 'nice.'

Right in the middle of me considering all that stuff, Mrs. Bidrall snapped her pointer down hard right across my knuckles and about scared the begeezers out of me. That's letting go of the part about how much it hurt.

"If you're intent on causing a ruckus," she said, "you might as well spend your time where no one can see you."

Mrs. Bidrall slapped the map pointer straight down, hard on her desk.

"Get under there," she said.

I opened my mouth to say, "What ruckus?" but she got one-up on me.

"No sass-back from you, mister."

I snapped my jaw shut and climbed under the kneehole in her desk. That was okay with me, 'cause about then, I wished I could drop on through the floor.

Just like most bad things, there was an upside, 'cause Mrs. Bidrall slid her legs right in beside me, like she forgot I was there. Her skirts smelled like the lavender sachet Mama put inside her stocking drawer. The only thing I could see was the white lace of Mrs. Bidrall's petticoat, slipping out from underneath all the black she wore: black skirt with tiny white dots, black stockings, and black shoes. I heard Mama call Mrs. Bidrall's kinda dress Dotted Swiss.

Mrs. Bidrall's shoes tapped, and I could hear her knees rustling underneath as she swiveled a little in that rolly chair she sits in. Her dotted Swiss sagged between her knees, as she called on one kid after another, trying to catch them in a slip, the way she likes to do. I put my face against the floor, with my hind-end almost touching the bottom of the middle desk drawer where Mrs. Bidrall keeps her ruler, but I still could only see a fringe of lace. I had an idea. I pulled my pencil outta my pocket and slipped it under her skirt, pulling it up ever so slow, so she wouldn't notice. I was just about to slip my head forward, when somebody came in from outside.

"I came about the text books."

Jeez-O- Pete's, it was Mama. What in blue blazes was she doing at school? Mama walked right up to Mrs. Bidrall's desk.

"I know we still owe you," Mama said.

I slid my face over to the other cheekbone. I saw the toes of Mama's shoes, then her skirt billow out around her as she stooped down and adjusted Itsy-Bets's coat collar. There was nothing wrong with Itsy-Bets's collar, Mama just does stuff like that when she's nervous about something. I pulled back a little, hoping she didn't see my shadow move under Mrs. Bidrall's desk.

"Let me check my ledger." Mrs. Bidrall left for a minute, then came back to her desk and I flipped back to the other cheek.

She rifled around pointing her shoes right at me, her dress floated around like it was hanging on the clothesline or something.

"My records say, paid in full."

She snapped the book shut, which sounded a whole lot like that pointer snapping down, just a little duller and thicker sounding.

"There must be some mistake," Mama said.

I slapped my neck around to the other cheek. All I could see was the toes of Mama's shoes; she was that close to the desk. I heard my heart pounding in the ear pressed against the floor.

I never noticed Mama's shoes had holes in the toes. From standing, no one was the wiser, on account of the black polish she put on top. Mama was so close to me, I heard her blow her breath out slow and even like she was blowing through a straw; the way she does when she collects herself. I watched Mama's skirt parachute out again, as she picked up Itsy-Bets, which was another thing she did when she was flustered. For Cripes sake, Itsy-Bets is five years old; Mama would probably be still picking me up, if she didn't have somebody littler to take care of her nerves.

I think about Mama and her shoes, and Mrs. Bidrall's ledger and her dotted Swiss dress smelling like sachet, and how her breath always smells like boiled eggs and cottage cheese, all the while I run toward Torrey Train Yard with Ephraim and Dallas disappearing behind me. All those thoughts going through my head, lickety-split, like in dreamtime, with a whole lot of questions attached. I wonder how those books got paid for, 'cause I heard Mama and Daddie talking about how could they pay for three kids in school with the year almost over and down to a three-day workweek, and what about what they owed Doc. I start thinking about Mrs. Bidrall and her white petticoat and how come she never told Mama I was under her desk for being bad, even though I never did a thing wrong. 'Cause for sure, Mrs. Bidrall knows I will be in hot water with Mama and Daddie too, for getting in trouble at school. Then I just start thinking about my pencil under Mrs. Bidrall's skirt hem, and how I almost got it lifted up and I feel my neck heating up.

I start thinking about Cecilea. Darn it all, no matter what I think about, it ends up I'm thinking about Cecilea. My whole body gets hot, and more than just from running. I suck in cold air that hits my tooth and heads straight up between my eyes. I have to stop. I never do make it to the Rail Yard.

CHAPTER 10
REMEMBERING HOW I GOT TOOTHLESS

There's Cecilea, just standing there, looking at me. I got one hand holding my side trying to catch my breath as I stand a ways off on the path. Me with my mouth clamped shut against the cold, my brain splitting in two. Pain stabbing up through my teeth like that reminds me about how stupid I can be sometimes. That, plus the plain fact that something can hit a fella out of the blue, when he's least expecting it. Like Cecilea standing there just a hitch and a jig in front of me.

Lots of the fellas think my tooth is keen, 'specially because of the gold rim and all. Ephraim is always asking me who I got in a scrap with; who knocked my tooth clean outta my head; and what the other joe looked like when I got done with him. I tell him to mind his own business.

Dallas was the only fella there when it happened. He's the only one knows what happened and he'd never rat me out. 'Course he might laugh his head off remembering it all. It was nothing keen like a fistfight. Thinking back about it, I s'pose it was a long time coming.

I never fought nobody. It happened right after Christmas, but it coulda happened any day that year. That's the year I got my first pair of long pants. That's the year Mama pretended not to notice Dallas and me lollygagging after school our first year at Hope, riding our wagon down Getter's Hill. That's the year I got in trouble with my old teacher, Miss Tedeman, for dipping Phyllis Smallee's pigtails in the inkpot.

I kept my hands off Phyllis's pigtails for almost two months. She sat smack in front of me, with those pigtail braids so darned long that they brushed back and forth at the top of my desk. A couple times her hair knocked my pen right out of the groove that holds it from rolling down in my lap. Plus, the hair sticking out below the rubber band looked a whole lot like a paintbrush. I kept thinking about dipping those brushes in my inkwell.

Miss Tedeman stood up front, pacing back and forth in front of the blackboard, telling us a pretty interesting story about Thomas Alva Edison, and how he never said a word until he was about four years old, and how he sold newspapers on a train, and that's how he went deaf, 'cause some guy cuffed him a good one right in the ear. Edison said that blocking out the noise helped him think. All the while, Phyllis's braids brushed back and forth across my desk, just missing the inkwell. Even Thomas Edison woulda been distracted.

I stared out the window at the leaves falling down all thick and yellow from the hickory nut tree out in the schoolyard. Just thinking about the smell of leaves in the fall always makes me feel relaxed. Walking along dragging my feet through a bunch of rustling leaves is about as peaceful as any prayer, even the ones you never say out loud.

Phyllis kept raising her hand to ask Miss Tedeman questions that she already knew the answers too, interrupting the story and making it last way longer than it needed to last. I started thinking that if I didn't have Phyllis's pigtails wagging in front of me all the live long day, I could probably think better, just like Edison without his ear working right. That's when I did it. I lifted up her braid with the nib of my pen and helped it over into the inkwell. I shoulda known; no matter how careful I was; she was gonna feel it. I guess my brain disconnected from my hands, and my stomach forgot to give me a warning lurch or two.

Phyllis whipped her head around so fast, the ink went a-spraying all over my desk and onto my shirt, and some even on my face. Everybody started laughing. Except for me and Phyllis, and Miss Tedeman.

Phyllis started to howl like a banshee.

"Miss Tedeman!" She whipped her head around to the front of the classroom. "Miss Tedeman!" Phyllis jumped up outta her seat. "Look what this little…little…little boy did." Spit flew out of Phyllis's mouth. She clenched her fists and bent over me, so I thought for sure she was gonna sock me.

Come to think of it, that woulda been way worse than what really happened to my tooth. I'd probably die if a girl, let alone Phyllis Smallee, had socked me in the mouth. A fella never wants to get hit by a girl. Jeez-o-Pete's. Still I sorta wanted to laugh about Phyllis calling me a little boy, like that was the best name calling she could do.

Miss Tedeman grabbed ahold of my ear and pulled me to the front of the room. She clamped her mouth closed tight, with her lips pushed forward, like there were words just behind them that she's holding back 'cause they're bad words, words you're not supposed to say. I heard those bad words before, but never from Miss Tedeman or any lady for that matter.

I never even heard Miss Tedeman shout either. She was quiet, like Mama, 'cept Mama never seemed to be holding back bad words; she just seemed to be thinking about what she wanted to stay. Miss Tedeman's quiet was more like one of those volcanoes she told us about with the steam and lava building up inside all quiet and still before, all of a sudden, birrrwhoosh, she explodes. When Miss Tedeman got in a volcano mood, her words were quiet, but they came out like steam hissing out of a teakettle. Even when Miss Tedeman's volcano stayed calm, her face gave away what simmered underneath. She had two lines permanently carved straight down between her eyebrows; the kind of lines only old people have, who are grumpy from rheumatism or some other permanent ailment and have a good excuse for pulling their face into a scowl.

Miss Tedeman whooped my bottom right there in front of the whole class. It hurt like the dickens, but I never cried a tear. At the same time, I felt my Irish rising up in my neck and face, and I felt like jumping clean out of my skin. I sucked in my breath and thought about Edison getting cuffed in the ear, and how that ended up a good thing for him.

After the whooping, the first thing I saw was Dallas all red in the face, tears brimmed behind his eyes and sneaked out of the corner. He turned away from me and looked out the window before he stuffed his knuckles into his mouth. It threw me off for about half a second before I understood that he was choking on a laugh.

Back at my desk, I saw why Dallas swallowed his laugh. Phyllis's neat dress back was all crisscrossed in blue India ink, like tree branches. The little flowers in the print could even be spring blossoms. It was my turn to bite my fist and hold back a laugh. I kept reminding myself what Daddie told me about getting it twice as bad at home if I got in trouble at school. He said he'd take me out to the woodshed. I never was out there, 'cept to fetch wood in for the fire.

"You get in trouble at school, son, and I'll beat you to a pulp when you get home," Daddie said.

He never did it. Still, this one might be enough to get him going. The only thing in my corner was Daddie working nights. For sure, a couple days would pass before he even heard about it.

I'm pretty sure he did hear about it, but neither he nor Mama ever said a thing. I took my time getting home that day. Anyways, as much time as I dared. Dallas and I went to Getter's Hill first.

Dallas and I were big enough to walk to school on our own. Like I said, that was the year I got my first pair of long pants. We told Mama we wanted to bring the wagon, so's we could give Nate a ride. I put my knee in back of Nate, and pushed with one leg, while Dallas pulled. That way I got to coast along and hitch a ride half the time.

"I'm not pulling you, too," Dallas said. He put one hand on his hip, like he was all grown up and in charge.

"I'm pushing like you told me to." I put my toe back on the sidewalk and pushed, so he'd think I was doing what he asked.

Getter's Hill was the best for pushing free and riding a wagon straight to the bottom. Dallas let me ride down alone. He might've just let me go because he felt sorry for me getting whooped, or maybe he got tired of walking back up the hill. He always did get tired out easier than me. Anyways, the day I dipped Phyllis's braids was the first day he let me go by myself.

"Hold the handle back like this," he said. "Don't let go." He showed me how to holds the handle steady.

"Do you think I'm daft?" I said. I got sore because he thought I never paid attention to what was going on.

"Okay, smarty pants," he said. "Off you go."

He gave me a hard running start and I went barreling down the hill. My stomach turned upside down, with all that speed and the wheels bumping along hard underneath me. At the same time, it was the best fun I ever had. Come to think of it, riding a wagon down Getter's Hill gave me sorta the same feeling as getting ink all over Phyllis's back. Only all I got was a whooping after the India ink disaster. Getter's Hill was a whole lot worse.

I barreled faster than I ever did when I was in the wagon with Dallas. Maybe he pushed extra hard 'cause I was giving him some lip about helping me. Or maybe it was just because all his weight added on to mine made the wagon drag more. I headed straight toward the white pine at Getter's lot line. I had never gone that far before. Plus, Dallas never told me how to steer or brake. I was so busy being all full of myself, I never even thought of asking how to stop at the bottom of the hill.

I saw I was gonna hit the tree. I shoulda bailed outta the wagon, but I only thought that one out later on. What I did do coulda got me a lot worse than it did.

I threw the handle forward. The rest went slow-motion in my mind's eye. The handle dug into the ground while the wagon and me kept on going. I was like one of those cartoon characters that gets launched up into the air and ends up splatted against a tree trunk with his body as flat as a pancake before it peels to the ground. Only my whole face slid down the tree trunk, leaving skin and a bit of my lip behind.

I know Mama pretended not to notice Dallas and me lollygagging at Getter's Hill 'cause she never said a word that day. She might've never noticed the wagon banged up, but my bloody lip and scratched up face was sorta hard to miss. She just got a pork loin out of the ice box and told me to hold it on my face. After that, she cut the loin into tiny pieces and cooked it with some leftover succotash.

"Well, I guess you won't do that again," is all Daddie said, when he saw me with a black eye and split lip still all swollen, even on Sunday morning.

I just nodded 'cause it hurt to talk, plus I had nothing good or smart to say for myself. He never said a thing about Phyllis or her braids or Mrs. Tedeman giving me a whooping. Mama never even asked me about the ink on my shirt. Maybe the blood covered it up some. Maybe she figured I had punishment enough. I never did find out.

I suppose Daddie should have been right. I was lucky I still had all my teeth, and my head was still attached to my neck. Least that's what Mama said. But I wasn't done yet. Christmas and snow was coming in a little over a month. I was about to prove I could still be stupid.

Back then, on Vermillia Street, Daddie worked five days a week. Still, he got to stay home all day Christmas Eve Day. Mama was out half the day, shopping. She had lots to do, 'cause Auntie Laura and Uncle Frank were coming Christmas morning, all the way from Pearl. It took half a day's light that time of the year for them to get to our house. Auntie Laura hates to be in a car at night, so they started out before dawn, Christmas morning and stayed until the day after. Uncle Frank slept on the floor and Auntie Laura slept on the davenport.

When Mama got home from shopping, she was so happy, I thought maybe somebody else got in her skin. She sat out sandwiches for lunch, all the while she hummed, "Bring a Torch Jeanette Isabella."

Afterwards, she told us all to get our coats on and she got Itsy-Bets wrapped up in blankets. Itsy-Bets was just a baby.

"Eldie, come over here." Mama wrapped a woolen muffler around my face, so I could hardly breathe.

Daddie got his big sled out of the shed, put Nate on top and reminded him where to hold on.

Mama put Itsy-Bets in the push-sled and Dallas took over the pushing, like a hot shot. Nate looked about as wide as he was tall, with all the bundling Mama did to him, and Itsy-Bets was just a ball of blankets.

Daddie said, "This is the best day to get a tree, son. Day before Christmas. We can get one at Getter's for maybe 75 cents. Tops, it'll be a dollar."

Daddie hitched up his leg and looked straight ahead before he gave the sled a big tug.

Mama's always fixing a poultice for Daddie's leg. I wonder what ever happened to his leg that makes it sore half the time and makes Daddie walk all wobble-legged, even when it's feeling good. I never asked him about it then and he never offered to tell me. Mama says it's bad manners to ask people about their troubles. People will tell you when they want, otherwise it's just prying and looking for gossip and maybe even trying to be high and mighty. Fellas ask all the time about my tooth, so I sorta understand what Mama's getting at.

Mr. Getter had the top of his lot all turned into Christmas trees. Except at Christmas, I sort of forget that Getter's Hill belongs to someone.

We looked at pretty near every tree until we found just the one we wanted, 'course mostly that's just the right one for Mama, but she pretended to listen to all of us, and Daddie pretended he had a say in the choice.

We got a giant Spruce for just fifty cents. Daddie was so happy it looked like he could skip, but he pulled his face all serious and grown-up looking until after he paid Mr. Getter.

Daddie's never that happy these days.

Dallas and me helped Daddie pull the sled 'cause the tree was way too big and heavy for just one man to handle, even if he had two good legs. My breath got hot inside my muffler so pretty soon the smell of damp wool took over the crispiness of the fresh cut pine. I hate the smell of wet wool, plus it chafes away at the tender skin under my nose, until I'm about to go berserk.

When we got back home, Mama sat out construction paper, scissors, paste, and cranberries. That's the first year I remember her letting me and Dallas help decorate the tree. She showed us how to make chains of colored paper–red, green, red, green–while she cooked up some popcorn.

Nate got bored and fell asleep on our mattress beside the stove. Nate was no good at cutting and pasting back then. Now, he'd be the star of that sorta thing. Mama sat down beside Dallas and me, and strung cranberries and popcorn with a darning needle and tailor's thread–six pieces of popcorn, one cranberry.

Mama cooked up some good sockeye salmon for our Christmas Eve dinner, drizzling some of the juice all over the mashed potatoes. I pressed my tongue against the roof of my mouth and sucked the flavor out of all that goodness until my stomach just begged my mouth to let it drop on down.

We never get salmon anymore, but back then I crunched the soft bones between my back teeth; my favorite part.

Daddie leaned back in his chair and rubbed his belly. A big grin slid up one side of his face. That's another thing I never see much of anymore: Daddie rubbing his belly and leaning back content as all get out like one of those *LOOK* magazines advertisements.

"Best sockeye I ever had," he said.

Dallas leaned back and patted his belly, too. He always did like imitating Daddie.

"You really outdid yourself tonight, Birdie."

Mama smiled, all big, before she stopped herself. Her fingers swept the back of her neck, sweeping her frizzy loose hairs up toward the back of her bun. "You should see what the boys made for the tree," she said. Mama nodded in the direction of the sideboard where the chains of paper and popcorn and cranberries sat like neat little nests. She got out her box of glass ornaments, which she must've brought from the bedroom.

"Can we have lights this year?" Dallas asked out in the air, not looking at Mama or Daddie. "I wanna have lights, like Middie's tree always had."

"No." Daddie says it right away, without any time to think it over, so I know he meant business, but Daddie offered an explanation anyway. "Remember, Doc Reeves's house burned last year? He almost lost everything. That's 'cause of those lights he had. The heat set the tree on fire."

Daddie's eyebrows squeezed the skin between them into two lines, the same way volcano Mrs. Tedeman did, when he said that last part.

"No lights," he said again.

I wished Dallas never asked, 'cause it kinda spoiled the happy mood.

Daddie brought the tree in after supper and sat it a bucket of sand before he pushed it into the corner by the radio. The tree looked so small on Getter's Lot, but now branches almost hid the radio.

All of us decorated the tree together. Daddie went out to fetch some wood for the stove. When he came back, he pulled an envelope of tinsel from his pocket. He gave Dallas and Nate and me a small handful each and showed us how to put it on the tree one piece at a time.

I got tired of the slowness of Daddie's way and I threw a handful of tinsel at the tree, trying to get it way up high. It landed in a glob on a low branch. Teensy ripples moved up along Mama's jawline on account of how hard she clamped down, but she never let a peep come out through her mouth.

Afterwards, snugged down on the mattress, Mama prayed over us, just like always, but that night my eyes were wide awake, and so was my imagination. Even Mama's quiet prayer-breathing failed to make me sleepy. I felt Dallas next to me fidgeting and breathing hard, which made sleeping even harder. I started thinking Santa would fly right past us on account of we're awake, which made me even more awake, so I kicked Dallas and he kicked me back.

Daddie sat up close to the stove, rubbing his bad knee. Mama was in the kitchen mixing up mincemeat for pie. I could see her working away, 'cause me and Dallas and Nate laid in our usual place keeping snug as a bug in a rug. The heavy scent of cloves, cinnamon, nutmeg mixed with the sharpness of orange and lemon peels. I sucked in the only-at-Christmas-smell of cherry brandy. My stomach filled up just from the smell alone.

The tinsel sparkled in the light from the kitchen and reflected the red from one of Mama's red Christmas bulbs. I hoped Santa would leave some of those orange candies that I liked to suck on all day long, like he did the year before. Those candies are still pretty near the best thing about Christmas. Raspberry, orange, lemon, and strawberry. Somehow they always show up. At the very center, they get soft and a little bit of juice comes out. I try really hard not to bite down, when the hard shell starts to melt. I can do it. Sometimes, me and Dallas and Nate try to see who can make it last the longest. My favorite is the one shaped like an orange. 'Course the flavor's not as good as real oranges, or even as good as Mama's jams and marmalades, but the sweetness makes up for all of that.

Maybe all that thinking about orange candy was the same as sugar plums dancing in my head. Anyways, the next the next thing I knew, I was waking up to Daddie's brand new Jew's harp vibrating out "Jingle Bells."

I saw my stocking bulging in the corner, behind the tree, but I knew better than to go for it. Everybody knows nobody opens gift until after church. My stomach jumped up toward my throat. How would I ever sit still through the service?

Cecilea says they go to church at midnight, Christmas Eve, and open gifts as soon as they get up, even before breakfast. Now that'd be the berries. I might even turn over to Catholic for that reason alone.

Christmas service is the one time Mama goes to church with us. That, and she goes to baptisms at the river.

Seemed like Mama pulled off her apron as she shut the door on the way to church and put it back on before she even took her coat off. The house filled up with the smell of roasting chicken with all the trimmings. Auntie Laura and Uncle Frank brought in the smell of frost and snow from their car. Mama had our icebox stuffed so full she barely had room for the ice.

Auntie Laura emptied her basket onto the sideboard; beside the mincemeat pie Mama made last night; she put down an apple pie, and stewed cranberries. Dallas and me and Daddie pulled the kitchen chairs into the frunchroom and our mattress got rolled up and tucked away in the bedroom, out of sight.

Inside my stocking, I found a Duncan yoyo just like I hoped for, and some of those hard orange candies, and for sure the raspberry ones Dallas loved the best. That's the year I got my Little Buddy Race Car, white, with a big R7 painted orange on the side and shiny red trim. Nate still plays with it, even though the seven looks more like a one and one leg of the R is worn off so now it says P1. He had it in his pocket the whole time we did the bucket brigade. Another silly thing that got saved and now that little car means something more than it ever would have.

At the very bottom of my stocking, stuffed way down tight in the toe was a real orange. One whole orange, all to myself. I stuffed the orange and the candies back in the stocking for later. Those little candies with the soft center and a whole orange to myself is still something I can always depend on at Christmas. I slipped the Duncan loop around my middle finger and palmed the yoyo. I'd be walking the dog in no time flat.

"Look, I got Little Buddy, too," said Nate.

He got a tow-truck, same size as my race car. Right away he tried to hook it to my racecar.

"No fair," I told him. "My car's not broken."

Nate backed away and started using the wood planks on the floor for a road, and pretty soon he's under the table, which Mama and Auntie Laura had all set up pretty for Christmas dinner, with the tablecloth that had the green tatted edges hanging down all around. I got down there on my belly, too, just for a bit, before I remembered I was in long pants. I was too big to play like that.

All that's gone now: all the good dishes, and the table, too, and the tatted tablecloth. Fire never cares what's special. It takes everything. Maybe we shoulda stayed in Pearl. Or maybe not, 'cause lots of folks lost their jobs when the Shop slowed down, because less cars bought meant less cars made, meant less screws and other parts needed. It's simple arithmetic.

"Santa left something for you behind the stove," Daddie said. "It was too big for your stocking."

I still wonder how Dallas and I missed the two Red Flyer sleds, one with my name painted right on it and one with Dallas's name. Now we each had a sled to take to school, like the other kids. I could hardly wait to get to Getter's Hill with my sled.

Something else was back there with the sled. Mama's sewing machine and a brown wrapper of dry goods just waiting to be made into dresses for Mama and Itsy-Bets. Daddie looked the same way he did when he got the Christmas Tree from Getter's. That hardly lasted a minute.

"Never thought I'd get a present that meant more work," Mama said.

She had her straight-lipped face on, and she made soft clicking sounds in the back of her throat. That's the only time I saw Mama with the same white-coals-simmering look as Miss Tedeman got. Still, Mama changed that right into a smile and a thank you as she stroked the bolt of fabric Santa brought her.

"Can we go to Getter's Hill?" Dallas always did know just when to get a question out so's he got the answer he wanted.

Me and Dallas took off for Getter's Hill right after Christmas Dinner. Mama looked sorta peeved at first, on account of Auntie Laura and Uncle Frank still being over and it being Christmas and all. Daddie got a Mama-melting grin sliding up over his face; the slow one that goes up one side, lights up his eyes, before it pulls his whole face into happiness. No one, especially Mama, can stay stern when Daddie's face goes like that.

A bunch of kids from school were there, too. We already knew how to steer a sled, which was mostly by leaning and some pulling on the crossbar, 'cause of watching other kids, plus Daddie gave us a quick lesson before we left the house. We steered clear of any kind of crashes. I'd be a moron to make that mistake again. Us fellas liked to take a running leap and plop down on our bellies to get the speed up. Dallas and me let Nate plop down on top of us, if he could run and catch us on the way down. His extra weight made us streak down like lightning.

We raced down Getter's Hill until it got too dark to see each other. I never got tired of sliding on my Flyer. Even on the way home, I ran and plopped down on the sled, just to see how far it would glide on the icy sidewalk. Dallas and I got a contest going, first him then me trying to beat where he came to a halt. If I won, Dallas tried to beat me.

That's when it happened.

I got a good run-up going and plopped down on my Flyer, but I was the only one who went flying. The blades of my sled stopped dead on a dry piece of sidewalk and my wool coat slid slick as snot over the Flyer's wood. I went airborne for a few feet before my face stopped me dead against the sidewalk. Dallas came running up to me, laughing his head off.

"You looked like a rocket," he said.

I tasted blood in my mouth and my lip felt like it filled up half my face.

"Man-o-man, that was the funniest thing I ever saw." Dallas split a gut laughing at me. He just kept on a blabbering. "You shot forward about six feet forward in nothin' but thin air, then k-blam. I never saw a fella stop so fast in my life. Your legs practically flew up over your head and made you do a flip like one of those circus clowns."

Nate never said a word. That's because he laughed so hard, he started to choke on his own spit. That kind of laughing is contagious. I got to laughing, too.

Only later did I understand I had a bigger problem that a thick lip. My front tooth started to throb like all get-out. Mama gave me cloves to suck on to take the pain out, but that hardly helped at all. After a few days, the tooth turned black, and Mama took me to Dr. Friese. I had to wait 'til the tooth went all dead and fell out. Until that happened, the only way I could bite a thing, was with my back teeth, and everything hot or cold or sweet, seeped in between my two front teeth and shot pains straight up between my eyes and into my brain.

The only way I could enjoy my orange candies was to hold them under my tongue, then suck the sweetness straight down the back of my throat. The best thing about that was no way could Dallas or Nate beat me on our "candy-lasting" contest. After the tooth got completely black and fell out, Daddie had Dr. Friese make me a falsie. That's how I got my tooth with the gold rim. Daddie said no son of his was gonna look like a toothless hillbilly, even if it did cost him an arm and a leg, and he had to dip into his savings.

Anyways, I never tell anyone how I got my golden tooth. I let them think whatever they want. For my money, the sharp pain it still sends up straight between my eyes just reminds me that some bad's gonna come into a fella's life no matter what. Some's gonna last for a little while, like crashing into the tree with the wagon. Others are gonna hold onto you forever, like Daddie's leg injury, like my tooth, or the fire on Vermillia Street. On the other hand, good things will do the same thing, like soft center candies on Christmas Day or lilacs in springtime. And you never can be sure which one is coming next. Like Cecilea standing right down the path in front of me.

CHAPTER 11
DOWN BY THE RIVER

At first, when I see Cecilea standing there, I think it's one of those figments of my imagination that Mrs. Bidrall's always talking about, on account of the pain knifing up between my teeth and through my skull, added to me trying to catch my breath with my mouth clamped shut. What was Cecilea doing out here on this dirt road to the Torrey, all by herself, looking at me, with her dress trying to escape underneath the hem of her wool coat, all pulled up tight around her like it's the middle of January, instead of near the end of March, with the smell of spring all around? I put my tongue against the back of my tooth to tamp down the pain.

Cecilea catches a couple of stray strands of hair and tucks them back under her kerchief and away from those eyes of hers. For some reason, that little thing makes my heart leap up in my chest.

"What are you running from?" she says.

"Nothing," I say.

I feel the blood empty out of my head and sink down somewhere under my stomach, 'cause the first thing that comes in my head is that night in late February when me and Dallas and Ephraim were out here by the Tamarack's house, and the second thing was lighting all those matches at Mr. Dibble's store. Funny how guilt sneaks into my lungs and tries to strangle me, just when I think I wrestled it into the past.

Right off, I'm thinking Cecilea knows what a bad person I am. Those thoughts wipe away the real reason I'm running: Trying to beat Ephraim and Dallas to the Torrey. I just stand there with my tongue practically lolling out of my mouth like an old hound dog, trying to think of something to say.

"I saw you running. I saw you all the way from the chicken coop," Cecilea says, which makes me feel real lame-brained.

'Course, she was talking about just now. I must look like a moron. I feel the red creeping up to my face and making me hotter than running can account for. Then I see she's got an egg in her hand, and I wonder if she's gonna chuck it at me. I heard Ephraim say he did that to houses of people he hated, back in Pittsburgh. That's back when people like him were flush with money and his Ma never even missed a few eggs and if she did, she just went out and got more and never gave a thought about people standing in bread lines, 'cause there were no bread lines back then. Anyways, none that Ephraim or me or Dallas knew about.

"Would you like to walk down by the river with me?" Cecilea says.

Her hand goes up to where I know those little bones are below her throat. Of course her throat's under about a half dozen layers, but she does it anyways, and I think about her Sunday-china skin underneath all those layers.

"Why not?" I say.

I look around behind me to see how far back Dallas and Ephraim are, 'cause one thing's for sure, I can do without those two tagging along making sideways remarks and jabbing each other in the ribs. With their two cents worth, Cecilea will think I'm a dope, if she even has a doubt left. Not a sight of 'em. They must've ran through the field hoping to cut me off, 'cause even if Ephraim stayed back with Dallas's slow running, which I doubt he'd do, they'd still be in my eyesight. The road between the school and here is flat as a tabletop and straighter than a barber's edge. Only thing to hide a person is the shadows of the trees.

Cecilea and I head out down the path she came on, which I know all about because it's the same path Dallas and Ephraim and I sneaked down a little more than a month ago. I just got caught up in all my rememberings and lost track of where I was, which is part of why Cecilea got me off kilter. 'Course if I'm as honest as I should be, that's only part of it.

The path winds down through her father's hayfield and past the pasture, which is pretty much empty 'cept for some new quack-grass poking through the ground and some violet leaves unrolling, and a bunch of stiff sticks of dead Queen Anne's lace from last fall. In a couple weeks it'll be all purple and yellow and green, and with the Tamarack's black and white cows tramping and chewing everything in sight. The place'll be peppered with brand-spanking new Holstein calves a-bawling 'cause they lost their mama in amongst them all, and the cows will be out here mooing low to their babies and throwing their heads against their stomachs, with a big old rope of spit landing smack on their backs. Daddie'll be sending me out here for dandelion greens. I feel lighter in the knees just thinking about all the greenness coming.

For now, Cecilea and I just walk, not saying anything. I try to think of something to say, but I'm empty, so I pick up a stick and switch at the dead Queen Anne's Lace and the new grass. Cecilea slips the egg into her coat pocket.

"I was gathering eggs for Mother," she says without turning her head to me.

She talks all hoity-toity like that, saying every syllable clear as a bell, same way as she plays the piano. Nobody ever says 'huh?' to Cecilea, even though her voice is soft.

"Oh," is all I can think of to say.

We just walk along like that, looking straight ahead, not saying a word. Sometimes she wobbles over my way and bumps her hand against my free one, or maybe it's me doing the wobbling; then quick, like there's static electricity between us, we both step away. I make a sort of 'sorry' grunt, and Cecilea says, "Pardon me."

"You talk so much when you are with your brothers."

I have nothing to say to that, so I just shrug and look at her sideways to see if she's looking at me, which she is, and that gives me the electricity feeling again, only stronger, like I ran chest-first into an electric fence. I start searching my brain for something smart to say. I'm still running on empty.

"My sister Theresa is leaving for the convent when the school year's out," she says.

I just nod. Dope.

"She's going to be a nun," she says.

I have no idea what she's telling me. I mean, I hear her words; they just make no sense to me. Least now I have a question to ask. In the back of my head, something Ephraim said is prickling at my brain.

"What do you mean, she's gonna be none?"

"No," she says, and I can tell there's a laugh underneath. "A nun. You know the women who wear the black and white habits?"

"I thought those were sisters." Ephraim's story about Theresa and Margaret going away to be sisters comes up to the front part of my brain. "Is Margaret going, too?"

"No." Cecilea looks at me; her eyes are the color of cool lake-water reflecting fall leaves. "I mean yes, sisters are nuns. But Margaret's staying here on the farm. Papa needs her help. What makes you say that?"

"Grape-vine, 's'all."

"You should wait to hear things from the horse's mouth."

Cecilea's eyes flash more green than blue at me. I think about saying she's not the horse's mouth, but I saw Daddie swing a conversation around to safe territory enough times, to know to tread in a different direction. He does it by asking questions, instead of offering opinions. Besides, I had so many questions popping up in my head, they just started spilling out.

"Why's Theresa want to do that? Seems like she already knows how to be a sister."

"She loves the Catholic Church. She'll be married to Jesus."

That sounds crazy to me, Jesus never got married when he was walking around on this earth, why would he marry a bunch of women all covered in black and white, looking like those penguins I saw in the National Geographic? I guess there's no accounting for those Cat-lickers.

"Why are they called sisters, then?"

"Because a nun's a sister to every person on the earth."

Cecilea seems so darned happy about her Theresa going to the convent, she just keeps talking about what it all means and when Theresa is leaving. Her eyes are back to gold flecks on blue-green again. I stop listening to the words and just watch Cecilea talk, her hand waving in the air, her cheeks all rosy, and her hair coming loose from her kerchief, fanning out around her, with the afternoon sun shining through it. She sure does look pretty.

I'm glad when we get to the river, 'cause now I have something to talk about. The river is all swollen and flowing fast, on account of all the snow thawing. Elderberry bushes are just turning pale green under winter's brown. The smell of wet clay and musty old cattails reminds me how alive this place will be before Easter comes along. Something about the smell of wet dirt makes me feel happy and hopeful.

I teach Cecilea how to skip stones. She's pretty bad at first, her stone making a fat kerplop right smack to the bottom of the riverbed. Still she catches on like nobody's business, and pretty soon, she's got the hang of it.

I ask her if she's ever been fishing, which she never was, so I can talk about that like it's a new invention. The sun dapples on the surface of the water, painting long shadows through the trees branches.

"Did you know my brother Nate caught a catfish in this river? He loved that fish and told Mama it wasn't supper; it was his pet. He taught it to walk on land."

"No," she said, just like I knew she would, 'cause nobody believes that story 'cept Nate.

"Yep. Nate even named that catfish, Whiskers. He kept it in a bucket and fed it breadcrumbs and little pieces of pork rind and johnnycake. Pretty soon, Whiskers learned how to leap up and beg like any dog I ever saw. He could even roll over for Nate. Every day, Nate took Whiskers out of the bucket while he fetched clean water for him. Pretty soon, Whiskers started following Nate on over to the pump."

"Are you fibbing me?" The flecks of gold in Cecilea's eyes sparkled like the light on the water.

"One morning, Nate went out to feed Whiskers and he was gone. Daddie said he must've leaped right out of that bucket and walked back down to the river."

"Did your Papa really say that?"

"Yep." I waited a second or two. I swallowed down the laugh that bubbled up out of my stomach. Nothin' better than a good story.

"Nate still looks for Whiskers every time he goes down by the river; he whistles and calls out 'Whiskers. Here, Whiskers.' He's sure that catfish will come back. Mama says Whiskers probably has a family and forgot all about Nate."

Cecilea laughs; the kind of laugh little kids do, with her whole body getting into it; the kind of laugh you know is real; the kind of laugh that loosens up laughter inside of anyone, no matter how grumpy. 'Course, I could barely keep my own laughing back, anyways.

"A fish with a family, now that's a good one," she says, and laughs some more. I laugh so hard; I have to hold my sides.

I bet my lucky Indian-head nickel that I never forget the way she looks sitting there beside me on the fallen trunk of the weeping willow tree, the one that got struck by lightning last September. Of course, I keep that bet to myself, 'cause saying it out loud would be just plain lame-brained.

I think I should get going. If Ephraim gets home before I do, his mother's gonna ask where I am. She'll be bellowing at one or both of us, that's for sure. I put my hand down on the willow trunk and my little finger, the one that doesn't bend proper, touches Cecilea's hand. Neither one of us wobbles or pulls away this time. I stay still, I don't even dare to breathe, and I think maybe my heart stops beating a second or two. I'm staying put as long as Cecilea does. Even if it means fire and brimstone from Mrs. Moore.

The shadows pull longer than long and both of us just sit there all silent 'cept for our breathing. Cecilea stands up quick, reaches in her pocket and pulls out that egg of hers. She brushes it off with her mitten, before she puts it back in her pocket.

"I better get home," she says, like that egg sent her some kind of message. "Mother will be looking for me."

"Yeah, I better hightail it too. Mrs. Moore's gonna be fit to be tied, if I'm late for supper. She hates that."

"Why do you live with the Moores?"

"My house burned down," I say. She probably already knows that part. Sometimes people do that: ask a question they already know the answer to, so they feel better about asking a tough one. I know what's coming next, 'cause I've heard it a million and one times, so I save her some breath. I already answered the tough question so many times I lost count.

"We're all split up, but not for long. Daddie's gonna find us a new house."

Cecilea just stays quiet. That's a new one on me. Pretty soon, I'm telling her all about the chimney fire, and Itsy-Bets getting lost, and how Daddie was working second shift, so it was all up to me and Dallas and Mama, and 'course the neighbors. I spill my guts like I never did to anyone before. I guess all that silent space, longer than the shadows pointing the way as we walk, just open me right up. I keep on a blabbing, right up until we get to the path leading to her place.

I'm sorry I told her, 'cause now I seem like a sad-soap, just thinking about what I lost, not what I have, like Mama tells me to.

"Lots of people have it way worse than me," I say.

"Sure they do," Cecilea says. "You're pretty lucky."

"Daddie says people lose way more than we did in the fire. We still have each other. Nobody got hurt."

"The Kerschkes had a barn fire once. They got all the livestock out, but they lost all the hay and grain. They put the hay up when it was still wet. Lots of barns burn down that way. You must be patient with hay drying and keep raking it. That's what Papa says."

"Good thing nobody was hurt," I say.

I'm wondering to myself why wet hay would just start a fire, but I already asked enough stupid questions, so I keep my wondering to myself.

"Their dog burned up to nothing but bones," Cecilea says. "They had it tied in the loft to keep it safe from other dogs. You know, because she was in heat."

Cecilea's eyes get all glassy lookin', and my own sting like blue blazes, way back behind the sockets. She lowers her head, and tucks her hair into her kerchief, and even in that near dusk light, I see the color rise up in her cheeks.

All the way home, I just keep thinking about the Kerschkes' dog burning alive, up there in the loft where she was supposed to be safe. My stomach feels like I swallowed a stone, and burped up bits of gravel and chewed up dandelion greens.

Life sure can take some sweet and bitter turns. Even in one afternoon. That's for darned sure.

Chapter 12
Remembering Butch

For as long as I can remember, I always did want a dog. I had one for a while, back on Vermillia Street, just a little while after we moved in. Butch was a hard time getting, then he was gone. That's sometimes the way it is with good things in life; just when you think you have something, it's gone. I just gotta remember that before I had Butch, I never did. Now I know the difference, and that's a lucky thing. Having a dog to pal around with is a good thing.

I was just minding my own business, walking alongside of Dallas up to Dibble's Five and Dime, with Nate hanging onto Mama's skirt, and Mama pushing Itsy-Bets in the carriage. That's back when I was getting used to calling Itsy-Bets something other than The Baby, and Daddie said Elizabeth was way too big a name for such an itsy-bitsy-baby. Everything at home still smelled like sawdust and new paint mixed in with the smell of iodine.

I stayed outside, thinking how I was gonna ask Mama for a dime to go to the movie show, which was a new thing for me and Dallas. Dallas was inside Dibble's with Mama, most likely thinking up a way to get some Lemon Drops or a Rainbow ice cream cone for a nickel. He loved those things more than anything. Same as now.

If we played our cards right and asked just at the right time, Mama almost always gave us a dime for the movies. The best time was right when Mama was busy feeding Itsy-Bets. If we got chores done beforehand, for sure, it was going to be a cinch. I looked down the street toward home, 'cause now that I had a plan, I was ready to hatch it.

That's when I saw the fancy lady with her dog, sitting on the bench outside of Woolrich's, next door to Dibble's. She was looking all down in the dumps. She had on one of those rich-lady coats with a circle of foxes around the neck; one biting the other's tail, like the tigers in that story, *Little Black Sambo* that my teacher read to us back in Pearl. Instead of eyes, the lady's foxes had glass marbles. I remember that because I coulda used a few new glassies and because I wondered why in blue blazes any lady would want a circle of dead animals around her neck. The lady was rich; for sure she was rich with that fur collar and the black felt hat with a little veil that looked almost new 'cept for some tatters around the edges.

Anyways, the rich lady just sat there studying the sidewalk. Butch laid down at her feet, all mangy looking, with his eyes blinking all forlorn, like he was the saddest dog in the world. 'Course I didn't know the dog's name yet. I just thought he looked like his name oughta be Butch, or something tough like Butch. I stepped over there and gave the poor dog a pat before I even thought about doing it. The rich lady sat there on the bench, staring, as if she forgot how she got there, let alone that she had a dog with her. Butch was all thin in the hips, with filmy, droop-eyes. I would have mistaken Butch for a stray, 'cept for the leash dangling all loose from the lady's hands laying lank in her lap.

"What's his name?" I said, just to be polite and because I was a little bit scared of so much quietness.

The rich lady never even took her eyes off the sidewalk. "Mitzy," she said. "She's a pure-bred German shepherd."

I never asked about what kinda dog Butch, I mean Mitzy was, and I never cared a lick about it either. Maybe I should have.

"He sure seems friendly," I said.

I was trying to be nice; Butch, I mean Mitzy, really seemed more like hungry. Butch's tail thumped against the sidewalk and he pushed his nose against my face. The lady kept on studying the sidewalk.

"Do you want her?" the rich lady asked. "I must find a home for Mitzy."

"Why? Does he bite?"

I was only nine, but I was smart enough to know that rich people never give away stuff just out of the kindness of their hearts. I heard Daddie say that rich people were some of the stingiest people around, and Reverend Zollar said it was harder for a rich person to get to heaven than for a camel to get through the eye of a needle, which meant it was impossible in Bible talk. Bible talk is never all that direct.

"I can't afford her anymore," she said.

The rich lady looked pretty, pasted on top of tired, in a dolled up sort of movie star way, with lipstick and rouge and spit curls spinning out around the brim of her hat and slicked to the sides of her face.

"She's a good dog," she said.

The rich lady lifted her head from her studying and looked straight into my eyes. I'm never gonna forget those eyes for the rest of my born days—all prettied up with make-up smudged around the rim because of the teardrops begging to be let loose; right there, filling up in her bottom eyelids, until she dabbed her pretty lace-edged hankie and sopped the tears up like Mama dipping the tip of one of her snowflake cookies into a teacup, her fingers all dainty and looking as delicate as Mama's Sunday china. The rich lady balled her hankie up, and I had to look away from those eyes. My own eyes darted around looking for a safe place to land, which is probably why I noticed the mismatched buttons and frayed edges around the cuffs of her wool coat and the hole making its way clear through on the toe of her boot.

"I always wanted a dog," I said.

"Well, take good care of Mitzy," she said as she handed me the leash.

"Sure will," I said.

I never told her I already changed his, I mean her, name to Butch. So what if Butch was more of a boy dog's name. It was gonna be my dog's name. I got up, so we could high-tail it out of there, just in case she had second thoughts, and for a bit I thought she did, because she grabbed me and Butch and hugged us both up tight against her chest, while she was still sitting there on the bench in front of Woolrich's.

"Good bye, Mitzy."

Right at that moment, I knew why any lady wanted those dead foxes up next to her cheeks. That fox fur was the softest thing I ever felt. I coulda stayed forever and a day with my face buried in that silky soft fur and wrapped up in her rich-lady hug that smelled like what I imagined was Chanel No. 5 from the advertisement in Mama's *LIFE* Magazine, because it was nothing I ever smelled before and my nose hairs just seemed to reach right out for more; and because Butch's sloppy breath panted warm against my arm.

The rich lady pushed at me and Butch, like she got caught doing something wrong, which sent a little shiver down my back. The kinda shiver that lots of times comes right before the Irish creeps up my neck and ears. I hate that so much. I pushed back from the rich lady, turned tail and started walking fast toward home. I felt my legs wanting to take off in a run, but I held a walk. I forgot all about Mama and Dallas and Nate and Itsy-Bets in Dibble's. I forgot all about the movie house, or wheedling a dime outta Mama. I never looked back; not even once did I turn around. Still, my mind turned back seven times a thousand times, maybe more, thinking the lady was for sure coming after me changing her mind, and wanting her Mitzy back.

He was already mine. I was never gonna give him up.

"Your name's Butch now," I said.

The dog thumped his tail hard against my thigh and I scratched under his chin. I swear I could see that dog smile, just like a real person.

Mama harrumphed around some on account of me disappearing on her. Still, she took a liking to Butch right away. 'Course so did Dallas and Nate, and even Itsy-Bets squealed and dug her fingers into Butch's fur. He never even whimpered. He was that good a dog.

"Butch is a girl dog," Mama said.

"Are you sure? He seems too tough to be a girl," Dallas piped in.

"Well, she might be tough, but she's a girl alright," Mama said with her no nonsense look on. "That's probably why her name is Mitzy."

"Well, she likes Butch," I said.

"Butch is a boy's name," said Nate.

"Well, there's a man named Sue in the Bible," said Mama. "There's no reason a female dog can't be named Butch. Besides, Lassie is really a boy dog. I read it in *LIFE* magazine."

Daddie was a different story altogether. Daddie worked nights, so he didn't see Butch until the next morning when we were all eating breakfast, and he got mad as a wet hen when he saw Butch all curled up on the rug beside the davenport. Daddie said we were way better off than most because Mr. Durant thought of his workers as assets, and tried hard not to put anyone out of work. Still, we had to be careful with our blessings, and not squander any money. Mr. Durant's assets only got so much to keep them going.

Daddie said I had to give the dog back, because he had enough mouths to feed. I figured I'd never find the rich lady again, because I never saw her before, and she was just sitting there on the bench. Now that I think about it, she probably came on the bus and was on her way back to the city, where I woulda never found her and besides that, I was forbidden to take the bus that far on account of the bus went through skid-row before it got to where the rich people lived. I was there before with Dallas, but no sense in letting that slip now. Besides, we never even got off the bus; just stayed on 'til it came back around and headed toward home.

"Now, you take that dog back," Daddie said. "I don't want to see her underfoot when I get up to go to work."

I nodded and concentrated on eating my johnnycake.

"I mean it."

Daddie grabbed me under the chin and made me look straight in his eyes before he turned and walked to the bedroom. Lying to eyes like Daddie's, the kind that peer right into yours, and practically bore into your soul, is about impossible.

"You and Dallas come home right after school," said Mama. "Then you two can walk Butch over to the Five and Dime and ask Mr. Dibble if he knows who Butch belongs to. After that, get over to Woolrich's and do the same thing."

Mama washed the corn meal mush out of Itsy-Bets's hair, flipped back the tray of the highchair and plopped Itsy-Bets on the floor.

"You can fetch the wood in when you get back. Now go. I got chores to do."

Mama bunched up her mouth, and her eyes searched around the room as if she misplaced her mending.

I had the luck I expected. No pretty rich ladies at Dibble's or Woolrich's. No foxes biting each other's tails. No smell of Chanel No. 5. Only some rag-tag men looking down in the mouth asking for odd jobs, and one woman tacking a sign up advertising her washing and ironing skills. She looked like she never saw the rich side of town, that's for sure. Mr. Dibble never even saw the rich lady in the first place.

"Let's go over to the Torrey Rail Yard," I said. "Maybe Butch knows some tricks."

"Maybe we'll see some hobos jumping a boxcar," said Dallas.

Dallas hitched up his left leg and breathed a cha-huff sound, slapped me on the back and headed for the Rail Yard. Butch held her head high and heeled like that radio police dog Rin Tin Tin.

When we got to the edge of town, I let Butch off the leash and she kept right there at my hip, just the way I knew she would. We played Cowboys and Indians with Butch helping me find the bad guys and hang 'em high. 'Course Dallas was the bad guy.

There were no hobos that day, and not a single train passed through the whole time that we played at the Torrey Yard. Still, the abandoned boxcars sat in the same place as they had last time. I kinda forgot they ever were boxcars: one was Robin Hood's and his Merry Men's hideout, another was Lady Marian's chamber, or the Sheriff of Nottingham's place. Of course Sherwood Forest surrounded them, but that took some imagining, because mostly fallow fields lay all around the Rail Yard.

Usually, if only me and Dallas were there, the boxcars were for playing at Lone Ranger and Tonto, instead of Robin Hood, because Robin Hood was better with a whole gang of guys. Today we had Butch, so we played *Wonder Dog*, starring Rin Tin Tin. Butch made the day about as perfect as a day can be. I never knew back then that Butch was the exact same kinda dog as Rin Tin Tin, 'cause radio shows depend a lot on the mind's eye. Maybe I had another idea about what the wonder dog looked like before I had Butch, but from then on, Rin Tin Tin looked exactly like Butch. Turned out he really did.

"Good dog," me and Dallas said at the same time.

That gave us both the belly laughs, so all the rest of the day we repeated "Good dog," just to see if we'd say it right in time again. Of course we did, 'cause for one thing, we said it so many times, and for another thing we are what some folks call Irish twin brothers, born in the same year and in the same grade in school. We almost thought the same thoughts at the same time. Back then, anyways. We forgot all about Daddie telling us we couldn't keep Butch.

Dallas and me headed home when the sun dipped behind the treetops at the west end of Torrey Yard. That's how we knew it was almost suppertime. I snapped the leash back on Butch's collar when we got to the sidewalk, and tied her to the porch when we got home, even though I knew Butch was staying put. Butch was my pal; she'd never leave.

"Come here boys," said Daddie, right the second me and Dallas came in the door, both of us carrying an armful of wood for Mama's cooking, just the way we were supposed to do every day before supper. This time without being reminded on account of knowing Butch was supposed to be somewhere else.

"Did you return that mutt?" Daddie said.

He was all dressed for work and had on his no nonsense look, which got me feeling jittery.

"She's a good dog. Heels and everything," I said. "No nipping, even when we were horsing around. She's a good dog."

"I could see she was a fine breed," said Daddie. "I said, did you give her back?"

"We couldn't find the lady," said Dallas. "Butch knows how to fetch a stick and jump high, just like Rin Tin Tin."

"I bet she'd make a good watch dog," I said.

"She's got to go. We can't afford to feed a dog. That's why the lady gave her to you. No dog."

Daddie took my face in both his hands. His steel blue eyes vice-gripped onto mine. I saw my reflection in Daddie's eyes, and I concentrated on that because otherwise, the tears were going to break loose; I felt them hot behind my lids, looking for a way to escape. I can sorta feel them now, just thinking about it. I tried to remember all the arguments for keeping Butch that me and Dallas thought up while we were at Torrey Rail Yard, but the depth of Daddie's voice pushed all my thoughts down somewhere below my knees. I felt my calves quiver right below where my arguments landed.

"I'll find a farmer," Daddie said. "Go wash up for supper."

I felt numb inside, and supper landed in my stomach like a rock. After supper I sat on the porch with Butch and cried. I just let all the tears fall right on her fur.

After that, I cried some more, until tears and snot ran down the back of Butch's neck and my breath came out in hiccoughs. Mama never told me not to cry and Daddie was gone to work. Dallas told me to 'cut it out,' but so what, who cared what Dallas thought, he was a crybaby himself, who was he to tell me to cut it out?

I had one more night with Butch, that's all; maybe I could stop crying tomorrow. I didn't. Even after Daddie took Butch away, and came back with a laying hen so we could have fresh eggs. I kept on a-crying the whole next day. Supper seemed like the same plate of rock as the night before.

Daddie sat by the stove, applying the hot compresses to his bad leg and listening to Reverend Zollar tell a story about God not giving his children a scorpion, when they asked for an egg. I thought maybe I got a laying hen instead of a dog because God thought fresh eggs were better for kids than a good dog. Maybe that's how prayers got answered, which was why it was so hard to trust that God heard prayers at all.

The next morning everything was just the same as always, 'cept something was different, like the feeling in the air when heat lightning was getting ready to light up the horizon. There was Itsy-Bets with cornmeal mush spread all over her face and in her hair, just like always. There was Dallas, walking along beside me one step ahead of me just like always. There was Mama sitting with Itsy-Bets's highchair wedged up to the corner of the table, between her and Nate, with Daddie down at the other end of the table.

"Get some firewood in boys," said Daddie.

His lip twitched up at the corner, like he was reading the funnies instead of the front page of the Journal, which never had good news, only stuff about hard times.

"We always do that before supper," Dallas said. "Can't we eat first?"

"Are you itching for a fight, son?" Daddie said.

Now his lip twitch was steadied, but his eyes danced like me and Dallas should be pleased as punch to fetch wood before breakfast.

The door clicked shut behind me, about the same time I let out a whoop, because there was Butch tied up to the front porch, just like the day she got taken away. I heard the screen door swish and clink again and there was Daddie, shifting his weight to his good leg.

"Thank you, Daddie. I'll take good care of him. He won't eat too much. Just some table scraps. I can collect some from the neighbors, too. And maybe walk up to Woolrich's and get some of the leavings from the sandwich bar."

All those arguments I planned, the ones that sunk down inside me, came spilling out of my mouth, without me even trying to remember them. For no reason at all, I felt like a rock got stuck in my throat, right there between my collar bones, and my eyes filled up with tears. I swiped a sleeve over across my eyes.

"She's your dog. You see to it," Daddie said. His blue eyes got all glassy looking and he cleared his throat. "What sorta name is Butch for a bitch dog, anyways?"

Daddie turned and walked back into the house. I buried my face in Butch's neck and let all the dog smell fill up my heart. The door slapped shut.

"I'll help, too," said Dallas, which should have made me happy as pie, but for some reason it seemed like my brother was horning in where he didn't belong.

It worked out okay for the next week: the two of us going to Woolrich's for table-leavings, which were sparse because for one thing, business was slower than molasses, and for another thing, the Taylor's pig got most of the leavings. Mrs. Taylor worked the counter, so she got first dibs on scraps. Still, pigs can die if they got too much salt, on account of pigs not knowing how to sweat, plus they don't eat meat leavings, so me and Dallas got just the kind of scraps Butch liked. Besides, playing Rin Tin Tin without Dallas would be no fun at all, even with a real live German Shepherd police dog just exactly like Rinny.

Sometimes things get taken away for no real reason. Sometimes I wonder why the heck Butch ever crossed my path, when the whole thing was going to end so bad. Just a week with Butch, that's it. One week.

Dallas saw Butch first, lying over by the stove, right by where Daddie warmed up his leg and Mama put the poultices on. Butch was all stiff, like that rigor mortis I heard about when something's dead awhile. Like a dead bird on the sidewalk, 'cept foam was bubbling out of her mouth, and her eyes rolled back in her head. Butch started to shake, her tongue lolling out of her mouth. I rushed over and held her head and tried to calm Butch by cooing like Mama did to Itsy-Bets. All the while Dallas held Butch's back legs, stroking her paw pads. It worked. Butch's fit turned into tremors, her eyes became clear and she threw her head back and looked right at me and gave my wrist a lick before she scrambled to her feet.

"She's alright," I said. "She's alright."

"Right as rain," said Dallas with his hands on his hips.

Butch licked my face, and then she licked Dallas's.

"Right as rain," said Nate.

For some reason, I looked around for Daddie.

"He's at work," Mama said.

I never even asked the question out loud.

When we headed for the Rail Yard, Mama just told us to get home in time for supper. She never said a thing about Butch.

"Did that dog have any more of those fits?" Mama asked at supper.

"What fits?" Daddie said.

It was one of his off days, no work, which meant after supper we were all gonna listen to Reverend Zollar and read the Bible. On Daddie's work nights, Mama listened to Rudy Vallee play the saxophone and sing with his Yankees, or Amos & Andy. I like them the very best; way better than Reverend Zollar.

"Just one fit that I saw," Dallas lied; it was really two more while we were at the Rail Yard. "Isn't that right, Eldie?"

Why did he have to go and bring me into his lie? I just nodded, keeping my eyes on my bean soup. Of course it never did any good to lie to Daddie. He always found out. Sure enough, that very night after supper, Butch went into a slathering fit right there in the middle of Reverend Zollar shouting on about how Jesus drove demons into a herd of pigs.

Daddie said he had to put the dog to sleep, if it kept up like that. Butch kept it up, getting worse every day. There was nothing Butch or Dallas or I could do about it, and Daddie said there was no use crying over spilt milk. Right before Daddie took Butch away for the second time, Mama laid her hand on Butch's head, closed her eyes and got all quiet and still, the same as she did when she was praying over her own children. Butch's tail went still and her panting slowed. I knew just the way Butch felt, because that's the same way I felt, when Mama put her hand on my forehead, right after I climbed between the covers at bedtime. Mama's hands could calm down a tornado or a blizzard or any other kind of storm.

That's the last memory I had of Butch. Just sitting there at Mama's feet, her tail thumping to a slow beat, and her head laying still in Mama's lap.

Someday I'll have a dog again. His name will be something other than Butch, that's for darned sure. There's only one dog good as Butch. She was the best. Besides, dogs gotta tell you their name. Butch taught me that.

Chapter 13
Washed in the Blood of the Lamb

"Step it up," Daddie says. "We don't want to be late for church, now do we?"

Daddie just got to the Moores' to get me for Church. He already fetched Nate from the Dibbles' and Dallas from the Pedersons'. It took longer to get to church, on account of being scattered around. Daddie had to be polite and visit with a 'good morning' and neighborliness.

'Course the answer to his question is already out there, squeezed tight between Daddie's eyebrows. When he pulls his face like that, it's as if a string is hooked between his eyebrows and his shoulders. Like one of those marionettes I saw in a Mickey Mouse cartoon when Dallas and me snuck into the movies.

Daddie's shoulders pull up a notch and get closer to his ears. His shoulders squeezing up is all I see from where I'm at. That's how I know what his face is doing. Nobody needs to say a word, the three of us boys just get our feet moving a little faster. Nate speaks up anyways.

"Of course we don't want to be late, Daddie."

Nate runs from me to Daddie and grabs hold of Daddie's hand. I notice Nate is starting to hitch his left leg, just like Daddie does, same as Dallas.

"This year, I'm gonna be saved. When Reverend Zollar has his baptisms on Easter, I'm gonna wade right in," Nate says.

Daddie squeezes Nate's hand. Nate tries to get a little taller in his Sunday wools. He's still in short pants, which maybe he's a little old for, seeing as he's almost ten. Mama says he should be happy with what he's got, Daddie still has a job three days a week, and not just any job, a good job at the Shop. Nate still has a roof over his head, to boot.

"Daddie," Nate says. "Is Mama born again?"

"Mama has her own way of knowing Jesus."

"What way is that?"

"Daddie, did you hurt your leg in the war to end all wars?" I say.

I know better than to ask Daddie about his leg. It just pops out of my mouth before my brain catches up to my tongue. I just want to get his mind off of Nate's question.

For one thing, asking Daddie about Mama and being saved and her staying home instead of going to church is a good way to get Daddie in one of his silent moods. One where all the strings pull tight inside him, not just on the outside like now when we're running late, and he wishes we are on time. I like it more when Daddie's in a talking mood, even if Daddie's talking mood is only a few words here and there.

Besides, something else is itching at my brain. I'm hanging back with Itsy-Bets, watching Daddie hitch his left leg, and I'm wondering how that all started and whether I hitch my leg, 'cause Dallas gets aggravated at me whenever I say something to him about it, and now here goes Nate limping for no real reason. I never asked Daddie about the war before, or about his leg.

I heard Mama say lots of men never came home from the war, and most that did left some of themselves behind. Maybe Daddie left a piece of his leg in France.

I almost forget I asked a question by the time Daddie answers.

"No, son," Daddie says. "I never got to fight, on account of this leg. I enlisted, but I couldn't keep up. The Army told me to go home and do my part here."

I see the strings relax a little around Daddie's shoulders. We walk along like that, with nobody talking. I just wait, hoping we hear more but not wanting to ask. I figure that's what Nate and Dallas are doing, too.

"I moved too slow for wartime."

All I hear is sidewalk scuffing under five sets of Sunday shoes. Itsy-Bets bats at bits of dust floating in the sunshine. I wish I never told her that was golden magic dust floating around in the sun. I press down on her shoulder and wag one finger in front of her nose to let her know this is no time for shenanigans. If we stay quiet, maybe Daddie will tell us more.

"I hurt it chopping wood for my Mama, when I was about your age. I was fooling around, pretending to be Paul Bunyan. I should have been paying more attention," he says. "Foolishness, that's all."

Daddie gets all silent again, and all I hear is Nate, kicking a stray stone down the sidewalk. He's run up ahead. I guess he really does want to get to church early.

"How come it still ails you?" Dallas asks.

He stretches his legs long to catch up to Daddie's hand where Nate was, but Daddie shakes it away from him. He lifts up his hat and runs his fingers through his hair, carving paths in it. I'm still hanging back holding Itsy-Bets's hand, and I see Daddie bend his head down toward Dallas, and Dallas looks up at him. He is pretty near as tall as Daddie; just a head shorter. The sun's shining through between them, so all I see is black blotches against all that sun. They look like one of those ink blot butterflies I saw Cecilea make with her India Ink, only Cecilea's butterflies are perfect and clean: one side looks just like the other. In the case of Dallas and Daddie, one side of the butterfly's wings is smaller, like it's still damp from the cocoon. Same hair is sticking out from the top of both of their egg-shaped heads. I never noticed their heads looking so oblong and bulging before now. Bits of dust that Nate kicked up dance between them in the bright sunshine. I run my hand through my own hair, and I can feel a lightness in my chest. I do like Sundays. It's almost like we're still on Vermillia Street, walking to church like we always did. I breathe in deep. Sunday even smells different.

"Sometimes, we just keep getting reminded of our foolishness, son," is all Daddie says.

He puts his hat back on and walks the rest of the way to church with his nose pointing straight ahead and his ears pulled up tall over his shoulders. That's the way he walks when he's in his no talkin' mood.

I keep feeling like I'm all these different people all rolled into one body. I gotta do all these chores around the Moores' house: fetching in the firewood, cleaning out the ash-can, collecting eggs from their Bantam hens and whatever else they think of 'cept chopping wood. Daddie made that clear to Mr. Moore, when they first said they'd take me in. I guess I understand why, and all this while I was thinking Daddie thought I was too much of a weakling.

After school most days, I come up with some reason I want to be alone for a while, so I can walk out on Potter Road, over by the Tamarack farm and maybe see Cecilea, where I get all tongue-tied and lame-brained.

I'm a whole different person on Saturday, when I get horsing around with Dallas and Nate, and of course Ephraim's always there, too. I can never get away from that guy, and most of the time I wish I wanted to, but then I get to feeling excited just seeing him, 'cause I never know what's going to happen. Like I say, I'm a whole different guy around Ephraim.

Most Saturdays he gets a dime to go to the movies. Times are harder now, so no dimes for me and Dallas and Nate. Besides, it's easier for folks to spare one dime for one kid, than when the folks have four kids; that's pretty near a half dollar just wasted on watching something that's pretend.

After everyone's settled in, concentrating on the picture-show, Ephraim goes over to the exit and sneaks me and Dallas and Nate in. We can stay all afternoon, as long as we're home for supper, just watching the movie over and over again, keeping a quick eye on the clock from time to time. First the newsreel, then *Popeye the Sailor Man* or *Betty Boop* or some other cartoon, then the feature presentation. Mr. Dibble plays the organ in between showings, while Mrs. Dibble minds the store. The movie house is right next door to Woolrich's, with the Five and Dime right next to that. Mr. Dibble plays the organ at the Roman Catholic church too. His movie music sounds just like his church music, or so Cecilea says. I never go in her church; Daddie would have a conniption fit if I even mentioned the idea.

Cecilea told me one day when we ran into each other on Potter Road, accidentally on purpose, that sometimes when she walks down that dark, quiet, aisle and hears Mr. Dibble playing, she almost forgets where she's at. It feels so much like church.

"Once Theresa genuflected before she went in to her seat in the movies," she said.

Cecilea covered her mouth so her laugh came out all muffled, like she felt guilty for thinking her sister did something silly. I had to ask what genuflect is 'cause they don't do that at the Free Methodist Church, and nothing about the movie house seems like church to me. All the stuff that Cat-lickers do seems way different than us Christians, like call the pastor 'Father' instead of 'Reverend', and having people called Sister and Brother that are no relation at all.

Ephraim's Second Baptist church and Reverend Zollar call everyone sisters and brothers. Still, it means something different for Cat-lickers. We don't go away to learn how to be a sister or a brother and be married to the church, we just are, well 'cept for the marrying part. Christians only marry real people. We never even need to be saved to be a sister or a brother. Jeez-o-Pete's, those hobos down at the Rail Yard are sisters and brothers according to Reverend Zollar.

"Do you get born again?" I asked Cecilea.

Now, I had to explain about sins getting forgiven and all the stuff about being saved. Cat-lickers don't get saved.

"We're already saved because we belong to the One True Church, starting with St. Peter, the first pope," she said, and then she told me that Catholics have Confession, instead. Cecilea and her sisters go every Saturday and tell Father Perotta every way they broke the Ten Commandments or the Church Laws. That way their souls get scrubbed clean and ready to receive Jesus in Holy Communion the next day at Mass. That's the word Cecilea uses for going to church, Mass. Free Methodists and Baptists only have to get their souls scrubbed once. Daddie says getting baptized is the same as getting washed in the blood of the lamb. If you ask me, it's more like almost drowning in an almost freezing Flint River.

I wish we all just used the same words; religion's more confusing than memorizing poems. Cecilea says poetry is easy, 'cause at least poems either paint a pretty picture or tell a story; plus, they all have a rhythm, which sorta tells you when you get off track. She has to memorize something called the Baltimore Catechism. As far as I can figure, that's a big book of rules about how to be a good Cat-licker. We just listen to Reverend Zollar. He tells us how to stay away from damnation. He tells us every single Wednesday on Church of the Air, and again on Thursday at the Soup Kitchen, then again at Sunday service, and afterwards, if we stay for Sunday School. Come to think of it, maybe all that memorizing of the Catechism would be easier.

Anyways, at the movies, Mr. Dibble sits up straight and stiff and follows music on a page, just like Cecilea does. The skin on Mr. Dibble's face flaps a little down by his jaws, and his mouth falls halfway open. Cecilea looks like an angel when she plays the piano; Mr. Dibble looks more like one of those gargoyles.

Lots of time, Mr. Dibble climbs up out of that pit his organ sits in and walks right by the aisle where I'm sitting. Sometimes he looks straight at me, and I'm pretty sure he knows me and Nate and Dallas sneaked in there, but he never says a word, he just walks on by. Just like he never says a word about us starting that fire in his tower of safety matches two months ago. He must know it was us. That eats at me, especially when he keeps being so darned nice to us all the time.

Nate says Mr. Dibble is a peach to him, and only makes him do little chores like empty the ashes into the ash-can every morning, and bring in the milk from the back porch.

Besides worrying about Mr. Dibble or somebody else catching on to us sneaks, my head loses track of everything but the movie. At first the clock over the exit shines bright blue numbers at me in a distracting way. I can hear people crunching popcorn in the dark, and the smell makes my tongue slide around in my mouth. Once I get into the story, I can forget all about the popcorn and the clock and even the other people in the movie house. A fella can lose track of himself at the movies.

Lots of times, we don't get there until the show's halfway through. I kinda like that. I almost always miss the first run of the newsreel and the cartoon. No matter what the movie is, it's like a mystery. I get it in my head how the whole story started, then we stick around 'til it starts up again and I can find out if I got it right.

I could watch *The Thin Man* a million times, even after all the mysteries are solved. That's because it's a mystery and funny as all get out. I'm pretty good at figuring things out. A whole lot better than memorizing stuff for school. My favorite is monster movies. Like *King Kong*. That girl, Ann Darrow, is pretty brave getting to know King Kong, the way she did. I got nightmares from that movie. I was a chicken-liver in my nightmare, running and squeezing under a mailbox to hide. I shook and shivered away with my hind end sticking way out for King Kong to see. In my nightmare I hoped and prayed Ann Darrow would come along and tame King Kong, but instead, I woke up with a jerk and a gasp. I had myself pulled up in a ball with all the covers thrown over on Ephraim.

Sundays are the best. Sometimes better than being at the movies with the fellas, and sometimes even better than the time I spend with Cecilea.

Daddie comes round with Itsy-Bets and collects us for church. First Nate, then Dallas, then me. Ephraim and his folks go to the Second Baptist church. Us Craines, 'cept for Mama, go to the Free Methodist Church. It's just like when we lived on Vermillia Street, walking to church, like we all still live together. Same church and everything.

Sometimes I forget that Mama's at the Taylors' instead of at home getting chicken dinner ready, with biscuits and maybe an apple pie to boot.

"Just ask Jesus into your heart," Reverend Zollar says, "That's all you must do. Then you'll be saved from eternal damnation." I did that once. I even got baptized in the river. So did Dallas. The same Easter as me. I'm sure glad that's over. I get a shiver just thinking about dipping down into that cold water and coming out gasping and spitting out the taste of muck, and clinging to Reverend Zollar for dear life. Seems like he's trying to drown the devil right out of a fella. Add to that, everybody in tarnation is up on the riverbank singing, "Let's go down, Let's go down. Down to the River to Pray…"

I'm happy Baptism's a one-time thing. So's Dallas. Even so, we're sorta glad Nate's all gung-ho. We tell him it's nothing at all, the water's warm as it is on the 4th of July, and it's just a quick in and out. I can hardly wait to see his smarty-pants head come up all google-eyed and scared, soaking wet and cold as all get out, clinging onto the guy who just tried to drown him. I suppose that's enough to knock the sin out of anyone. At least for a while, anyways.

I would hate Cecilea's Confession. I'd have to tell all about the fire and what we did at Dibble's and about what me and Dallas and Ephraim did at the Tamaracks' house back in February. Probably have to keep confessing about sneaking into the movie house. I'm sure I'd never be able to look Father Perotta in the eye after that. It's bad enough when somebody like Mr. Dibble already knows what I did, it would be a hundred times worse if I had to say it out loud to someone who thought I was towing the line, especially if I had to go back every week and give Father Perotta the low-down on all the things I did wrong, even the things I thought about and never actually did. Pretty soon, I'm sure Father Perotta would see I'm a hopeless case.

Chapter 14
Remembering Forbidden Fruit

For the life of me, I will never figure out why me and Dallas agreed to go along with Ephraim's lame-blamed plans back in February. It was stupid; I was stupid; we were all stupid. Knowing that doesn't make it any better or change a gosh-darned thing. Once a fella does something like we did, there's no taking it back.

Ephraim has an itch about him. That's what Daddie calls it anyways, like it's a bad thing. He tells me not to go jumping off a cliff just 'cause Ephraim does. He says I gotta use my own head, think for myself, and keep off of that road paved to hell and damnation.

Daddie might be right, but Ephraim sure comes up with some fun stuff on his road to hell. Daddie and Mama read the newspapers and worry about the Lindberg family and how they're holding up at the kidnapper's trial and talk about another year of black blizzards out west, and factories and banks closing and Durant doing his best to keep the unions out, and men working at least part of the week, and poor people getting poorer and Hoovervilles all over creation, with or without a New Deal and the poor Zyber brothers in danger of closing up their grocery store next to Woolrich's on account of their kind hearts giving everybody credit, and now they've got next to nothing. That's not even counting Auntie Laura worrying about crazy folks blowing up schools like what happened in Bath, which was way the heck back when I was in first grade. Every year on the anniversary of all those kids getting killed, the newspaper reminds everybody about crazy Mr. Kehoe and how hard times can make a fella crack.

Ephraim picks up the same newspapers and magazines and reads about Rudy Vallee and Benny Goodman, and thinks about joining up in a dance competition, and he talks about Popeye and Wimpy or Dagwood, and people doing crazy stunts like sitting on flagpoles, and the Loch Ness monster over in Scotland. Ephraim's eyes just dance with that itch of his until he's found some way to make the excitement all his.

Sometimes Ephraim's excitement hurts next to nobody, like making a Dagwood sandwich out of the last of his Ma's bread: piece of bread, some summer tomatoes from the garden, a fried egg, another piece of bread, a slab of ham from the icebox, a cut up cucumber, another slice of bread, some cheese and mayonnaise and one more piece of bread to close it all up.

"How does old Bumstead eat a sandwich like that?" Only Ephraim says sammich.

Neither one of us could get our mouths open wide enough to take a bite.

"Maybe he squishes it flat," I said.

"Naw. Look at the picture."

Ephraim points to *Dagwood* in the funny papers. He sure did have a big mouth. We tried again, but it was hopeless. I pressed down on top to flatten the whole thing out, but still it was too big. When Ephraim picked it up, cucumber slices slid on the floor.

Mrs. Moore came in about then and got on her high horse. "You went through most of my bread making that monstrosity," she said. "You're gonna eat it."

"Ma, some of it's been on the floor."

"We've been blessed with food. Some's got none. You're not wasting it playing some sort of game. As it is, I gotta get more of that bread made before tomorrow morning."

I did what I was told. So did Ephraim. Least, we did when we got caught. That was about the best sandwich I ever had, but Mrs. Moore wasn't done with us.

"Popi got that ham in exchange for fixing floorboards at the Five and Dime. They had a fire in there. Started by the safety matches. What, in the name of God, kind of safety is that?"

Ephraim and I just got busy eating our sandwich and kept our heads low.

Ever since I met him back on my first day of school at Cronk, that itch Daddie talks about Ephraim having is sorta catchy. I know cause I catch it from him all the time. Same way with Dallas, only Dallas sometimes likes to be the one getting it started, like that day at Dibble's.

Ephraim got a good gag going last fall using throw-aways from Zyber Brothers Grocery. We got callin' it Ghost Groceries. Us three Craine boys and Ephraim were walking home from Torrey Yard, when Ephraim spied some old boxes. His eyes lit up with that itch of his. After that, any piece of trash got looked at extra close, as a contender for Ephraim's new gag. An after dark sort of gag.

Ephraim and I have no trouble getting out at night. We just climb out the window and down the elm tree. His folks' bedroom is on the other side of the house, so they're none the wiser. Dallas is the same way over at the Pedersons'. Mr. and Mrs. Pederson got the zzzzzz going up over their heads, like Donald and Daisy Duck.

If we plan a night outing, we keep mum with Nate because for one thing, Nate is all goody-two-shoed, and for another, Mr. Dibble sleeps with his ears wide awake, so's he can keep an eye on his store. Anyways that's what Nate said Mr. Dibble told him. It makes no sense when you think about it, but on the other hand, it sorta does.

We get empty boxes and cans and weigh them down a little, so they stay put, then we put everything in a box tipped on its side, smack in the middle of the road, so a car coming from either direction is sure to see it. Sometimes we get a flour or sugar sack filled up with old newspaper, or dried out leaves.

"It's gotta look natural," Ephraim said.

Funny about how a fella's gotta work at making a box look like it just fell off the back of a truck and got left in the road. Seems like random accidents fall in a certain sort of order.

"We gotta be sorta near the edge of town, but near some houses, so's we have someplace to hide."

I gotta hand it to Ephraim, when he gets a plan cooking, he's got all the ingredients he needs.

"Hurry, here comes somebody," hisses Dallas, as if somebody coming in a car three blocks away can see or hear him. Sometimes he gets jumpy and a car is nowhere in sight; it's just his imagination running wild.

Most times, Dallas's the first to scramble behind some bushes. He gets jumpy easy. He's sorta slow footed, but his nerves jump extra fast. Ephraim holds on 'til the last second, making sure everything is all right. It seems like the last second to me anyways, 'cause when the itch gets jumping inside me, a second seems like half a week.

We hide out in the bushes until a car comes. I never saw a car pass by a box spilled out all over the road, looking like groceries dropped right in their path, straight from heaven or something. We watch the poor sap get out of his car thinking he is lucky, just to see him kick that box to Timbuktu when he finds out it's empty. Most times, it's just a milk toast of a guy, but sometimes a man and wife get out and we can hear 'em low-talking as they get close to the boxes, getting excited about their good fortune.

I tell you something though, as much as Ephraim's itch is catchy, Dallas's laugh is. I can feel his hoot rising up out of him, and spreading across my skin, before he makes a sound.

Hiding in the bushes, playing that gag on folks was the berries. I clamped my hand over my mouth, and swallowed hard to keep what I knew was rising up outta Dallas tamped down inside my own belly.

Most the times we got through 'til the saps drove away, but sometimes we busted out laughing, so's we had to skedaddle out of there.

I sorta lost my taste for that gag though, the night Mr. Kerschke came through with his wife and kids. He was driving his rattle-trap Ford pickup. The brakes were half broke, so he had to pump 'em hard to get the truck to stop. He never saw the boxes quite in time to stop fast enough, and the left tire crunched over an empty Heinz catsup bottle. The door groaned open as Mr. Kerschke jumped out of the pickup.

"Look, Sophia, it's a box of food," Mr. Kerschke said.

He waved his hand for her to come. She had their youngest in a blanket, with the rest of the kids sleeping in bundles in the back of the truck. Who knows where they'd been or where they were going.

"What'd you say Ray?"

"Groceries. All over the road."

The two of them picked up a can, an empty cereal box, another can. They even shook out every dry leaf from the empty flour sack and turned it inside out. Seemed like Mrs. Kerschke got smaller and smaller standing there with the truck's headlights shining through her dress sticking out below her coat. Mr. Kerschke went through the whole box of trash, even though he had to know by then it was just a gag. His wife sat right down there in the middle of the road and buried her face in her baby's blanket and cried big blubbery sobs. Mr. Kerschke looked around like he was lost.

"It's just some kids pulling our leg," he said.

She looked up at him, her face all slobbery, nothing but sobs coming out of her mouth.

"It's just some kids, Sophia," he said. "Probably watching right now. It's sorta funny if you think about it."

Mrs. Kerschke ran her fingers over her eyes and squeezed the top of her nose.

It's strange how feeling are catchy: Ephraim with his itch, and Dallas with his laugh sending out sparks before I even hear it, and right then Mrs. Kerschke's sadness sinking into my guts like I swallowed a rock.

Mr. Kerschke helped his wife get to her feet, took his handkerchief out of his pocket and wiped her face. She gave up a smile and hugged the little one in her arms. One of the kids mumbled something from the back of the truck, and Mrs. Kerschke shushed him as she climbed back into the truck.

After that, I lost track of why we liked the Ghost Groceries so much in the first place. We never stopped sneaking out and playing that gag, but it was old. Even when some fella made a fool out of himself, Mrs. Kerschke's face snuck into my mind and that rock-swallow feeling hit me full in the gut.

Anyways, nothing stayed with Ephraim for too long, and by the end of February, he was itching for some new excitement. He was sure as shooting ready to find out what the Cat-lickers did with those beads they carried. That was before I got to know Cecilea, before she started explaining things to me, before I ever looked her straight in the eye or knew the way her hair smelled like oat mash, chicken feathers, and dumplings. Before I knew that straw and chicken feathers and dumplings would be smells that made my heart race more than anything Ephraim or, for that matter, Dallas could ever think up, even if they had a month of Sundays on top of a blue moon to connive.

"I heard they have some sorta of voodoo thing going with those beads," Ephraim said. "They conjure up spells and put hexes on people with them."

'Course I know better now. Back then I was as wet behind the ears as the next guy.

"Naw," I said. "Those girls don't seem like the conjuring type."

"Exactly. That's how they get away with it. Looking all innocent and proper. No one suspects a thing."

I gotta hand it to Ephraim, he makes a good argument.

"Besides it's bath night," he said. "You never know what we might get a peek at."

I never even asked him how he knew it was bath night.

I can say it was Ephraim's pearly white teeth smiling that smile of his, that made me think everything was alright. Or I could blame Dallas, jumping on Ephraim's bandwagon so quick. I could do that, and it'd be half true. Still, nothing was gonna change the fact that I was lying there on the icy ground in a late February thaw, hiding in the leafless verbena and honey-suckle, just outside the Tamarack's farmhouse, close enough to see right in their windows.

The frozen stubs of Queen Anne's Lace poked into my overalls and clumps of snow, which had half melted and re-froze, clung to my socks and mittens. The clean, fresh scent of snow seemed wrong against the taste of fear in my mouth.

Funny how that taste comes back to me, clear as day. Just like biting down on a penny, that's what fear tastes like. My jaw clenched tight against it, made my head start to pound, and my front tooth ache like blue blazes.

Cecilea and her sister Analie had just finished the dishes when we got there. Dallas squinched his nose at me, 'cause of the cabbage smell leaking out the chimney right along with the smell of Applewood. I buried my face in my arm, just to keep from laughing out loud. I got to trembling. I like to think it was from the cold, but I know better. I was scared we was gonna get caught any minute.

Let's go home. I felt the words rise up in my throat. I swallowed hard to keep my thoughts to myself. No one was gonna call me a chicken liver. I heard my heart beating fast in my ears telling me to get the heck out of there. I breathed out a long cloud of steam, which made me even scareder, 'cause for sure someone would see my breath from the window if they happened to look out.

Mrs. Tamarack lit candles in the frunchroom. Small candles in little red glasses. Mr. and Mrs. Tamarack knelt side by side with their backs to the wood stove. Cecilea and her sisters formed a circle joining them. Each had what looked like identical black beaded necklaces clutched tight in her hands.

"The hexing beads," Ephraim hissed over at me.

Each of the Tamarack girls, and their parents, all kissed the dangling end of the necklace then touched forehead, chest, and each shoulder. All together, right at the exact same time, like they had some sorta secret signal. Even Lucy did it, and she was no bigger than Itsy-Bets. The whole family recited some chant together in a strange language that I know now was Polish 'cause that's the Old Country Cecilea's folks came from. 'Course, back in February, I was clueless about all that.

They touched each bead, then moved on to the next, repeating what sounded like the same words. I looked over at Dallas, and his eyes looked like saucers. The whole whites showed around the colored part.

Mrs. Tamarack's eyes were closed and she swayed slightly to the sing-song. Holy mackerel, Ephraim was right, they were putting a hex on someone.

"Cat-lickers," Dallas mouthed silently across at me.

Ephraim nodded.

Theresa rubbed her back, right above where her dress gathered up below her waist. My spine tingled. When all that chanting ended for what seemed like no particular reason, Mrs. Tamarack dragged a big old wash tub from behind the stove and poured in hot water, which was waiting. I guessed it was heating up during the hexing.

I thought maybe they were gonna cook up a Jewish baby. Ephraim said that's another thing Cat-lickers do, on account of them blaming all the Jews for killing Jesus. 'Course, I know better now, 'cause Cecilea 'bout spilt a gut laughing when I told her.

She said, no that's the gypsies. They're the ones who roast babies. I asked her if she thought a gypsy took the Lindbergh baby and she just rolled her eyes. No, those were evil people, not gypsies or Jews or any other types of people. She sure must think I'm a numbskull.

Anyways, what happened next took less than half an hour. Sometimes I think it must've been longer, like the whole world slowed down. Lucy undressed, stepped inside the tub and got bathed by Mrs. Tamarack. She splashed and giggled in the tub, all pink and soft in the candlelight.

I never saw a naked girl, not even my own little sister, Itsy-Bets. Never-ever. Not even when she was a tiny baby.

More hot water, and in jumped Analie all naked and smooth. She's ten, same age as Nate. Mrs. Tamarack added more steaming water from the stove. Mrs. Tamarack rubbed Lucy dry. I swear the blood drained straight out of my head and my face started to freeze in the damp February air. I felt my bad tooth throbbing. That's how I knew I was all slack-jaw, staring at those girls. I bit down hard, and closed my mouth, which sent a pain up through the top of my head. At the same time, my heart was a steam engine pounding away in the station with nowhere to go. I tore my eyes away long enough to see Dallas and Ephraim like zombies in some sort of trance; faces frozen 'cept for jaws that looked like their tongues were about to loll out.

I heard the tea kettle whistle on Mrs. Tamarack's stove, clear through the stillness. Cecilea's turn was next. I knew right then and there, what we were doing was dead wrong, but at the same time, my eyes were glued on Cecilea.

There she was all naked and white as a lily, stepping into the tub. Her hips curved into a tiny waist; so small, I was sure I could circle my hands around and touch thumb-to-thumb, fingers to fingers. As she curled her body down into the tub, I saw her nipples standing at attention, not much bigger than a tiny brown burr from a burdock gone to seed; the kind that sticks to a sock and pricks the skin just enough to be a constant bother. She bathed, rose, covered herself with the towel and scooted out of the kitchen and out of our sight.

I heard Ephraim let out a slow, long sigh and imagined the stream of smoke-breath curling up toward the sky. He had his own train engine waiting at the station. I wanted to punch him in the face, right then and there. I hated him for that long sigh, 'cause I knew his heart was pounding away just like mine, and I hated him for coming up with the whole lame-brained plan, and I hated him for taking something away from me.

Next, there was Margaret, slipping her dress down around her knees and stepping out. Same as Cecilea only rounder and taller.

Margaret bent to swirl her fingertips in the water. She looked out the window and smiled. My stomach woulda dropped right outta my body if I'd been standing up. Jeez. I felt like she must've known we were there. I still wonder about that. Ephraim says no way because of the reflection on the window. He showed me from his own frunchroom how any light at all on the inside, makes reflections on the glass so no one can see out. It's like that one-way glass that the police have.

Mrs. Tamarack added more hot water to the tub before Theresa stepped in. Each oval hip came together to form a perfect heart shape. I saw for just a flicker of a moment, a dark hour-glass shape right at the point where Theresa's hips joined up with her legs.

After all the girls had their bath, Mrs. Tamarack unbuttoned the back of her own cotton housedress. Up and over her head, she removed everything in one swoop, dress and under things, and hung it all over a chair. I swear to this day, her dress coulda made three for her girls. She shifted her bulk into the tub.

"Don't bite your tongue."

Ephraim's voice hissed like a snake in my ear as he tapped my jaw up hard with his open hand. The salty taste of blood filled up my mouth. I was sorta glad 'cause now I had something real to pin on the pain filling up my chest. I sucked in my breath and crawled out of sight of the farm house. My heart was pounding like I just ran five miles at break-neck speed.

Just like pheasants flushed from the field, we all rose up off the ground and flew for safety, never looking back. My legs beat the ground. My mind's ear heard the front door open and somebody step out on the porch. I never looked back to check if that was my imagination or for real.

If God was like Reverend Zollar said he was, the three of us were gonna be smote off the face of the earth right then and there and thrown down into hell.

Maybe God was crueler than Reverend Zollar knew, 'cause hell might have been the easy way out. Least then, I would be spared looking at Cecilea every day and knowing what I know and thinking about her, plus her sisters all naked, and wishing I could wash that memory out of my skull. At the same time, I hope I never forget, and knowing that wish is one that, for sure, will come true. I can see why someone like that H. G. Wells fella thought up a contraption like a time machine, that's for darned sure. Mrs. Bidrall makes us read some real lame-brained stuff sometimes. Still, if I had a Time Machine, there's a whole lot of stuff I'd go back and change.

Chapter 15
The Promised Land

"Out for a Sunday stroll?" Nate asks, catching up to me on Potter Road.

I hear him panting a mile away. I'm just walking along easy-like, so he has no problem catching up to me. He bumps his shoulder against my ribs.

"Yep," I say. "Wanna come along?"

Of course he does. For once, Ephraim is nowhere in sight. I feel my hands unball before I even realize I pulled them into fists.

The whole world is full on green now, just like I pictured it in my head, back on the first day I ran into Cecilea on Potter Road. The cows are out in the field with their calves bawling every time they're a few feet away. Scaredy-cats.

Guess they never heard President Roosevelt say, 'The only thing we have to fear, is fear itself.'

I believe him. So does Daddie. No other President, ever, anywhere, took the time to talk to just regular folks like us. I can see him in my mind's eye: President Roosevelt sitting by his fireplace, and us boys sitting around the radio at the Taylors', with Mama and Daddie and Itsy-Bets, or just me sitting with Ephraim at the Moores'. Either way, there's a fire going in the stove and all across the land folks are listening in the same way. That makes me think he's right. He's gotta be right. I wonder if anybody told the hobos that there's nothing to be afraid of.

I believe President Roosevelt in my heart, but still, in my guts I'm scared to death of one thing. Bats. Maybe Roosevelt's right. Still, bats give me the willies. Ephraim says there's bats up in his attic.

I hear them scritch-scratching right before they fly out: a giant sigh into the night air. I'm just lying there, thinking, or sometimes that scratching gets into a dream before it wakes me up.

Bats give me the heebie-jeebies. Sometimes I wake Ephraim up and tell him to explain his plan about getting away to Chicago and playing the piano there, where everyone will come to see him and his name will be on everybody's lips. He's gonna have his own radio show, like Reverend Zollar, 'cept no talk about hell, only songs and tap dancing. Ephraim says tap dancing's the only kind of dancing people can appreciate on the radio. I do love the sound of tap dancing. Sometimes my legs seem to jump, trying to get up and dance. I never do. Get up and dance, I mean.

Anyways, Ephraim's Ma sings this song about life being a bowl of cherries and a mystery nobody can figure out. That makes no sense at all to me, 'cause cherries are as straightforward as all get out, nothing like life at all, which gets more confusing by the day. Still, I like it when Mrs. Moore sings. She gets her wide hind-end a swinging, and next thing you know, Ephraim's pounding on the piano. If his Popi's home, he'll get out a couple of spoons and bang 'em against his knee, making his own kind of music. I swear my legs start twitching to all that music. I can imagine Ephraim' music drifting out of radios all over the country and legs just a-jumping out of sheer happiness.

Daddie says dancing and singing like that's the devil's work. Still and all, Ephraim's Ma sings Bible songs that make my legs twitch the same way. I gotta believe something that makes me feel so good must be good for the soul, too.

"Are you scared of anything?" I ask Nate.

"What would I be scared of?" He puffs out his chest like Mr. Dibble's rooster. Seems everyone has a handful of chickens and a rooster these days.

"Bats?"

"Them tiny things? I could squash one with my boot." Nate stamps his foot down, as if to prove he can do it.

"You're not afraid of the rabies? I heard bats have rabies."

"Naw, a crazy bat would get eaten by a fox or something before it had a chance to bite a person."

That Nate is a real smarty-pants. He has an answer for everything.

"What about losing all our money? Are you scared of that?"

"What money? Daddie says we never had any."

"What about never getting a house again?"

"Daddie says we will. He already had that land to build on from before the fire. It's just a matter of time."

"What about dying?" For sure I got him on that one.

"Mama says we should look forward to heaven when all our strife is over."

Easter Sunday and getting baptized is still puffing Nate's chest out.

Sometimes I get sore at Nate for no real reason. He just seems so cock-sure about things. It makes me mad as a wet hen when he's like that.

"What strife do you have? Seems like you're living on Easy Street over there at the Dibbles'. Mrs. Dibble dotes on you like you're her real son. Look at those fancy clothes you're wearing. Still in your church clothes."

That makes Nate's Irish come up and I'm sorry I said anything.

"Let's cut across the Kerschkes' field and get to the river faster."

I start running through new Timothy-grass, the kind that's still soft and feathery. It's about halfway to my knees and Nate's tangling up some, so he shouts out "hey, no fair" from behind me.

I slow up a little, but not enough to let him get ahead, or even suspect I slowed for him. Next thing I know, I'm Robin Hood and Nate is Will Scarlet and we're in Sherwood forest robbing from the rich and giving to the poor, and pushing knights and stuff into the river with our long balancing poles that Robin Hood and his Merry Men always use to fight people on bridges. Nate wants to be Little John. He's too small for that. Besides, Dallas is always Little John. It's not too hard to figure out who's poor, but robbing from the rich takes a little more imagination.

We make our way back to the riverbank, 'cause that's where Robin Hood and his Merry Men do most of their work. I guess in merry old England it's big sport to push people in rivers with poles. Here fellas mostly get in fistfights until one guy eats dirt; enough dirt to cry "uncle."

Elderberry blossoms line the riverbank, pushed off the branches by new green berries. I'm thinking of elderberry pie this fall when out of nowhere, Nate lets out a scream and high-tails it up the riverbank. I tell you, I never saw him move so fast in my life. I take off after him.

"Did you see that?" he says. "Did you see it?" He turns and lets me catch up a bit.

His face is as white as bleached muslin.

What? See what?"

I start to get the goose bumps just looking at Nate's face, 'cause it's like Bella Lugosi drained all the blood out with his vampire fangs, and Nate's got the crazy eyes darting from left to right and round and round, like he's gone flappers.

"A huge snake," he says.

I laugh so hard, my legs give out and I'm in danger of rolling down the bank into the river. Nate just runs off through the Timothy-grass, legs a-churning; chin leading way out in front of his shoulders. When

I get up, I have to spint just to catch up to him. I try to apologize, but I keep busting out laughing.

"I thought nothin' scares you," I say.

I'm down in the Timothy-grass laughing all over again. Nate flies at me, fists flailing, which stuns me for about a half-second, and then I start laughing all over again. Green fills up my nose and bits of Timothy-grass blossoms sink into my mouth and nose, 'til pretty soon I'm coughing and gagging. Even that can't stop my hoots.

"Take it back. Take it back," he says with his face all blustery red.

His eyes are popping out of his head again. I can see the spit spraying out of the corners of his mouth on account of the sunshine in back of him. I just keep laughing, 'cause he looks more like one of Walt Disney's mouse cartoons than a Jimmy Cagney tough guy. All my laughing and thrashing around stirs up the sweet greenness of the Timothy-grass even more, which gets me sneezing.

"Hey, what you guys playing at?"

I know that voice like it's my own.

Me and Nate both jump up. Sure enough, there's Dallas holding his side from trying to keep up with Ephraim's smooth, long-legged strides. Ephraim's switching a big stick low in the Timothy-grass. He looks like a swashbuckler of some sort.

"Hallo. What do we have here?" Ephraim says and he points with his stick out over my shoulder.

I get goose bumps and feel the blood start pounding in my ears all at the same time. He's got that itch of his again. I can feel it.

Those words, 'what do we have here?' can mean a bunch of different things, depending on who says it and how. Ephraim's mouth is stretched in a grin that shows all his teeth, and his eyes spark. Mama calls that a Cheshire Grin. Ephraim's up to something and for sure me, and Nate, and Dallas will join right in. I can feel it in my gut.

Nate hangs on Ephraim's every word. He almost looks like a pup, his tongue is practically lolling out of his mouth and his eyes fix on Ephraim's face like he's waiting for a command. I half want to make up some reason to turn tail and head up to Potter Road and at the same time, I know I'll wish I'd've stayed if I end up hearing all about it from Dallas and Nate, 'cause all Ephraim will say is 'you shoulda went with us.' Or worse, all three of them will call me chicken liver.

Part of me wishes I was the one thinking up all the fun stuff Ephraim does, and another part of me wishes he'd move back to Pittsburgh or maybe get goin' to Chicago like he's always blabbing about.

Ephraim points out across the field to what looks like a barn, a chicken coop, a pigsty and a big white house. Anyways, I can tell it used to be white. Now it's more like a grey house with white paint falling off around it like after a bad sunburn.

"That's the Kerschke farm," Dallas says like he's telling us something new. 'Course we know the Kerschke farm, even before we moved from Vermillia Street. Still, I sorta lost the connection, with everything that happened between then and now.

"Looks like nobody's home," says Ephraim. "Let's go."

We do. No questions asked. Ephraim jabs his stick in the ground and pulls his shoulders back like a colonel of an army leading some kind of mission. The rest of us follow along single file.

Cecilea told me about Raymond and Sophia Kerschke and their three kids and their troubles. Sarah Kerschke was their oldest, and she was the same age as Itsy-Bets. The other two, I forgot. It's hard for me to remember people if I hardly ever see them. I never knew the kids' names before, but just listening to Cecilea made me think back about Mrs. Kerschke holding her baby tight in the middle of the road; the rock-swallowing feel hits me in the gut.

Cecilea said the bank tried to foreclose on the Kerschkes and put them out of their house, but Father Perotta got wind of it and all the men of the parish, and some of the women and even some kids, went over there and blocked the bank men from going in the house.

Parish is the same as church in the Catholic language, near as I can figure. Anyways, the bank men never came back, so the Kerschkes got to stay.

"There's nothin' here," says Dallas. "No tractor. No cows. Not even a chicken. No machinery at all."

Dallas pushes at the barn door, yawning open and hanging by one roller. It screeches across its warped metal runner. Behind the door is a skeleton of charred wood that reminds me of the story Cecilea told me about the Kerschkes' barn burning. That's another thing I shoulda known. A fire like that'd light up the whole sky for miles. All red and pink and yellow in a night sky is something a fella never forgets. Maybe it happened in the middle of the night.

Somehow the closed barn door makes me feel sad, 'cause it's standing there, tired and sturdy, with no use at all. I push it back, so it yawns open again.

"No sense of closing the door after the cows are out," I say and I force a laugh out.

The fellas all laugh at that, and somehow that floats the heavy feeling out of my guts.

"Where is everything?" Nate says.

That's the first I heard his voice since he got here. He's looking up at Ephraim with that same lolling puppy look on his face, which gets me aggravated, like Ephraim's the only one who knows a thing or two around here. So I pipe up and tell Dallas and Nate and Ephraim what Cecilea told me about the fire and the foreclosure and how the parish helped out. It was good to see Ephraim with his mouth shut for once, even if it lasted just about two seconds after I finished. That pushed the hollow gut feel clean out of me and left behind a good full-of-myself feeling.

"Let's go see if anyone's home," Ephraim says.

He marches right up the porch steps, punching each step with his stick.

"We could get in trouble for trespassing," says Nate.

For once, the know-it-all makes some sense.

"Not if nobody's here."

Ephraim has a point. I knock on the door, 'cause for one thing, that's neighborly, and for another thing, I'm on the verge of being called chicken-liver. My mouth has that old copper penny taste. I suck in my breath between my teeth, so my gold tooth sends a pain up between my eyes. That gets my mind off of being scared.

Nobody comes to the door. I knock again.

"Hello," I say. "Anybody home?"

Dallas pushes past me and traipses right inside. He's just showing off, I can tell he's scared 'cause I see goose bumps popping all over the back of his neck.

The whole house is empty. I mean nothing's left. No clothes, no food, no rugs. Our boots thunder on the oak floors in all that emptiness. Everything is scrubbed out clean, like Mrs. Kerschke just finished the spring-cleaning, 'cept she forgot to knock down the cobwebs around the chandeliers. Still, rainbows dance around the dining room walls on account of the afternoon light coming through the dangly-down things around the empty candleholders. I feel a heaviness in my stomach that makes me want to heave up all my full feeling. Jeez-o-Pete's, if my guts could talk, I'd be an open book.

"Let's get out of here," I say.

"Why?"

"Might as well explore."

"Don't be a chicken-liver."

"We're trespassing."

"No one will know we were even here."

Everyone has something to say one way or the other.

We go through every inch of that house. I start daydreaming about living in a house like this. Maybe this is just the kind of house Daddie has up in his head.

Upstairs are so many bedrooms. I never had a bedroom of my own. Heck, I never even had a bedroom at all. Downstairs is a kitchen and a dining room and a frunchroom. The Kerschke house is bigger than the Taylors', maybe as big as Cecilea's house, which I never went inside, but seemed as big as a hotel from the outside. I keep walking around from room to room and forget all about I'm trespassing. I forget all about Dallas and Ephraim and Nate. I wonder what it would be like to live out here and have a garden bigger than we ever had or dreamed of having. I start thinking about my dog, Butch, and how Daddie said if we ever got a bigger place, I could have a dog.

"Hey, Dallas," I say.

I'm gonna take him aside and put a bug in his ear about this house. No answer. Everything is quiet as death.

"Hey, Nate."

I start down the stairs. Still nothing. I stand still and hold my breath at the landing. Those guys high-tailed it, while I was upstairs. I can see the three of them running back to the river from the window on the landing: Ephraim up front, pointing that darned stick straight ahead of him while he runs, Nate at Ephraim's heels, and Dallas holding his side, about six paces behind, trying to catch up. Jeez-o-Pete's. Forget it.

My heels crunch the stones in the dirt driveway down to Potter Road. I was out past here with Cecilea before, on one of our walks. I can see the three of them running back to the river. I head on back to town, which just happens to take me by the Tamarack farm and Cecilea. Seems like I'm always heading in this direction when the shadows are pulling long in front of me.

Chapter 16
Chicago Bound

"Whatcha got against Reverend Zollar's Tabernacle?" I say.

Mrs. Moore is cleaning up the supper table. A warm May breeze is bringing the sound of early June bugs hitting the screen on the back door. I hear Popi harrumph down deep in his throat and a wheeze comes out of Ephraim as he scrapes his chair against the floor and busies himself clearing dishes off the table.

Wednesdays after supper, wherever I am, I listen to Reverend Zollar bellow out about hell and fire and brimstone. No matter whether it's from the Moores' radio or over at the Taylors' with Mama and Daddie.

"Nothing. I just don't want to go there, that's all," Mrs. Moore's eyes bug out at me so's all the white shows all around.

"It's the church alliance," pipes in Mr. Moore. "She's mad because the Second Baptist Church never gets invited."

"Us and the Cat-lickers," Ephraim says.

"You can go with me," I say.

I'm sore about Ephraim still calling them Cat-lickers, but I keep quiet about it. No sense in riling Ephraim up.

"It's just churches visiting back and forth. Nothing special," I say.

"Some people's just up on their high horses, that's all," says Mrs. Moore.

"If you go to The Tabernacle on Thursday, you can help feed the hobos and the drifters and even some people that live around here that are down on their luck," I say. "Even some Catholics come and help out."

I say the word Catholic extra clear, so Ephraim gets my point.

"We got enough helping out to do at the Second Baptist Church," says Mr. Moore.

He harrumphs up outta his rocking chair and clicks the volume knob all the way around to off. He turns and looks down his nose at me, which is as much a scolding as any words from him.

Two things Mr. Moore and Daddie have in common: they both work at the Shop and they both listen to Reverend Zollar every Wednesday night. There's probably more, but that's the two main things I see. Oh yeah, they both love to play horseshoes. If I stop to think some more, I'll probably think of lots more things alike about those two fathers, but I got better things to do than sit around all day and think.

One thing, for sure, that is different as to and fro: Ephraim's folks will never go near the Tabernacle where Reverend Zollar preaches, no matter how many times I tell them everyone is welcome. I see all sorts of people there. Still, Ephraim says his folks will never go there.

"Come on boys, let's get some hymns a-going," says Mrs. Moore.

"The Catholics don't want any part of the church alliance," Ephraim breathes in my ear.

He's the sorta fella that's gotta get the last word in, even if only one person hears it.

Mrs. Moore gets up outta her rocker with a big harrumph, same as Mr. Moore, like they both gotta get their engines cranked up to move their big bodies up outta their chairs. Once she gets her engine revved, Ephraim's Ma sure can move and I know she's getting revved right now, 'cause at the Moores' house, praying gets followed by singing and singing means swaying.

Most Wednesdays, I'm at the Taylors' listening to Reverend Zollar, with Mama and Daddie, and Itsy-Bets, and the Taylors. Everybody sits in their spots, like someone put their names there, quiet as field mice, and Mrs. Taylor serves some elderberry pie or yellow cake afterwards. If I'm lucky, Mrs. Taylor insists I take some, even if I say I'm too full. At the Moores', everything Reverend Zollar says gets loud Amens and Alleluias from Ephraim's Ma and Popi. It's like periods and exclamations marks at the end of the sentences in my grammar lessons, only out loud instead of on paper.

Mrs. Moore says she's taken by the Holy Spirit. Ephraim's Popi says I gotta be born again and get my sins washed away, then I'll understand, on account of I'll be saved. Ephraim just rolls his eyes at me behind his Popi's back.

"Come on brother let's go down." Ephraim bangs out a song on the piano. "Down to the river to pray."

I get all balled up inside, 'cause of Daddie saying dancing is a sin, and here's the whole Moore family dancing and singing about Jesus and Baptism and praying all at the same dang time. I feel like scramming outta there, all the while my insides are jumping and my feet start a-tapping, so of course I stay. Anyways, the song is in my head already, so's Ephraim's piano playing and his Ma's big hips swinging back and forth, and her hands a-clapping, and her feet a stomping. If I leave, it goes right with me and I'll be wishing I was right back here seeing and hearing it all for real.

"Popi, I been baptized," I say to Mr. Moore. "I'm saved." He likes me calling him Popi, now that I'm living there. In my head, he's always Mr. Moore.

"What does that mean to you, son?"

"It means I been baptized," I say. I'm trying to figure out what Mr. Moore wants.

"Is Jesus your savior?"

"Why sure. He saved everybody."

"But, did you ask him into your heart? Did you get a calling?"

I'm stumped now. Mr. Moore's talking English and all, but it's like my head thinks he's talking a foreign language, 'cause the words make no sense to me.

"Me and Dallas got baptized at the same time. Down at the Flint River, on Good Friday," I say.

"Why'd you do it?"

"Because," I say. "That's what you're s'posed to do when you're old enough."

I'm searching around Mr. Moore's face, trying to figure out what he's getting at, and at the same time, my thoughts get interrupted by how big his nose is, and how I hafta practically look up into it to meet his gaze head on, and how no matter whether he's sad or happy or mad as all get out, those eyes, always seem half-closed. His nose is about the same size as my fist, that's for darned sure. It fits him right though. Mr. Moore is a mountain of a man. I understand why the iron mines in Pittsburgh were sorry to see him leave.

Daddie always wants him on his team for the tug-o-wars at the Shop picnics in the summertime, plus Mr. Moore sure can sling a horseshoe; he's about as strong as Sampson. That gets me thinking.

"Why would Reverend Zollar want the Second Baptist Church out of the church alliance?" I ask. "Folks come from all over. Lots of folks that go to our school, and some that work at the Shop and go to the same parks and picnics. I bet there's some men that plays horseshoes with you, Popi."

"Stop asking questions about the church alliance." It's Ephraim in my ear again.

"I told you already," says Mrs. Moore. "Some people are up on their high horse."

"Let it lie, son," is all Mr. Moore says. He gives me his down the nose look again.

Mrs. Moore sings out "Amazing Grace, How Great Thou Art," and Ephraim joins in on the second line with the piano. Mr. Moore presses his finger to his mouth in the shushing signal at me behind his wife's back.

I'm snugged down under the covers almost asleep when Ephraim starts to talk about the church alliance again. He does that a lot. Talks in the dark, I mean. I guess the dark frees up Ephraim's heart to come out of his mouth.

"It's not the church alliance so much," he says. "It's that the church alliance reminds her of the same things in Pittsburgh, and Pittsburgh reminds her of Thomas. Not like she really needs anything to remind her of Thomas."

I guess sadness comes out all crooked sometimes. I just say, "Hmm," down low in my chest, 'cause that can mean yes or no, or go on, or what, or anything Ephraim wants it to mean. I figure the most important thing is I'm awake and I'm listening. Besides, I'm keeping as quiet as I can, so I can piece together the puzzle he's spreading out.

"In Pittsburgh, we had the Second Baptist Church and the First Baptist Church. The white folks went to the First Baptist Church. We never got invited to any of their doings. Ma said the First Baptist Church was high-class, up on top of the hill. She wanted to get invited up there. Some of the people in that congregation were the same people as worked side by side with Popi in the mines: went to the same picnics, and shared the same food. Mama says how come their houses and their families and their sorrows were good enough to share, but not their churches."

"Holy Mackerel," rolls up out of me soft and low from down below my belly button.

I breathe in slow and out again, like Mama does when she's giving a blessing. My eyes were drifting off toward sleep, but now they're wide-awake staring up at where the ceiling must be in the darkness.

"Did I ever tell you why we moved here?" Ephraim says.

I feel Ephraim roll over toward me; I just keep staring up where I know the ceiling is. Sure he told me before, more'n once. Still, I know enough to listen to a story when it needs to be told, even when it's been told before.

"Tell me about Thomas," I say, so I can keep from lying straight on. I'm willing to live with a lie that means I left something out.

"Thomas just got old enough to work in the mines, with Popi. Ma said no, he can't work there. Ever. It was too dangerous. She called the mine a widow-maker. If someone got killed down there, the foreman took the union workers out to the bar, which was before prohibition, of course. The foreman kept the drinks a-coming and asking new questions until the miners told the story the foreman wants to hear. They wrote down the story, then gave a ham and her man's week of wages to the widow. The other miners' families helped out what they could."

"Sharing sorrows?" I ask.

"Ma never wanted that for Thomas. She said we had to move and get safer work. That's how we came here. But Thomas was dizzy for a gal named Bette. He refused to come with us. Bette was sweet on Thomas, too. Asked him to the school dance and everything. She had the bluest eyes I've ever seen. True-blue, Thomas called them. Almost got Thomas in trouble until Bette's folks found out it was she who asked Thomas."

My mind went right to Cecilea, and Bette got to looking a whole lot like her in my mind's eye. Mama and Daddie would be sore as all get out if I went to a dance. They'd give more than two hoots whether it was me or Cecilea doing the asking. Still, I'd probably go if Cecilea wanted me to. Never mind what anybody thought; even Mama and Daddie. That gets me thinking about our night in February, spying on the Tamaracks'. I sure have a tough time keeping my mind in one place.

Ephraim starts to talk again, so my head's pulled back to where it belongs.

"Anyways, Thomas wouldn't move with us. Popi already quit the mine. He figured more cut-backs were coming soon, so's he could maybe keep someone else working if he volunteered. We had to leave. Thomas took his saxophone and moved into an apartment above the Bee Hive. Bee Hive's a gin joint. He plays his sax in the gin mills and honky-tonks, and makes lots more money than Popi ever did in the mines or here in the Shop."

Ephraim stops talking and I hear his breath suck in and hold for a long time before he lets it out again. I hear the bats rustle around overhead and swoosh out into the night air.

"Ma hates Thomas playing in the honky-tonks."

"What about Bette?"

I never heard Ephraim tell these parts of Thomas's stories before.

"She stayed with her folks. They'd have nothing to do with her as long as she's doe-eyed over Thomas. Said, he wasn't her kind; no matter how much love they had for each other, being together wasn't natural and her life would be tough as nails going out with a fella like Thomas."

"That's tougher than nails," I say.

"Thomas loves the saxophone more than anything."

I hear Ephraim suck his breath in and hold it again before he continues.

"More than Ma or Popi or me, that's for darned sure. 'Cause he stayed."

I feel a hard rock in my throat and my brain plugs up thinking about what Ephraim must be feeling without his only brother.

"Soon as I can, I'm going to Chicago and join up with somebody like Al Jolson. Somebody classy."

"You're not going to work in the Shop? Or go back to Pittsburgh and be with Thomas?"

Just about every guy's dream around here is to work at the Shop, on account of the good wages and because Mr. Durant tries his hardest to keep everybody working, even in these hard times. Mama says he gives tons of money away down on skid row. He looks just like one of the drifters down there, walking around in his patched overcoat until he finds someone he wants to help, then he pulls out a roll of bills and tucks some in the poor sap's pocket and lickety-split, Mr. Durant's out of there, before the lucky stiff has a chance to say thank you.

"No. I'm going to Chicago."

"Why not back to Pittsburgh with Thomas?"

Even though I'm sore at Dallas and Nate half the time, I gotta have those two close at hand; I need them with me way more than even Mama or Daddie.

I say to Ephraim, "Brothers have the same history is what Daddie always says, so you gotta keep 'em close and take care of them. For sure Thomas would lend you a hand back in Pittsburgh."

"Naw. Chicago's where it's at. That's where I'm going. Maybe if I get a toe in the door of a real night club, Thomas will come out there with me."

Ephraim starts flapping his jaw about Pinetop Smith and Meade Lux Lewis, and a hoard of boogie-woogie players, I only know about through him. He tells me Pinetop is dead and gone, but he's living forever through his music. Ephraim's gonna play piano with the best, or so he says.

I drift off to sleep dreaming about Al Jolson playing his trumpet on the lift of a mine shaft, only the lift looks like that giant sea snail called the Chambered Nautilus tipped on its side with a rope threaded through. Ephraim and Cecilea hang onto the rope for dear life 'cause everyone on that lift's gotta be in perfect balance or the snail-platform will tilt and someone will fall down the shaft. Cecilea's got on a blue dress and an old-fashioned bonnet and one of the sheep's crooks like Bo Peep hooked over her wrist. Her eyes are wide and wild looking.

Chapter 17
Father Perotta

At first I think the black sedan on Potter Road is one of those Sunday drivers Cecilea told me comes around every once in a while, 'specially now that summer's in full bloom and school's almost over. I guess some people have time on their hands and not enough chores to do.

Mrs. Moore says he heard the President say we gotta get out and breathe some fresh air. According to her, he said it in one of his fireside chats. 'Go for a drive in the country. It's good for the mind and the body.' Maybe Mr. Roosevelt's right, maybe fresh air can heal. I never get sick; neither does Dallas or Nate. Itsy-Bets gets protected from pretty near everything, and stays right by Mama's skirts. She's sick all the time. I never see Cecilea or her sisters missing school, so I bet they never get sick either. Those girls are outside pretty near all the time, on account of all the farm work they do.

Cecilea says some Sunday Drivers must be from as far away as Detroit, 'cause they stop and stare at deer in the field, like they're at the zoo looking at animals from Africa. Cripes, some folks are mighty strange. Once I saw a fella at Genesee Park studying a snail. He acted like it was the most interesting thing he ever saw. And that fella was a grown man, too.

The black sedan stopped right at the path where I always run into Cecilea. My blood rushes up through my neck and pounds at the inside of my ears. My legs give a wobble for no reason, and I feel my left leg give a hitch as I move forward. Just like Daddie, I think, like I'm somebody outside of myself, watching me. There's a big man in a fedora behind the steering wheel and I see a few strands of blond hair drifting out the window on the passenger side.

"Hey Eldie," Cecilea turns and sticks her head out the window.

A wave of hair the color of wheat slides out over her shoulder as she halloos at me. Cecilea's face is golden-rose on account of the sun being low in the sky. Maybe that's what Midas's daughter looked like after he touched her. I'm still feeling kinda like I'm just watching myself.

"Is that you?"

She salutes, shading her eyes, so she can see me better.

"Of course it's me," I holler back. "Who else would look just like me?"

I feel all the muscles in my back relax before I even know they were knotted.

"Dallas. Maybe."

Cecilea tips her head to one side and puts one finger on the side of her head, like she's studying me.

"Or Nate."

I can tell she's holding back a giggle and she's teasing me. Funny how Cecilea's teasing seems like honey. All the while Ephraim ribs me, it leaves a bitter taste like dandelion greens picked too late in the season.

Whoever's in that car must be fine and dandy, or Cecilea wouldn't be so darned happy looking.

"Come on over here, I want you to meet someone," she says, as she jumps out of the sedan.

I'm already on my way. Still, I feel good that she invites me like that. I would probably go just about anywhere she asked me to go, even over that cliff Mrs. Moore's all the time asking Ephraim would he go over if his friend asked him to. I would go over a cliff for Cecilea or down the river. Maybe even for Dallas, too. I'd tell Ephraim he's gotta show me how, first. He would, too. He'd jump feet first and holler while he's falling to come join in the fun.

Right away, as soon as he's got one leg out of the car, I know who the fella is driving the sedan. It's Father Perotta. He's the only guy I know with spit-polished black shoes, black socks, and black pants on at this time of day. Everybody else is changed out of Sunday clothes and into their everyday clothes. I see him all the time walking around town and cutting the grass around the Catholic Church or sitting up on his big wide porch. Always dressed like that. All black 'cept for the white ring around his throat.

'Course. Now I recognize the car, too. Who else has a car spiffy as that? Still and all I never saw Father Perotta up close, and I never saw him out driving. I only saw him out by his shed with the car pulled out in the drive, and him running a chamois cloth over the hood and fenders, keeping all the dust off, which never even had a chance to land on all that black shininess.

"Cecilea's told me a lot about you," Father Perotta says, and sticks his hand out at me just like I'm a grown man.

The first thing I notice is Father Perotta's eyes. They're the same color as the wild violets growing along the path, and they peer straight into mine from underneath his jet-black eyebrows sitting up high on a shelf of a forehead. I could never look away, even if I wanted to, which I don't. He could be searching right into my soul for all I know, one hand holding onto mine and the other one grabbing my elbow.

I know right away why Cecilea likes Father Perotta so much. I never saw anyone who looked so happy, for no reason at all. Maybe it's all that thick straight hair that kept sproinging up like black wire, or his white-white skin, or those violet eyes. Father Perotta's skin crinks up around the edges of his eyes and his mouth pulls into a smile that stays serious at the same time.

"Yeah, she's told me about you, too," is all I say. I'm pretty lame-brained when it comes to meeting people.

"Cecilea's on her way home and I'm on my way back to the Rectory. Do you want a lift?"

The Rectory is where Father Perotta lives, right next to the Sacred Heart church.

"Sure," I say.

I'd rather stay with Cecilea and tell her about the Kerschkes being gone and the house being all spic and span clean, with not a crumb left anywhere, even if it means Mrs. Moore's gonna be hollering at me for being late again. Still, Cecilea's standing there, tucking her hair behind her ears and smiling at me sideways, and I know she thinks the world of Father Perotta. Like I said before, I would jump off a cliff if she wanted me to.

"See you at school tomorrow," she says and gives me one of those shoulder high waves girls always give.

I just nod and get in the car.

Tung's oil fills up my nostrils and makes my nose hairs stand on end. Father Perotta's car is "slick as snot," as Ephraim likes to say; the seats all oiled up. It's hard for me to stay on my side when he swerves to miss a pothole or turns a corner.

"How long you have this car?" I say for no reason 'cept to break the silence.

"I don't drive it much," he says. "I keep it in the shed, most days."

"I sometimes see you cleaning it."

I hold my tongue from asking why. It's probably because of money, and it's bad manners to ask people about things that might be scarce, or eat the last biscuit on the plate, or comment about the holes in their shoes, or ask for credit. That's what cads do. A fella with good manners waits for people to offer. That's how you get known as a gentleman.

We ride along in silence, so my mind wanders around about cads and gentlemen and how sometimes it's hard to tell by looking which is which. Thoughts can travel halfway 'round a year in a couple minutes; same as dreams.

Last Halloween, me and Dallas and Nate and Ephraim all went trick-or-treating around town. Mama hates trick-or-treating on account of it being like begging. Cecilea and her sisters have to stay home 'cause her Mother says Halloween is for devil worshippers.

Anyways, most people are good-natured about kids begging for treats and give out popcorn balls or apples or Bit-O-Honey and sometimes even chocolate. Some people just turn out their lights and pretend no one's home. Then there's Mr. Pritchard. He's got a sign out front says he's a lawyer. A fine looking man who wears a tweed suit. Looks like a gentleman.

"Well, hallo there," he said, friendly as all get out.

"Trick-or-Treat," we shouted out.

"I'll be just a minute," he said, and clicked the door shut.

We just stood there on his big porch, looking at each other. Maybe Mr. Pritchard got caught off guard and had to go rustle something up. That happens sometimes with people who have no kids. They forget about what time of year it is. Once an old widow invited us in while she made us popcorn balls. That was really nice, 'cept for trying to think up things to talk about to someone that old. 'Course the popcorn noise sorta helped out, filling up the silent space where words should be.

Thinking back on it, Ephraim musta figured something was amiss with Mr. Pritchard 'cause he sorta stepped to the side and peeked in the window. I saw Mr. Pritchard's outline through the lace curtain over the door-window and whoosh. We got doused with a bucket of cold water. The door slammed on our faces, before my brain even registered it opened. Nate got the worst of it. He shivered the rest of the evening in sopping wet clothes. He sure was a good sport about it, though, not wanting to miss out on a thing.

Getting back at Mr. Pritchard is the one thing Nate took off his goody-two-shoes for. We started small with our revenge. Just a potato in Mr. Pritchard's tailpipe. More fun than Ghost Groceries ever could be because Mr. Pritchard deserved it. Us boys hid in the bushes, and watched Mr. Pritchard pump up his gas pedal and get his Model A revved, only to have it stall out before he could get it into gear. He opened up the hood, and fiddled around with the carburetor and the spark plugs and tried again. We had to run for the hills, just to keep from being found out.

Next thing you know, Ephraim got the idea to move Mr. Pritchard's outhouse over, first a few feet forward, then a few feet to the left and next a few feet to the right. We got that going once a week, after all his lights were out, and moved it back again before dawn.

We siphoned his gas out one night, and put it back the next. We even made ourselves a list of pranks to pull on that high-and-mighty cad for the rest of the winter. 'Course when summer came, we sorta lost interest in Mr. Pritchard.

"Cecilea tells me your house burned," Father Perotta says, making my mind do a U-turn and come back to right now.

He's looking straight ahead at the road. I look over at him and his hair is still roostering out of the top of his head. I can see he tried to oil it down with some Brylcreem or something, but all that did was stick hairs together so they seem like short stiff cables. My stomach lurches up a laugh, which I swallow down fast. I hold my eyes straight ahead on account of I'm afraid I will bust out laughing if I have to see his hair flopping around in the breeze.

Maybe it's because the only sound is the trees swishing by as he drives, maybe it's the goofy feel I have from the Tung's oil, maybe it's the way Father Perotta's eyes crink up and he looks so happy even as he's driving along with nothing in particular to be happy about; maybe it's because ever since I went out to the Kerschke farm I hope we can just move in there. Just until they get back. All my hope is mixed in with sad feelings about them leaving, and maybe a little guilt about feeling happy that the house is empty. Anyways, I start spilling my guts: about the fire being my fault, and all of us split up at different people's homes, and me staying with the Moores, and Ephraim. I tell him about Mr. Prichard's mean spirit, and our Ghost Groceries game, and how I feel sorta bad about the Kerschkes, especially now that their house is empty. I even tell him about the fire Dallas started at Dibble's and how I skedaddled out of there with *LIFE* in my hands, which I haven't said a peep about to anybody, not even Cecilea. Everything comes spilling out in no particular order, like I'm some sort of booby. Inside my head, I'm telling myself to stop, but I keep a-going, like a rail car outta control until I clap my mouth shut like I have a brake on it, 'cause maybe I'll let slip what me and Dallas and Ephraim did out at the Tamarack farm back in February.

Besides, we're sitting in front of the Moores' house.

Father Perotta puts his car in neutral and pulls back on the brake. He slides one leg up on the seat and his arm stretches out across the back. His violet eyes look right into mine. They're cow-eyed wet, and at the same time, his face is holding a happiness underneath the sad eyes.

"Are you sorry for what you did?" he says.

"'Course I am."

"You believe God forgives sins?" he says.

"I've been saved for over a year. Me and Dallas got baptized by Reverend Zollar last Easter."

"Sometimes it's easier to ask God for forgiveness than to ask people."

"I s'pose," I say. Father Perotta's eyes lock on mine and his eyes crink up again.

"Something to think about," he says. "Especially when that person is yourself."

My stomach gives a lurch and I'm half wondering if I'm hungry and half wondering if I'm gonna be sick.

Father Perotta swivels back around, releases the brake and waits for me to get out. I hear him pop the clutch in and shift into first gear. The sun's nothing but a red line stretching across the end of the street, lights popping on in every house, and the smell of all those suppers cooking in everybody's kitchen seeps out to join the night air as I step off the running board to face Mrs. Moore and the chores I'm late getting done.

Chapter 18
Remembering Vermillia Street

I get a sick feeling in my gut a lot. Sometimes it's something I smell, or something I eat, or even something I'm just thinking about. I get feeling like I'm gonna throw up when Mrs. Moore makes me drink milk with the bean soup she makes. I can feel the milk curdling up underneath the beans and all the side-pork grease floating around on top inside my stomach. Daddie says me and Mama are the only people he knows who can tell where their food is in their body and what it's doing at any one time. Anyways, sometimes I have a hard time telling right away whether a jumpy stomach, Mama calls it the turvy-tummy, is something worth mentioning or not.

The first springtime after we moved to Flint, everything made me feel sorta sick. For one thing, everything smelled like sawdust and burnt metal and the kind of glue that holds linoleum together. Even two years later, the air still smelled like that on account of so many new houses still getting built

"My stomach feels sick," I said to Mama.

"You're feeling poor nearly every day," she said.

Mama was barely listening; she was that busy. She had a serious, sad look about her, like she does when she's figuring something out. She had times back then, when she was more sad than happy. She got a deep, sadness going, the kind where even her eyes seemed clouded over and deeper than eyes should be. Even her happy look was sorta pasted on top of the sad, and she couldn't clear her eyes free of it.

Daddie was happy as a clam. I never saw him so happy, before or since. Daddie is happiest when new things get his juices jumping. New places, or new people, or new tools. Anything new.

Mama likes things the same. I suppose she missed Auntie Laura, who stayed in Pearl. I know I still missed Middie a little bit. Still and all, I had Dallas and Nate to keep me company and new friends at school. Daddie had all the new men at the shop, like Mr. Moore, who was an old hand there, seeing as he'd been there a year before Daddie started. Daddie got to know Reverend Zollar, really well, just about as soon as we moved to Vermillia Street. Mama had Isty-Bets and putting the house just the way she wanted it. Plus, I was getting the turvy-tummy all the time. I guess I sorta got on Mama's nerves on top of everything else.

Getting on Mama's nerves was different than the way Ephraim or I get on his Ma's "ninth nerve," as she calls it. Mrs. Moore's whole body gets in a stir and a hum. She's like a teakettle coming to a boil. One of those whistling kinds. She gives a whole lot of warning before she blows. It only takes a fella one time hearing that ruckus; when the signs start a-coming, Ephraim and I start scurrying around, doing anything to keep her gasket from blowing.

Mostly Mama's calm and quiet, and the only way I can tell she's mad is her lips disappear into a line, and she tucks her fly-aways up the back of her neck. 'Course she tucks her hair up for all sorts of reasons other than being mad. I gotta look at all the signs together.

The year we moved to Vermillia Street was different. Looking back, Mama was sort of sinking into sadness, like those safari fellas in the

Tarzan movies sink into quicksand. The more she tried to fight it, the deeper down she sank. And all the while, my stomach kept acting up; sometimes feeling like a rope got tied around with a hangman's noose.

Good thing Auntie Laura came to visit; for Mama and for me.

Auntie Laura hated changing up things even more than Mama. Daddie and Uncle Frank never could talk her into moving to Vermillia Street so Uncle Frank could work at the Shop, even though the pay was better and she'd have her pick of brand-spanking new houses, with linoleum in the kitchen and indoor plumbing.

"I heard tornadoes rip through the houses there," Auntie Laura said to Daddie.

"Sure," he said. "That's true. There's tornadoes in Pearl, too."

"Never been one where I live," Auntie Laura said. "Our house's been there a hundred years."

No arguing with logic like that. Even I could see that.

Anyways, Auntie Laura came visiting with Uncle Frank, and stayed all weekend. She came in like a basket of Blood Root flowers after the last snow, dragging Uncle Frank along like last fall's oak leaves. Everything got dizzy happy for a while.

"What you need is a new dress," Auntie Laura said.

"What's wrong with my dress?" Mama asked.

"Nothing," Auntie Laura said. "But look at this rose garden linoleum prettying up your kitchen. You don't need that either. A plain wood floor is just as good."

Mama palmed up the back of her neck and looked down at her hands warming up around her teacup. When she looked up, Mama's eyes were all wet and glassy, and her teeth held on to one side of her bottom lip. She nodded at Auntie Laura. "Perhaps you are right."

"I usually am."

The two of them took off right after dishes. Leaving me and Dallas and Nate with Uncle Frank and an icebox full of cold ham and cheese and Auntie Laura's apple pie.

Most times, I could feel my stomach begging to send down Auntie Laura's food, but that day, my stomach lurched just listening to Auntie

Laura giving Uncle Frank instructions, just in case she and Mama got back after lunch, which is exactly what happened. My stomach seemed to be telling me, if you send food down here, you'll be sorry. Uncle Frank got sorta miffed when I refused all the good food that Auntie Laura was so kind to prepare and bring all that way for us to eat, and that he had to put on the table because both Auntie Laura and Mama got to lollygagging somewhere.

They got back just in time to fix supper and kiss Daddie goodbye before he went off to the Shop. I'll never know for sure, 'cause Daddie never said, and I was too green in the gills to pay attention to him, but I think he got confused by the way Mama looked when she got home.

First off, she was happy as all get out. So happy it was like she was somebody else in Mama's body. Her cheeks looked all rosy, sorta like Middie's did when she came over to our old house and Daddie was home. Plus, she had a new dress, store bought, and a brand new hat that looked like something out of *LOOK* magazine; a hat sorta like a football helmet only softer and girlie looking, with a big wide ribbon around. Mama's fly-aways peeked out all around the sides like they were plastered down with wallpaper paste in neat penmanship capital Cs all around her face. Those two things were enough to set us all back on our heels.

When Mama took her hat off, I swear, Daddie tilted back in his chair so far, he 'bout tipped over, and a knife sliced from my lurchy stomach and came out my side right above my hip. Mama's hair was gone. I mean it was short as I ever seen a woman's hair.

"Now ain't you a sight for sore eyes," Daddie said.

He pulled his mouth in a wide grin that looked real as can be, 'cept his eyes never lit up like usual. No stars; not one twink.

"You look like you just stepped outta a magazine," Dallas said.

"She's sure is pretty as a picture, isn't she?" said Auntie Laura.

She was as proud as if Mama was her own pretty baby, instead of her little sister. Mama blushed bright, put her hand to her neck, where she used to have hair and looked at Daddie.

"What do you think, Lew?" Auntie Laura said.

"I'll tell you what I think," Daddie said, and he pulled Mama up close and gave her a big bear hug. I never saw him do that before. Mostly Daddie just patted Mama's hand, or kissed her light as a feather. "You seem happy as a school girl," he said.

"Lew." Mama said. "The children." She pulled away and smoothed down her new dress. "Supper's waiting." Mama tied on her apron and got busy.

I stopped paying attention after that, on account of the knife pains going from my stomach out my side. I never wanted to spoil Mama's good day, so I sat at the table and picked at my food, pushing it around, and putting it to my lips and back on the plate again. I recall Daddie hitching up his leg and heading for the davenport with Uncle Frank while Mama and Auntie Laura cleaned up the dishes. Daddie tuned in "Press-Radio News." Mama put a hot water bottle on Daddie's knee and tucked the afghan around his lap.

After Daddie left for work, we listened to "Colonel Stoopnagel and Budd." Mama switched off the radio and started chatting away with Auntie Laura and Uncle Frank. Most of the rest is kind of blurry, on account of fever setting in.

"Good Lord, you're burning up," Mama said when she came to pray over me at bedtime.

"Did you go to bed on your own? How long have you been feeling poorly?"

"Off and on all day, I suppose."

Next thing I remember Dr. Friese probed and prodded me and asked me when I ate last and what, and when I last had a movement. I wanted everyone to hightail it outta there and leave me alone.

Dr. Friese looked up at Mama. "It's appendicitis. He needs an operation."

"No," I said as loud as I could.

I remember that clear as day, I never wanted an operation. Never, ever, on account of Itsy-Bets getting an operation on her neck when she was just big enough to crawl. Dallas and me saw it all through the window. We just got home from school and found the door locked, so we went around to the side of the house and peeked in the kitchen window. There was Itsy-Bets laying on the kitchen table still as dead, a cloth over her face, and Dr. Friese with a knife up to her throat. Mama told us later, it had to be done because of Itsy-Bets's thyroid got so big she was choking on it. Still and all, I never wanted to be splayed open like a fish getting cleaned.

"No," I said again.

"Is there something we can do until Lew gets home?" Mama said.

"We can pack him in ice," Dr. Friese said.

"What do you think, Frank?"

I could hear Mama and Uncle Frank and Auntie Laura talking things out by the davenport in the next room. Of course it was better to wait until Daddie got home. Of course it was.

I never knew ice could burn and freeze and hurt and feel good all at the same time. One minute I was hurting like blue blazes and the next minute everything was numb. I drifted in and out of sleep, thinking how I ruined all Mama's happiness. Even her slicked down curls all framing up her head had come loose and fly-aways stuck out all around her head. She kept smoothing them down, but with no bun to hold them in place, her fine coppery hairs sproinged up all the more.

By morning, when Daddie got home from the Shop, I was feeling right as rain in April.

"Can I have pie for breakfast?"

"Of course not," Mama said. "Fried oatmeal, today."

"I should've known."

Daddie scratched his chair back, harumped himself up out of his chair, and patted me square on the back. "Looks like you're feeling better."

"No operation. Right?" I asked.

"Let's see what today brings," Daddie said. "Appendicitis is nothing to fool around with."

"I'm good now. No pain at all."

"Dr. Friese says it must come out," Mama chimed in.

"I saw what they did to Itsy-Bets. I never want to be splayed out like that."

"We'll see what you think when you're in all that pain again, and ready to split open on your own," Mama said.

"No need to get melodramatic, Ida," Daddie said.

Daddie gave Mama a sorta one-handed hug and she leaned into him and patted his belly. I never could put my finger on it, but it seemed like my appendix reset something. Mama was like her old self again; the real kind of happy, the way she was before we moved; rather than giddy-happy like after she went shopping with Auntie Laura. Daddie's eyes matched his slow smile. He no longer had that pasted on smile look about him.

I ate up my fried oatmeal and headed out to get the ashes dumped in the ash can out back, pick the eggs, and maybe bring some wood in for Mama's cooking needs. For sure, I planned to prove I was good as ever. No need to call Dr. Friese or start getting the kitchen table ready for another operation. No need, at all.

That's the way it's worked ever since. Whenever I feel the appendicitis kicking up a storm, I get packed in ice. Ice calms the fire down. Only thing is, sometimes I have a hard time knowing whether it's the turvy-tummy, the jitters, or the real thing. In the summertime, I gotta wait until I feel the knife stabbing, on account of ice costing upwards to thirty cents in the summer, which is more than a good cut of meat. My appendicitis treatment could feed the whole family. Still, it was loads better than Dr. Friese operating on me.

Mama's sadness got pulled clear of the quicksand. Maybe Auntie Laura was right; Mama just needed a new dress. Maybe worry about appendicitis shook the sadness out of her. Sometimes she sank down a little, but never again did her eyes go fish-eyed dead. Daddie always says if you're feeling sorry for yourself, look around for someone who needs a little help. Mama did get to watching me like a hen with a chicken hawk hovering over her chicks.

I know she loved the hat Auntie Laura helped her pick out. Mama wore it everywhere she went. Seemed like she'd wear a hole right in it.

Sometimes she forgot to take it off in the house, she loved it that much. I guess she wore it until her hair got long again. Her bun made the hat lump out queer, so she put the hat up on a shelf in her bedroom in one of those round hatboxes. Even though Mama never wore that hat again, it's sorta makes my heart sad to think even that got taken away by the fire.

Chapter 19
Dibble's Five and Dime

"Let's get out of here," says Ephraim.

He comes up between Dallas and me and shoves us like he always does. I'm sure glad Nate was on the outside edge of us three brothers walking on the sidewalk, 'cause for sure, he would of gone flying.

"Sorry, I gotta run some errands for Mama," I say.

I keep my eyes straight ahead, so's I can keep away from Ephraim roping me in. I'm heading over to Dibble's Five and Dime, but there's no reason Ephraim has to know everything I do.

"What kind of errands?"

"Just stuff. You know. Stuff mamas always want you to do."

"Yeah, I gotta pick the worms off Mrs. Pederson's tomatoes," says Dallas. "She's fit to be tied, with those ugly cusses chewing up half a plant before she or I even notice they are there."

"I hate the horns," Nate says.

I swear I see him shudder.

"She slices off their heads with her thumbnail."

I feel sorta queasy thinking about green blood on Mrs. Pederson's apron.

"See ya later," Dallas gives his sideways grin at me and waves.

"If you're lucky and I'm lazy," says Ephraim and he heads off for home.

I gotta make up excuses for everything these days. Most days after school, Dallas and Nate and Ephraim want to go to Torrey Yard. Mrs. Moore wants me home to feed her chickens and gather the darned eggs, which would be okay, 'cept for the sitting hens, which peck the living daylights out of my hands and arms. She should let those hens have some chicks instead of insisting on the eggs. Still, she sells the eggs for 2¢ apiece, less than the grocer and fresh that day. The Moores need it too, because the Shop is down to two days a week now, which stretches pretty thin according to Daddie. He reminds me to be too full for seconds on even Mrs. Moore's meatless meatloaf, and to leave a few crumbs on my plate so she'll be sure to believe me. The first part is easy, but leaving scraps behind pains me, especially if Ephraim starts banging on the piano before the plates are cleared away. Sometimes I got my fork in my mouth, with that last bite I meant to leave behind, before my lips even know they opened up.

Daddie tells me to come to The Tabernacle to help feed all the hobos soup on Thursday. I get something to eat there, just for helping out. Cecilea and her sisters came there all winter long, with milk and dark bread.

All I really want to do is take a walk down Potter Road and run into Cecilea, which hardly ever happens now that summer is in full bloom and the calves are born. She says there's tilling and still some planting chores to tend, and the first mowing of hay to get raked and dried. There's no time for lollygagging.

Besides, there's one other thing I want to do. I gotta square things up with Mr. Dibble. My stomach knots up, just thinking about admitting everything to him. Especially since so much time has gone by and he's gotta know it was us fooling around in his store. He might be clueless about Mama's magazine. Maybe he never even missed it.

Father Perotta gave me the idea about fessing up to my part. Anyways, he got me thinking about making amends somehow. The thoughts niggled in the deep parts of me already; Father Perotta just got the thoughts out of dark clouds and into thoughts I can put into words and action.

I'm tagging along with Nate on his way to Dibble's Five and Dime like I just want to be with him and keep him company. I plan to see if Mr. Dibble will let me work some, to pay him back for the damage from the fire Dallas started. I got to thinking on it after talking to Father Perotta. His words about forgiveness stuck right up in my brain, and they keep pestering at me pretty near day and night. Maybe I needed to earn some forgiveness from Mr. Dibble. Okay, sure, it was Dallas started the fire, but I never did a thing to stop him, or the fire, and I never took Mama's *LIFE* back, or paid for it or anything. Maybe it's not God's forgiveness that's weighing on me.

That whole business of starting a fire is way different than any other pranks we pulled. Sure I feel bad about the Kerschkes and our Ghost Grocery game, but still and all, nobody got hurt, or nothing was taken away from those folks. Good Lord, both Dallas and I know how much a fire can take away from a fella. I never want to think about being responsible for something like that. Never again in my life. Never ever.

Maybe I should feel bad about Mr. Pritchard, but the fella had it coming and then some. Besides, seeing his face all contorted and angry as all get out, with no one he could be angry at; well that was the berries, that's for darned sure. It almost made it worth getting sopping wet on Halloween night.

I keep mulling around on Cecilea and her sisters and what we did back in February. Father Perotta comes up all over again, and how he said, you gotta think about what good saying sorry does and who it's for anyways.

All that remembering gets me right up to Dibble's Five and Dime. I push all my worry about Mr. Dibble down inside me like an old davenport spring. The little bell over the entrance rings out so's he knows someone came into the store.

"Whatcha doing here?"

It's Dallas that I see first inside the store. He's pulling Mrs. Dibble's feather duster behind his back and getting his Irish up at the same time.

I feel the blood drain out of my head and settle in around my guts making me feel sorta full.

My brain is in slow motion, 'cause at first I try to think of some reason to tell Dallas why I'm at Dibble's, then I try to think of some reason Dallas is here, and how he got here so quick on account of him being so plod-footed.

While all that slow-motion thinking is going on, Mrs. Dibble comes in from the back room with a plate of oatmeal cookies with real raisins in them. Nate's trailing right behind her, fist already full of cookies. I guess he went straight back there without me even noticing. I see the raisins poking out of the sides of the cookies, all plump and juicy. Mrs. Moore uses currants instead of raisin. I hate currants, 'cause of all the seeds. There's more crunch than taste to a currant. I can smell the tartness of those raisins and something else.

"You got black walnuts in there," I say.

"How'd you know?" says Mrs. Dibble. She smiles straight at me. That's one thing I learned from Daddie. Women love to talk about their cooking.

"I can smell them," I say. Nothing covers up the smell of black walnuts.

My tongue gets all wet in my mouth and all my thoughts go out of my head, so all that's left is an empty hole in my gut that wants to be filled up with Mrs. Dibble's cookies.

"Whatcha doing here?" Dallas says again, still all red in the face.

"You're lucky and I'm lazy," I say.

Dallas laughs, even though I can see he's trying hard to keep serious. His laughing makes the feather duster bop around, peeking out from behind his shoulder. That makes me laugh right out loud. Nate just sits there looking at the two of us, first me, then Dallas, all the while chewing on his cookie. Jeez, he sure is spoiled.

"How about some cookies and milk, boys?" says Mrs. Dibble to me and Dallas. She already knows the answer.

Nate goes in back to fetch the milk pitcher from the icebox. Dallas gets around in back of the counter and eases the feather duster down on the shelf. I know he's hoping I never notice. What a dope. For sure something's up, 'cause he should never go behind Mr. Dibble's counter, let alone with a duster that I already know he's got. Still, I just keep still. I want Dallas to keep his dander down. No ruckus is gonna come between the cookies and me.

Soon as I bite into one, my mouth fills up with the musty bitter of the black walnuts, along with the sour-sweet of raisins. I just want to hold that cookie bite in my mouth as long as a can to suck out every last bit of goodness, the black walnut flavor oozing up into my nose. My stomach wants the cookie too, and I swallow before my mouth is ready to let go. I take another bite.

I'm off daydreaming about the Kerschke farm and the black walnut tree between the house and the skeleton of a barn, with nothing else there 'cept dandelions poking through the burnt timbers and the cement sidewalk that led out to the clothesline. One thing about nature: it never seems to care what's happening to people or what happened last year, or what's gonna happen next year. It just minds its own business and keeps on popping up new growth.

Itsy-Bets could have a swing on the thick branches of the Kerschkes' black walnut tree. I'd put pieces of old, worn out tires over the branch first, like the swing out back at the Pedersons'. Mr. Pederson put that up for his son back when he still wore short pants. Dallas told me how sad Mr. Pederson looked talking about his son off in California, now that he's all grown and seeking his fortune. Dallas says the rope isn't one bit frayed 'cause of the rubber between the tree branch and the rope, and it's still strong enough for Dallas to sit on, even though he's almost as big a grown man.

"Is there something you need?"

Mr. Dibble is standing behind the counter where Dallas was. Dallas is nowhere. He must've moved while my eyes were up inside my brain imagining the Kerschkes' house.

"Yes," I say.

My throat goes all dry. All the words are going around in my head, but they won't get down in my mouth for some reason. I'm just sitting there looking at my hands gripping the edge of the counter. I take a last gulp of my milk.

Mr. Dibble just stands there waiting, looking straight into my eyes, like he's trying to bore into my thoughts.

"I came here to talk about the fire you had in here a while back."

"Uh-huh." Mr. Dibble closes his eyes and holds the lids shut for a moment. I see his eyeballs move under the lids before he opens them back up again."

"I was here that day," I say.

"I remember that day like it was yesterday." Mr. Dibble rocks back his heels and pushes his fists into his pocket.

"I got something to tell you about that day."

Mr. Dibble closes his eyes real slow again. When he opens them, they look clouded over, like he's got a touch of the rheumatism.

"Go on."

"I was here that day, getting a *LIFE* magazine for Mama,"

I gulp and take a breath and start over. This time all my guilt spills out of me like the bottom of a bag of groceries letting loose. I probably make about as much sense as that, too. Words tumble out of my mouth, bumping into each other and scrambling up like eggs in a bowl. Somehow I manage to leave Dallas and Ephraim out of the story. I'm not a squealer.

Mr. Dibble just stands there, with his hands planted in his pockets, with his cloudy eyeballs drilling into mine, just listening and listening until I stop to catch my breath. Jeez-o-Pete's, I bit my tongue in all that. I can taste blood.

"Do you want to work it off?"

"What?"

"Do you want to work to pay for the damages?" Mr. Dibble says. "I could use some more help around here."

Mr. Dibble opens the cash register, removes the money tray and pulls out a sheet of paper. All the damages are listed right there: matches, floorboards, ceiling paint, and all the sundries that got destroyed by the fire. Beside each line item, Mr. Dibble wrote down a cash figure. All the numbers are lined up in a neat column with all the decimal points in a neat column, 'cept for the last one, which is scribbled in like an afterthought: *LIFE* 10¢. I look up straight into Mr. Dibble's eyes.

"Lucky all those matches burned bright and cool," Mr. Dibble says.

I just stare. I never heard of a cool fire.

"I got the fire out with a couple of buckets from the washtub in the storeroom."

"Oh." I hafta say something, just to let him know I'm listening.

"Well?" Mr. Dibble says.

"Yes sir?"

"Are you ready to work it off?"

"Yes sir."

"Good to hear. Now come on back here and you can help your brother."

Right then a key turns in my head and I know Dallas has been coming to Dibble's Five and Dime after school ever since Nate walked down into the Flint River on Easter Sunday.

A strange thing happens. Poetry springs into my head, clear as if Mrs. Bidrall is standing next to me and Cecilea's reciting in her angel voice:

> Wrecked is the ship of pearl!
> And every chambered cell,
> Where its dim dreaming life was wont to dwell,
> As the frail tenant shaped his growing shell,
> Before thee lies revealed,
> Its irised ceiling rent, its sunless crypt unsealed.

I never even knew I memorized that poem and here it is springing out in my head. That poem still makes about as much sense as reading a book on a summer Sunday. Still, I smile 'cause it seems like I learned something when I wasn't even trying.

Chapter 20
Kerschke Farmhouse

"Psst."

It's Ephraim. I tell you, Dallas and Ephraim are worse at keeping still in school than I ever thought about being.

I glance sideways at him, so Mrs. Bidrall's none the wiser. Next week I will be free of this place. This is my last year at Cronk School.

I slap at the back of my neck where I feel a fly-bite, and come away with a wet wad of something.

Ephraim's got a loony grin on his face that makes him look loony, especially since his eyes are straight ahead. Even so, I can see those dark eyes glisten with his mischief, even from the side of his face. He gives me a palms-up shrug without looking over at me. Mrs. Bidrall watches Nate put the Six-Times tables up on the blackboard, which gives me plenty of time to scan over the room and find the pill who shot a spitball at me.

Dallas's eyes train on Mrs. Bidrall with his ears all going red. He slips something under his behind. Yep, it's Dallas all right, hiding the peashooter he got from Mr. Dibble when he got the debt all paid off. He's still going every day after school to work at the Five and Dime, because he wants to help pay Nate's way, on account of Nate is still pretty much a little weakling and does next to nothing around there. Besides, Mr. Dibble gives Dallas things like that peashooter.

Sometimes Dallas can be a dirty dog to me for no reason at all.

Mrs. Bidrall calls Cecilea up to the board to do the Twelve-Times tables. That's the hardest of all, if a guy just tries to memorize. Memorizing is sort of lamebrain, if you ask me. I got an easier way: 12 X 12 is the same as 12 X 10, just add a zero, and add on 2X12. Two easy as pie multiplications added together. One hundred forty-four. A simpleton can do it. Teachers sure can make things tougher than they really are.

I'm sick of being inside when bees are buzzing outside, and the smell of the honeysuckle blooms comes in from the schoolhouse window so's my whole brain fills up with outdoor thoughts and nothing else can get inside.

Mr. Dibble treats Nate good and all, and Dallas loves getting cookies from Mrs. Dibble. 'Course I do, too. Still, I plan to get a job on a farm, so I can be outside all day. I hate being cooped up. Besides, I'm kinda sore at Mr. Dibble since he told me to help myself to a sandwich that got thrown in the wastebasket. I'm not that hard up that I have to eat somebody else's trash.

"You're looking like you can use some meat on your bones," Mr. Dibble said.

He saw me standing there with the sandwich in my hand. Me just wondering why the heck somebody threw a perfectly good sandwich in the trash; not even a bite out of it.

"You can take it. It's okay."

"Naw," I said.

"Somebody must have dropped it there, coming in from Woolrich's lunch counter," he said. "Still looks fresh."

My stomach feels all clenched up just thinking about it two days later, sitting here in the classroom, wishing the end of the week was here. The look on Mr. Dibble's face, like he just did me the biggest favor in the world. Thinking about it makes me feel sorer than the day it happened.

I hear a fake cough behind me. The kind that comes out way louder than any real cough. It's Ephraim. I can tell without turning my head.

"Want to go to the movie house?" he whispers.

"Can't," I say out of the corner of my mouth.

"Why not?"

"Gotta get over to the Taylors'."

"Why?"

"Shush," I say outta the corner of my mouth.

Ephraim thinks he needs to know everything about everything. Sometimes I feel like giving him a poke in the nose. He deserves it for being so nosey. I smile a little at my own joke.

I turn a little toward Ephraim and roll my eyes toward Mrs. Bidrall. I mouth "Dynomite" at him. I feel a jumping feeling in my guts that's partway between excited and afraid. Ephraim gets the hint and leaves me alone. Now I'm halfway between sorry and relieved. Mrs. Bidrall pulls the map out, getting ready for geography class.

I look over at Cecilea already getting her book out, like she loves geography more than anything in the world. Her blue-green eyes seem bluer, now that the sun's put even more streaks of wheat color through her chestnut hair and put the roses in her cheeks, like Mrs. Taylor likes to say about Itsy-Bets.

Cecilea must've felt me looking at the back of her neck. She turns, looks straight into my eyes, and gives me one of her halfway, lips-only smiles. I stare down at my hands, 'cause I can feel the heat rushing up my neck. Mama can wait. I'm finding some reason to walk toward the Tamaracks after school, and get away from Nate and Dallas and Ephraim, too.

Turns out, it's no problem at all. All I see is the backs of Nate and Dallas. Ephraim gives me a half-shove, his shoulder bumping mine.

"See ya, wouldn't wanna be ya."

"If you're lucky and I'm lazy," I say back.

I realize too late, with what Ephraim said, I sound lame-brained. He sure is quick. I make no sense at all. Ephraim is already laughing his head off and waving with his back to me. Good, I think, no need for excuses or lies.

Cecilea is half a block ahead, but walking really slow, so I catch up in no time. I feel so comfortable walking along quiet with her, just listening to the jays and the grackles arguing and the breeze rustling high up in the tiptop of the trees all around us.

We get to Potter Road. The sidewalk disappears and the fields start up; everything's flat and open. It's like we just walked through some sort of doorway to freedom. I get to thinking maybe this is the way Daddie feels walking along, quiet and relaxed on Sunday morning.

I'm talking without thinking about what I want to say. I tell Cecilea about Mr. Dibble and the sandwich I found in the wastebasket. I was planning to keep that all to myself, never tell no one.

"He makes me angry, thinking I'm that poor, I have to eat out of a wastebasket."

"Maybe Mr. Dibble was trying to be kind," Cecilea says.

"Maybe he was trying," I say. "It don't matter what he was trying. He was a long way from kind."

Now I'm feeling sore at Cecilea for taking Mr. Dibble's side.

"You are rather thin," she says.

Cecilea takes my hand, turns and looks up at me. I try to hold on to what she said that made me sore at her. We start walking again, but I keep ahold of Cecilea's hand. Her hand is velvet inside of my burlap bag hand.

"Father Perotta talked about kindness, just last week," Cecilea says. "You know Mr. Dibble is Catholic."

I just nod. Part of me is thinking that 'course I know, everybody knows what church people go to, and only Cat-lickers play piano or organ the way Mr. Dibble and Cecilea do. Darn it all, sometimes I still think Cat-licker, but least I never say it out loud anymore.

"Father Perotta says if you're feeling blue and feeling sorry for yourself; if you think you're in a bad situation, look around for somebody to help."

"Daddie says something just like that."

"Maybe Mr. Dibble listened to what Father Perotta said."

We walk along silent. Somewhere in that silence I think about Reverend Zollar and the Tabernacle and the bread lines on Thursdays.

"Is that why you help at the bread lines?"

"Maybe. Why?"

"I have to. Daddie says so."

"My Papa, too. Still, when I get home, I feel so lucky. I have everything I need. More than I need. I have enough to share."

"Yeah, me too."

I'm not just saying that to please Cecilea. I do know what she means. Even if my family is living in other people's houses, we still see each other, go to church every Sunday together, and we all have warm beds and clean clothes.

"That Father Perotta has a lot of smart stuff to say in a few words," I say.

Cecilea stops. She still has ahold of my hand, so I twist toward her. She looks up at me again. Her hair is coming loose and the breeze fans it out around her head, with the sun shining through. She's so close to me I can feel her breath. She smells like cloves. Cecilea squeezes my hand. Her eyes dart back and forth like she's searching my face for something.

"He is so wise," she says.

"Listen," I say. "I better hightail it. Mama's waiting for me. She wants me to help her get all the ironing and laundry sorted. She gets tired out easy these days."

"Why's that?"

"Every time I ask, Daddie changes the subject, and Dallas just rolls his eyes and calls me a dope."

"Oh-ho," she says.

I see in my mind, a funny papers' light bulb over her head.

"What 'oh-ho.'?"

"Is she getting big in the belly?"

"Why are you asking that?"

Cecilea cheeks look like they're on fire and she looks at her toes.

"Better ask your Mama."

Now I feel the heat coming up my neck. Why the heck does everybody want to talk like riddlers? I turn and start running back toward the Taylors' house and Mama. I imagine Cecilea is watching me run away from the sun. I don't turn back until I get to the sidewalk. Cecilea's nowhere in sight.

I make out Father Perotta standing at the Taylors' porch from two blocks away. He's got one foot on the first step, his fedora in his hand. I know it's him, 'cause it's the middle of the week. Father Perotta's the only man I know that dresses like it's Sunday every day of the week. He's talking to Daddie, which scares the begeezers out of me. For one thing, ministers only come to houses in the middle of the week with bad news, like somebody died. Even I know that. For another thing, nobody living at the Taylor house is Catholic, not us, and not the Taylors.

I cut through in back of Mrs. Taylor's lilac bush, and head for the back door. The lilac branches bend low, heavy with blossoms; the smell almost makes me keel over. Daddie is listening so hard to Father Perotta, he never even notices me. Something must be wrong, that's for sure.

Inside, Mama's got her thin-lip face on, which is another reason I know something is wrong.

"Where have you been?" she says. "I expected you here right after school."

"Sorry."

I start helping her bundle up the piles of her laundry pieces according to family. Everything smells like Ivory flakes and starch, all crisp and mended, and folded in neat piles. Mama can make a patch next to invisible. Either that, or she makes the patches look like they're meant to be there all along. Mama is the best at setting everything in good order.

"Get the string," she says.

We tie up the bundles, me putting my finger on the crossover, so Mama can tie the bow nice and tight. By the third bundle, her tight-lip face is gone, and pretty soon, her face looks almost as relaxed as when she's praying over us.

"What's Father Perotta talking to Daddie about? And why are you tired all the time?"

I'm risking the tight-lip again. Still and all, if I spit out both questions at once, I'm bound to get one answered.

"Curiosity killed the cat," is all Mama says.

Drat, less than one answer. No sense in pushing any further. The two of us just work quiet; the only sound is our breathing, the rustling of the brown paper, and the low voices of Daddie and Father Perotta riding on a wave of lilac perfume. I feel so content, I think there's no way those two men can be talking bad news.

The screen door slaps. Daddie comes across the dining room and stops in the kitchen doorway.

"Birdie," Daddie says. "We're moving."

Mama ties my finger into the bundle. She's all tight-lipped again, and for no reason at all I think of her and Daddie in the train station back when Nate was still in the baby buggy.

Daddie stands there trying to look all serious. He keeps his mouth steady, but Daddie's eyes are twinking away like the skies on a clear night. Those blue eyes never can hide how Daddie is feeling.

Something peculiar happens to Mama, just then. Her mouth gets all slack-jawed and her eyebrows shoot up. She just stands there, one hand on the package with my finger stuck in the knot, like she's frozen or something. My brain keeps popping out questions faster than I can ask them, so nothing at all comes out.

"It's the Kerschke farm," Daddie says. "Father Perotta arranged it."

"What?"

"Father Perotta. He says we can stay there until the Kerschkes come back or the bank sells it."

"How?"

"He convinced the bank that it's better for them to have a squatter who works right here and plans to stay in the community, than to have drifters roll in and maybe burn the place down."

"What?" Seems like Mama is just a one-note woman.

We can start moving in today if we want." Daddie takes a step toward Mama and me.

"What?" Mama sweeps her hair up toward her topknot.

"There's room for all of us."

Daddie picks Mama straight up and swings her around right off her feet. Mama throws her head back and laughs right out loud with all her back teeth showing. Daddie's laughing out loud too and swinging Mama around like something in a Cary Grant movie. I never saw Mama and Daddie like that in my whole life, up until this day. I plan to make this a memory I take out and hold onto, 'cause I bet I never see it again, if I live to be as old as Methuselah.

Chapter 21
4ᵀᴴ of July Picnic

"Get yourself ready for the 4th of July picnic," Mama says to me and Dallas.

She's got Nate on the chair cutting his hair with her mixing bowl on top of his head.

"What's so funny?" Nate says.

"Stop wiggling or I'll make a mess of your hair."

"Nothing," I say, pulling my hand across my jawbone.

"I can see your eyes laughing."

"Just reminds me of Pearl, is all."

'Course that's far from what's really funny, but it's part of it. Me remembering Pearl, and Dallas and me in a chair getting our hair cut before another 4th of July picnic. The picnic when my Kiddie Kar kept pinching my taliwacker; the day me and Dallas sneaked off to Middie's house. 'Course, we were way littler than Nate. Heck, we were littler than Itsy-Bets. Least I was.

"Remember how you all slept on the same mattress by the stove?" Mama says.

Her eyes look shiny-wet. Her tight-lippedness is nowhere in sight. "We'd never fit now," Nate says.

"Now us boys have our own private room, just the three of us. Out of your hair," Dallas says.

"And I have a room all to myself," says Itsy-Bets.

She's starting to get that holier-than-though attitude Nate had for a while. Now Nate's all settled down and more like one of the guys. Next year he and Itsy-Bets will be the only ones of us Craines at Cronk, and Dallas and I will be in 8th Grade at the High School. Me and Dallas and Ephraim, too. We could stay another two years at Cronk, but Daddie says we gotta transfer to the High School, 'cause of better opportunities. Ephraim's gonna go wherever me and Dallas goes, that's for darned sure. He's keeping mum about High School, but I know; he'll be with us. He's practically like a brother now. Well, like a brother that gets on my ninth nerve.

"You're not gonna believe who's coming up the drive," says Dallas.

He lets the screen door slap behind him as he steps out on our porch.

Our porch. I'm still getting used to thinking that way.

Nate and I follow. Right off, I guess who it is, but it's like my mind created one of those mirages people see in the desert. I try to think of someone that looks like her as she gets closer, right up until she says 'hallo boys,' and I know from the voice, it's sure as shooting, Middie Sterling.

"I hardly recognized you two," Middie says, squinting at us. "You're so big."

The three of us stand there, mouths half-open, looking at Middie, like we're deaf and dumb.

"Do you remember me?"

"Why should we?" Nate says.

Middie laughs, "You were not much more than a baby."

Nate gives Middie Mama's straight-lip look, and pulls his lower eyelids up just a little.

"You're different, too," says Dallas.

He says what I'm thinking, 'cause Middie looks the same. Sorta. I mean, for sure, she's got the same hair and the same smile, and she's even smoothing down her dress, like I remember, only just with one hand, on account of her other hand being busy with a cake carrier. Still, something's missing from how she used to be.

"Is your Mama here, too?" I say.

"No. She's still in Pearl. Is your Mama here?"

The screen door sproinks open and Mama's hugging Middie, before I have time to turn around.

"Middie Sterling, I heard you were coming."

"It's Middie Reeves now. I'm married to John Reeves. Dr. Reeves's son?"

"You grew up to be a teacher and a doctor's wife?"

"Not exactly. John's never finished school. He's helping with birthing the farm animals when there's trouble. 'Course there's not much of that. Animals seem to find their way on their own, for the most part. He can shoe horses, too, but there's not much use for that either."

I just stare at Middie. She's a teacher? No. I never would have guessed it in a million years. Well, mulling it over, maybe it does make some sense.

"Looks like you're growing, too," Middie says to Mama.

Mama smooths her hair with one hand and touches her belly with the other. She is getting sorta round. Her Irish creeps up her throat and leaves a red splotch between her collarbones.

"Some things stay the same," she says. "Come on in."

Mama and Middie talk grown up talk. I stick around just long enough to find out Middie's going to be teaching at Cronk school on account of Mrs. Bidrall will be "showing" before school starts in the fall, and Middie and her new husband will be at the picnic with her chocolate cake. It seems "showing" is against the rules for teachers.

"My Mama taught me how to make her best chocolate cake," Middie says.

She tells Mama all about how she made it, starting with eggs and butter. Mama smiles at her, like it's the best news she heard in a long time. Middie opens up the carrier and cocoa smell surrounds my head and seeps into my nose, so I can almost taste it. Lickety-split, Dallas wipes a dollop of frosting from where the plate meets the cake. Mama swats at Dallas, but his hand is faster, and he pops his finger straight in his mouth. Middie laughs the way I remember her. I can almost taste the bitter-sweetness of the frosting Dallas swiped, that's how clear the memory of Mrs. Sterling's cake is in my mind.

Holy Mackerel, I hope I never get all dull like Middie, thinking a recipe is the most interesting thing in the world. She's the same Middie with all the vinegar and vim hidden somewhere inside her; nothing left on the outside but ladyness. I start to wonder if Mama ever had some sass in her. Did she skip rope or play hopscotch or rough-ride a wagon down a hill? I hope to high heavens Cecilea never gets so that all of her sunshine is hiding behind a cloud of adultness. I'm sure as heck never gonna forget what it's like to be a kid. I got the best memory for things I want to remember.

Dallas and Nate and I hightail it outta there, and tell Mama we'll meet up at the picnic at Kearlsey Park.

"Don't get dirty," she calls out, as my feet hit the bottom step of the porch.

"Jeez-o-Pete's, she still thinks we're little kids," Nate says.

"Wanna go take a look at the Tamaracks' pigs?"

Dallas looks sideways at me and raises up one eyebrow. He finally learned that trick of Ephraim's. I bust out laughing, and Nate just looks at me all queer. He's one of the guys now, but he'll never catch up to all the memory me and Dallas share. He'll never be an Irish twin. For half a second I think about tricking Nate into kissing one of the Tamarack piglets, but no sense in getting Mama all riled and making Nate go back home before the picnic. With my luck, she'll make me go with him.

We head over to Zyber Brothers and rummage around in the back for some boxes. The store's closed on account of it being a holiday and all. We stash the boxes in back of Ephraim's house, behind the chicken coop. Ephraim and Popi and Ma are nowhere in sight. Probably over at Kearsley Park already. Daddie left early to get his tug-o-war team together: the Shop against the merchants. After that the farmers team plays whoever wins. For sure, Popi's on Daddie's team. Popi's the strongest man working at the shop.

By the time we get over there, blankets and picnic baskets are set up all over tarnation.

"Where's Mama?" Nate says.

"Same place as always, I'm sure of it," says Dallas.

I know he's right. Mama likes things the same. I can see Itsy-Bets sitting on the tablecloth that Mama laid down, up at the top of the what hill there is. Anyways, that's the best place to have our picnic and watch everything that's going on, and see the band.

Somehow, everybody's got lots to eat when it comes to picnics. We might be having milk toast or bean soup for dinner near every night, but today, we have a feast. It's sorta like that story about the stone soup. Somehow, everyone finds the best food to lay out at picnics. Mrs. Moore's fried chicken, Mama's sourdough bread, Mrs. Taylor's pie, Mrs. Pederson's potato salad, Mrs. Bidrall's deviled eggs, and Mrs. Tamarack always brings the ham. The Tamaracks have their own smoke house. This year, there's Middie with her Mama's best chocolate cake. 'Course the fathers make ice cream, even though ice is precious. It's 4th of July. Even the littlest kids get a turn at the crank. My mouth starts to feel slippery inside just thinking about all the good food.

"Come on back over here where you belong," Mrs. Zyber grabs ahold of a tow-headed girl with a blue ribbon in her hair.

"It's fine," says Mama. "The girls just want to get to know each other."

Mrs. Zyber relaxes her grip a little.

"What's your name?" says Itsy-Bets. She's got an embroidery hoop on her lap. Mama's teaching her to make daisies with French knot centers.

"Rita."

"I'm 'Liz'Beth. Wanna be friends?"

I never heard Itsy-Bets say her name like that, almost as formal as church. I mean I know her real name's Elizabeth, but I never hear anyone call her anything but Itsy-Bets, least of all her.

"No," says Rita.

Itsy-Bets, looks at Mama. Mama just smiles at Rita.

"Wanna learn to make flowers?" Itsy-Bets says.

I'm thinking Rita's way too little for a needle and thread. Still and all, Rita nods her head and plops down beside Itsy-Bets. Mrs. Zyber sits down beside her. Mama gives Rita a needle and thread and a square of muslin. Itsy-Bets shows Rita how to push the needle in and out and loop the floss around the needle. I start to say something before I see nobody's listening. I gotta hand it to Mama; she knows how to keep little kids busy and at the same time teach 'em how to be good helpers. I guess that's the same way all the fathers do with the ice cream.

Rita's and Itsy-Bets's necks are craned over so their heads almost touch, with Mama's and Mrs. Zyber's bent over above the girls. Sunshine dances off loose hairs floating up in the breeze like spun gold dancing around hearts inside of hearts that are really bodies bent over in work.

"She'll be in school next year," says Mrs. Zyber to Mama.

"She's so small."

Mrs. Zyber nods. "She is a slip of a girl, and she's young yet, but smart as a whip. She already knows how to read." Mrs. Zyber straightens her back so she looks taller sitting there. Now Mama's smile shifts from Rita over to Mrs. Zyber.

"Rita's going to school next year, even though she will still be in her fourth year on this earth."

"What a blessing," Mama says.

She smooths Itsy-Bets's needlework between her thumb and first finger, so her daisies lay flat. Mama keeps mum about how Itsy-Bets can read, too. Even if pride is a sin and all, sometimes it's better just to let people be a little puffed up and feeling special. I bet Mama feels that way to.

"What did you bring for the picnic?" Mama asks. I think she's just being polite.

Mrs. Zyber looked down at her hands, and says nothing for a bit. "We eat our own food."

"Well, you're welcome to join us. The families from the Shop potluck our picnic. Lots of the farm folks join in, too. You're more than welcome."

"We better get back to our own."

Mrs. Zyber stands up and bunches her skirt in her fists. She clucks to Rita to get a-going. Rita puts up about a half-second of protest, before she looks up at her mama. She's got the brownest eyes I ever saw next to Ephraim's. Just like Ephraim's; so brown they're almost black. I never saw such brown eyes on a tow-headed kid before.

I hear the band starting up on the other side of the park. Without saying a thing to each other, Dallas and I head over there. We walk along comfortable like that, without talking or even looking at each other.

"Wait for me," comes from Nate, behind us.

He brushes up next to me and falls right in step with the two of us. I see Ephraim galloping down the hill from where his Ma's got her tablecloth spread, just a few feet from ours. He's flapping his arms at us, and hallooing away, as if it's been ages since we last saw him.

"Going to listen to the band, strike up a march?" he says pushing up between me and Dallas. Even that seems comfortable and right nowadays.

"Sure thing," says Dallas.

"We put some boxes behind your chicken coop," pipes in Nate.

"I can hear Sousa, already."

"Who's Susan?" I ask.

Right away I wish I had Mama's way of smiling and keeping quiet, 'cause there's Ephraim with his head thrown back in a wide mouthed guffaw.

"Sousa. Not Susan," he says. "Just the most important march composer in America."

I can feel my ninth nerve start to throb at Ephraim. I tell you, sometimes he can be a real music snoot. Dallas looks at me over the back of Ephraim's shoulder and gives me the one-eyebrow up look, and at the same time he pulls the down-eyebrow side of his mouth down. Nothing in this world can keep my nerve twitching with that booby hatch look.

I feel the Zyber brothers' tuba and bass drum down deep in my guts before I hear a melody. Already my legs twitch underneath me. But different from the way Ephraim's music make my legs twitch. Sousa's music makes me wanna get up and go somewhere, or do something. Rita's marching in place in front of the bandstand and wagging a tiny flag in the air. Her Mama looks happy as all get out, no longer holding her skirt in stiff-armed fists.

"How come the Zybers have their own food?" I ask Dallas.

"Same reason they don't work at the Shop." It's Ephraim talking.

"I heard the Shop asked the brothers to come work there on account of they want their own band," Nate's putting his two cents in.

"He can't work at the Shop," says Ephraim.

"Why not?" says Dallas.

I get distracted trying to figure out how Nate knows what's the what's up. 'Course it's because he's still working at Dibble's Five and Dime. All sorts of news comes through there.

"The Shop won't hire his kind."

"Shopkeepers?"

It's the second time Ephraim gives me his head thrown back laugh with all his back teeth showing.

"He's a Jew," Ephraim says. "Don't you know anything?"

"Mr. Dibble says he's a good Jew," says Nate. "He never cheats anyone and gives more credit than he should. Sometimes his own family goes hungry."

"I heard the Jews steal and eat Christian babies," says Ephraim. He pulls a face that looks surprised and at the same time scared as all get-out look.

"You told me the same thing about the Catholics," I say.

I feel laughter bubble up below my Adam's apple and I let it burst right out of me. I see the folks from Zyber Brothers' setting out their picnic. Going up the side of the hill is Father Perotta and the Tamarack girls carrying baskets of food.

"One of them two does, the Cat-lickers or the Jews. Maybe both. Plus, the gypsies. Don't forget about those folks."

"Well, look at that little bit of a girl, Rita. She looks like she could blow away in a summer wind."

Dallas and Nate slap their knees; they laugh so hard.

"Maybe the Zybers are from Transylvania like Dracula," hoots Dallas.

"They're just people, is all. Look at 'em, Ephraim," I say.

I sling my arm over Ephraim's shoulder and swing him around toward the band. The Zyber brothers are puffing and working so hard to make their music that beads of sweat stand up on their foreheads and run down into their ears. Rita grabs a hold of her mama's skirt and dances in place until Mrs. Zyber picks her up and marches her around in time to the music, pumping Rita's little arm up and down all the while.

"Just people," Nate says.

"Just people," Dallas says.

One thing's for sure about Ephraim, he can never stay mad with good music in the air. And Sousa is in the air, and beating through the ground, into my legs, and out my chest. I doubt there's a fella in this world can stay mad with Sousa making his heart beat the same as everybody else's around him.

Chapter 22
Another Kind of Fire

"Hey Ephraim, wait up."

I strong-arm Ephraim right between his shoulder blades. He turns and gives me a Hollywood slug in the guts. Same as always. Ephraim is my best friend, when I'm not hating him. Next to Dallas of course, who is the first friend I ever had. Nothing can make that different. Daddie was right about brothers sharing the longest history with a fella. That's what makes them the best friends in the whole world.

Mostly I'm done hating Ephraim. He's different now that I got my family all back together under one roof. Maybe it's me that's different.

"Wanna go to Dibble's?" I say.

"Nah. I gotta get home."

Ephraim gives me one of his full-out grins.

"How 'bout the movie house?"

"Nah. Ma's expecting me."

"Aw come on." I bump my shoulder against his. "You can charm the honey from the bees."

I learned that one from Ephraim, so for sure I got him there.

"Nah. I got things to do."

"Like what?" I want to know.

"Like none of your business."

He's still grinning that toothy grin of his, and shaking his head at the ground. If he gave any of his down in the dumps looks, I missed it. He just looks happy, and for some reason a little embarrassed.

"Whatcha keeping?" I say.

"Nothing you need to know or care about."

That sorta hurts, 'cause it seemed like just last week Ephraim had a hard time holding one thought behind his tongue.

I head off toward home. Home. We have one. All of us Craines together, spread out in the same house, feeling like we're living in a mansion, even if there's no indoor plumbing and no electricity. Holy smokes, it's the best house in the whole wide world.

"Eldie," I hear Cecilea's voice behind me.

"Hey."

"Where are you going so fast?" Cecilea brushes her hair behind her ear.

"Home. I got chores to do."

"Me, too. How's your pup?"

"Named him Prince," I tell her.

"How's he doing? Does he miss his mother and his family?"

He's happy as a clam, but I soften it a little on account of Prince is from Cecilea's bitch dog, Patch. Daddie brought him home just after we moved into the Kerschke farmhouse. 'Course, he thinks it's a secret, but Dallas and me know it was him and I know it's one of the Tamarack's pups. I found Prince inside the ash can, whining and a-whimpering, when I went out to do my chores.

Where'd that mangy cur come from?" Daddie said.

He pulled his hand down over his mouth, and rubbed at his chin. Still and all, he never can get the smile out of his eyes. Mama closed her eyes and let her breath come out slow. She wiped her hands down the side of her apron.

"Looks like a pup's found you," she said.

"How'd a pup get in an ash-can?" Nate said.

"How'd your fish learn to walk on land?" Daddie said.

Right then and there, I knew for certain, even though I already had a strong hunch: Daddie put the pup in the empty ash can. I looked at Dallas and his eyes matched Daddie's, with the same solemn face. I got to wondering if Dallas was in on it. Later on, when I got him cornered, he convinced me he never knew; he was as surprised as me. I still think he was keeping mum 'cause he was afraid of jinxing it.

"You better give that pup a name," Daddie said. "And teach him to mind. A dog's got to pull his weight in a family. There's no free ride."

"Prince," I said.

I knew it the first I laid eyes on him. Besides, I saved up that name ever since I lost Butch. Right off, Itsy-Bets and Dallas and Nate started calling to Prince: "Here Prince, come here Prince." The poor pup looked all confused and he peed right on my lap, which got everybody but Mama laughing their insides out.

I tell Cecilea, "He whined and whimpered at first, but he's gotten over it. Mama put a clock in his bed and a water bottle,"

Cecilea nods. "A heartbeat and a warm belly to cuddle up to."

"He's a good dog. Smart as I can hope. He already knows how to stay and sit and come."

"You need a good watch dog."

"That's just what Daddie said."

We walk along together, 'cause home is in the same direction now, so it's natural as natural can be. We don't go straight home though; we go down by the willow tree that's half in the river. The same place we went the first time we ran into each other out walking back in March. Only now I know why she was standing there at the end of the lane leading up to her barn. Cecilea told me all about it, once, when we were out taking a walk on this very same road. Potter Road. The road Cecilea, and now I live on; almost neighbors.

Back in March, Jeez-o-Pete's that seems about as long ago as living in Pearl. Cecilea saw me running from way up on the hill where her chicken coop sits. She was just finishing up the gathering, and she saw me. Eventually she told me she came down here on purpose hopin' she'd meet up with me.

I like to turn that one over in my head from time to time, just to bring back the way my stomach reached up to meet my heart when she first confessed it to me. I do that now as we're walking along. 'Course we walk straight on over to the river. We never even ask each other if we want to go there, 'cause we both know. I like that about Cecilea and me. Lots of things get understood with no words uttered.

New growth sprouts up smack dab out of the dead willow, springing up where life was before the lightning hit it. Twigs are coming to life right from the trunk and some are sticking straight out of the riverbank. The bark from the downed tree is crumbled and rotten all around below the trunk half-sticking in the water. Pieces are flecking down into the water and washing away to somewhere else.

"I never told you, but we had a fire at the farm, too," says Cecilea, her back getting even straighter than usual. "Not like your house burning down."

Cecilea gets all quiet, waiting for me to ask her. That's what she does: says a little then waits. At first I thought she had nothing left to say, like me. I got all jittery 'cause I felt like one of us had to fill up the space where silence fell. Now I know she always has lots to say, she's just polite and waits to be asked before she blurts things out.

"What happened?"

"I was very little, maybe about Itsy-Bets's age or Lucy's. You know Lucy? My littlest sister?"

'Course I know Lucy; she's the same age as Itsy-Bets. Someone else might think Cecilea is part daft asking a question like that. I know she's just working up her nerve to tell me something important. That's another one of those things we never put into words 'cause we both already know.

"Mother told Margaret and Theresa and me to hide under the bed."

She stops and waits again, but I don't have a question, so I just wait too. The willow branches make a soft hushing sound.

"Mother and Papa locked the doors. I smelled the smoke and heard men's voices in the front yard. Margaret tried to stop me, but I had to see what was going on, so I came out from under the bed and looked out through the lace curtains."

"The barn?" I say. "Was it the barn, like over at the Kerschkes'?"

"No. Someone made a huge cross out of timbers and stuck it in the ground in front of our house," she said. "That takes a lot of work. You know. To sink a big timber cross in the ground so it stays upright."

"What?"

"A timber cross burned there. Black smoke covered up the sky. Flames licked up so high, I thought the oak tree would catch."

"A timber cross?"

I never heard of such a thing.

"Mother said men brought it there and burned it on purpose to scare us. I never saw a soul. By the time I crawled out from under the bed, they were gone. All I saw was the cross and the smoke and the flames."

"Why would someone want to scare you?"

"Mother and Papa never said. But Father Perotta says sometimes people do hateful things out of fear."

"Afraid of what?" I asked.

"Catholics moving in."

"What?"

My mind is trying to make some sense of grown men being afraid of a farmer and a house full of girls. Most of 'em little girls. A farmer who can hardly talk English.

"Catholics." Cecilea says a little louder.

I guess she thinks my 'what' means I didn't hear.

Cecilea turns and gives me that darty-eyed look of hers. The one where her eyes search my face for an answer to a question she never asked. My stomach's all knotted and my heart pounds up in my throat.

I kiss Cecilea square on the lips without even thinking about it.

Maybe I wish all her sad thoughts could be erased, like Mrs. Bidrall's blackboard after lessons. Maybe I wish I could protect her from ever getting hurt. I'm not thinking about any of those things, to tell the truth. I'm not thinking at all. When I pull away, she's looking at me with her mouth kind of wet and quivering between a smile and a frown. Just before she looks down at her hands, her green-blue eyes lock right on to mine.

Father Perotta's words rings in my ears, just like he said 'em to me instead of Cecilea. I suppose he's right about people doing hateful things when they're scared. Cecilea sure learns a lot from him. For some reason I think of Father Perotta's eyes fixing on Cecilea's dancing eyes, and how she must have felt all calm inside with his simple words and lots of room to let them roll around and sink down into her heart. My neck gets all tight and my scalp starts to tingle for no reason I can think of.

"Sorry," I say.

"Don't be," she says.

She looks straight into my eyes like she's studying them. She pulls in her breath, deep, almost like a yawn and holds it there a couple seconds before she lets it out slow. She gets up and heads down the path toward her house.

For some lame-brained reason, I just sit there until she disappears.

I get up and walk along the river to my new home.

Mama's doing laundry at the riverbank where I climbed up that day a couple months ago and saw the Kerschke house and met Dallas and Nate and Ephraim. Without electricity or a washer, Mama's laundry and mending business is all dried up. She's down here with a washboard, doing our own laundry. She puts the last of Daddie's workshirts in the basket just as I get there, so I pick up the basket and carry it for her. Mama tries to smooth her escaping curls up toward her topknot. She's red in the face.

I think of Cecilea pushing her hair behind her ear like she does. Pretty near everything still makes me think of Cecilea.

"Did you ever hear about people being afraid of Catholics?"

Somehow it's easier to talk to Mama or Daddie when we're walking side-by-side.

"Why do you think people call them Cat-lickers?" Mama asks me.

"Just 'cause it sounds funny."

"It's hateful."

"Did you know about the cross-burning at the Tamaracks'?" I ask her.

"Who told you that?"

"Why does that matter?"

Mama glances at me. "I thought that trouble was all in the past. Especially since the Moore's moved here without a fuss. I thought we were done with that trouble, and you had no need to know about the hatefulness."

"Is Mr. Moore a cross-burner?"

"No."

Mama looks off at the sun sinking low in the sky, sitting just above the tree-tops. The smell of our very own tomato vines stings in my nose. My mind starts to wander to Dallas and wondering what he's up to, when Mama starts talking again.

"Come help me hang the laundry. I'll try to explain The Klan to you."

Anyone else would've told me, I'd've never believed it. The Klan is something like out of the movies, like King Kong, or Frankenstein, only scarier, 'cause none of the people are pretend, they're all real, and they think of themselves as good God-fearing people.

"Do you know people in The Klan?" I want to know.

"It's a secret group."

"You mean it could be anyone?"

Mama turns and looks at me, one hand on a clothespin she's clipping onto the line. She says, "By their fruits you shall know them."

She picks up the laundry basket and moves it down along the line a little, puts a clothespin in her mouth, picks up one of Daddie's shirts and gives in a hard snap before she starts clipping it to the line. The clean smell of Boraxo fills up my heart.

"Good gravy. I gotta ask Ephraim if he knows about The Klan."

"Of course he knows about The Klan," Mama says.

"Why do you say that?"

"His kind knows all about the Klan from the Civil War."

"Ephraim says his family never were slaves. They lived by Pittsburgh and never even saw a cotton field. They're musicians and artists on his Ma's side, and miners and foundry men on his Popi's."

"Makes no difference to blind folks."

"Blind folks?"

"I mean their eyes are shut. They can't see the truth. Their ears are shut, too. Can't hear the truth. I suppose a closed heart starts to shut out the truth in every way."

Mama's got her back to me, hanging up the clothes. For some reason that makes it easier to talk to her. Even easier than when we're walking.

"What's the truth Mama?"

Mama considers for a moment. "God's spirit is in every single soul. There's an Inner Light in each of us, no matter what we look like, or where we come from."

"Can you see folks' Inner Light?"

"Sometimes I must trust it's there." She snaps another shirt before she starts talking again.

"Sometimes it's easy. Stillness helps me see."

I think of Mama putting her hand on me at night when I was little, not saying a thing, and how her hands on mine makes me still feel all quiet inside.

"What about Father Perotta?" I ask.

"Of course he has an Inner Light. Just like everyone else."

"No. Do you think he can see?"

"Sure seems that way to me," Mama says. "He's a gentle man. And he leaves plenty of room for people to understand how important they are."

"That's for sure," I say.

Mama smooths back her curls again and rubs the back of her neck. She seems tired. Even more tired than yesterday.

Prince bounds out from under the porch and pushes his muzzle into my hand. Dallas must still be at Dibble's Five and Dime, working late.

I get a-going and leave Mama alone. I got chores to do. I got our own chickens to feed, and some weeds to get out of the garden. I don't need a crank to get me started. 'Sides, I got a lot to roll around in my head.

Chapter 23
A Land of Milk and Honey

"Finish your johnnycake," Mama says. "Get on your shoes."

She kneels down to fix the bow at the back of Itsy-Bets's dress, but she's talking to me. Morning sunshine comes in through the open window in slanty rays like those pictures of heaven. I look at Dallas, who pulls a face at me, a bit like Daddie does sometimes, which makes me flat out laugh.

"What did I say?" Mama says.

It's not really a question.

"Why do I need my shoes on?"

"Because I'm going to work. You're going over to the Tamaracks first. With me and Itsy-Bets."

"What?"

"You keep talking about going over there. Now you're going."

"I do?"

"I've got ears."

Mama sorts beans now, over at the cannery, on account of her mending jobs stopped about the same time she stopped doing laundry. Those two go hand-in-hand, Mama says. Mama says we need the extra money because Itsy-Bets gotta have a snowsuit by winter, 'cause she's starting school. She's gonna be sorely disappointed, 'cause all she talks about is getting a pair of shoes with a pocketknife in the side like me and Dallas and Nate got when we started school.

Heck, she was just a twinkle, as Daddie likes to say, when me and Dallas started school; still, she talks about it like she does remember. Maybe she remembers Nate starting school. Maybe, if Itsy-Bets's got a memory like mine. Mama will never let her have a pocketknife. Pocketknives are just for boys.

"I can walk Itsy-Bets over to the Tamaracks," I say. "That way you have all the time in the world to get to the Taylors'."

Mama's always worrying about hitching her ride to the cannery with Mrs. Taylor. Being late would just about be the unforgivable sin.

"Don't call me that. I told you I'm 'Liz'Beth. Itsy-Bets is for babies." She sticks her bottom lip out at me.

"Itsy.. 'Liz'Beth," Mama says, turning Itsy-Bets around to face her. "Better pull that lip in or a bird will perch on it."

Itsy-Bets looks up at the ceiling before she pulls her lip in. Mama looks up at me; her lips are pressed together so tight all the pink is drained right out of them.

"Get your shoes on," she says. "We can get started together."

Of course that's just what I do, and so does Dallas, 'cause he knows what Mama says to me is for him too. Nate just studies his johnnycake, resting his chin on his hands.

"Elbows off the table," Dallas says at the same exact time he swats Nate's arm out from under his chin.

Nate's chin hits his plate and johnnycake flies up and lands on the edge of the table, spewing clumps out every which-away.

"Shush," Mama says. "Daddie's sleeping. The least we can do is let him rest on the days he's home. Now get your shoes on, while I get your dishes done up."

Mama's lily-of-the-valley smell fills up my heart as she clatters the dishes to the kitchen sink. Itsy-Bets sticks her tongue out at me from behind Mama's skirts.

"I could walk Itsy-Bets over to the Tamaracks by myself," I say to Dallas. "Why do you suppose Mama says no?"

"Mama never lets Itsy-Bets out of her sight, 'cept when she goes to church. It's a wonder she's even taking her over to the Tamaracks."

"All they have over there is girls, that's probably why. She'd never even get a scraped pinky finger over there."

"That or she thinks you'll take Itsy-Bets fishing, and never make it to the Tamaracks at all," chimes in Nate.

"You mean 'Liz'Beth?" I say.

All three of us laugh at that one, but into our cupped hands, to keep Mama from hearing and so Daddie stays sleeping. Dallas slugs my shoulder.

"Do you suppose Jesus was a shouter?" I say to Mama.

We're walking along all silent and everything, which makes my mind wander around to a bunch of stuff: Cecilea first of course; asking Mr. Tamarack about working on the farm; which gets me thinking about Father Perotta, Daddie and last off, Reverend Zollar.

"What?" Mama says.

Dallas bumps his shoulder against mine and gives me his one eyebrow up look that makes me swallow down an out and out donkey-laugh. I want Mama to listen to me.

"Do you suppose Jesus was a shouter, like Reverend Zollar?" I say. "Or do you think he was more like Father Perotta?"

"What's Father Perotta like?"

Mama already knows Father Perotta, from when he came to tell her and Daddie about the Kerschke farm.

"How do you know Father Perotta?" Dallas chimes in.

"I talk to him sometimes. Ever since he gave me a ride into town once when I was out walking on Potter Road, before we moved out here."

"When was that?" Dallas says.

He's all the time trying to catch up on the stuff I did when I lived at the Moores' and he was busy hanging out with Ephraim, like Ephraim was his new best friend. Funny how that worked out, me living with Ephraim and Dallas hanging out with him all the time, and me wishing I never met Ephraim. I sure was sore at him back then. Maybe at both of them.

I answer Mama's question and ignore my brothers. Dallas gives me another screwball look; this time I feel more like slugging him than laughing. Nate's already skipped ahead, kicking a stone along the road.

"Well, for one thing, Father Perotta has violet eyes. I never saw anything like those eyes of his."

"Violet eyes?" Itsy-Bets says.

She gives a skip while still holding Mama's hand, which kicks dirt up on account of she's just learning to skip and it's a lot more of a skid than a skip. Mama just listens.

"When he talks to me, he looks right into me, and I never heard him shout. He just says a few words; words that make me think."

"What kind of words?"

"Mostly about sin and forgiveness: God's and people's. Reverend Zollar got me thinking about whether God shouts, with all his fire and brimstone and casting into hell talk, which is all kinda scary. Father Perotta makes God sound a whole lot more like Daddie: stern and quiet and protective and a maybe a little scary sometimes. Always there even if he never tells you right out that he will be. Still, Daddie loves to listen to Reverend Zollar and the Tabernacle, and people come from all over to the bread lines and get saved."

"What does Father Perotta say about forgiveness?"

"Sometimes it's easier to get forgiveness from God than people. And sometimes God forgives us before we forgive ourselves. We have to make things right with people, even if God forgives us."

"Is that why you started working at Dibble's?" Mama says.

Dallas perks right to attention. My knees feel loose under my thighs. I'm pretty sure that neither one of us knew she was on to us on that one. Dallas sticks his hands deep in his overall pockets and kicks a stone down the road.

"Yeah," I say, "but Father Perotta never told me to do it. He just got me thinking."

We just walk along quiet for a while, so my mind jumps around again and I forget Mama never answered the question I asked her in the first place about Jesus shouting. I smell the dry-green of fresh-cut hay in the fields and hear the click-shweew of the red-winged blackbirds, and I'm off thinking about Cecilea and how she's afraid of red-winged blackbirds diving at her head, which makes me think of Mrs. Bidrall and my first day at Cronk School.

"What if a person can't come up with a way to make amends for something he did wrong?" Dallas says.

Holy Cripe, it's like Dallas and I have the same mind. I wonder if he's thinking about what we did way back in February. I wonder if he's been mulling that over the same as me, just like he did the fire at Dibble's. I look over at him, but he's still got his head down, kicking at stones and pushing his fists deep in his pockets.

"Maybe it's better just to keep that between you and God," Mama says.

I search her face to get a read on what she knows, but she's just looking straight ahead, face all relaxed, 'cept for her eyes squinting in the morning sun.

"Perhaps you need to ask yourself, who are you helping: the wronged person, or yourself by confessing," she says.

I feel like scrambled eggs inside: my legs are jumping trying to make me run, my brain is thinking up excuses in case she says something about the Tamaracks' and February, at the same time I'm trying to mull over the words she says, and coming up empty about anything else to say.

Dallas must be feeling at least part of what I am, 'cause he takes off running shouting over his shoulder. "Race ya!"

He slaps Nate's shoulder making him stumble a bit, and Nate's after him, shouting out, "No fair."

I almost run too, but then I remember something: the question I had in the first place. "What about the shouting, Mama?"

"What shouting?"

"Did Jesus shout like Reverend Zollar?"

"Maybe. Why do you care whether Jesus shouted?"

"I'm just wondering who sounds more like God talking."

"I think God talks to us the way we need to listen. If we need shouting, he shouts."

"Does God talk to you, Mama?"

"All the time."

Mama combs her fingers up through the back of my hair and grabs a handful right at the crown, before she gives a little tug that feels sorta good, kinda like the hugs she used to give me when I was small as Itsy-Bets.

Mr. Tamarack crosses right in front of us, coming in from the barn with a big pail of milk. I never even notice him up until this very minute on account of my mind pulling all my attention inside my head, so I see nothing but my thoughts. I forget all about how scared I am to talk to Cecilea's Papa.

"Do you need a hand?" I say.

"Thank you."

Mr. Tamarack says it, without the 'th,' so it comes out 'dank you,' just the same way Cecilea pronounces his words when she tells me what her Papa says. The milk sloshes around way too much, so I spill some out on the ground.

"Hold like this."

Mr. Tamarack shows me how to hold the pail in one hand and stick my other arm out to balance and stop all the sloshing around. He has the same color eyes as Cecilea.

It's a start, I think, 'cause somehow I gotta tell him I mean something more than just carrying in a pail of milk, which I can hardly do by myself. "Where should I put the milk?"

"There." Only it sounds more like 'dare.'

Mr. Tamarack points to the drain board by the sink. By the time I get to the sink, I got it in my head just what I want to say to Mr. Tamarack. I spit out how I'm strong and a hard worker, and a fast learner, before I turn around to face him, so I can keep my nerve up.

"Start Monday," he says.

Gold flecks smile in Mr. Tamarack's blue-green eyes, while the rest of his face stays as serious a funeral.

"Be here at dawn. Ready to work hard. Eat breakfast, lunch here." 'Work' comes out as 'verk.'

Mama lays her hand on my shoulder. I can tell she's smiling at Mr. Tamarack just by the sound of her voice.

"See you this afternoon," she says and, "You be a good girl," to Itsy-Bets, with a little less smile in her voice.

Mama and us boys walk down the drive together until we get to the corner where Dallas and Nate walk into town, and I head back home. I watch their backs walking side by side. Mama will take leave of Dallas at Dibble's Five and Dime, where he works now for lunch and some pocket change. She'll head on over to catch a ride with Mrs. Taylor to the cannery. Nate'll probably head home after he gabs with Mrs. Dibble and gets his fill of cookies and milk.

I guess that's the way family goes; swirling like leaves down a stream. Floating together and apart, hitting an eddy that pulls everyone together before some force spits them further down the river. Just like that crazy poem Mrs. Bidrall made us memorize, and I never thought I'd remember, 'cept for it keeps popping back into my head in bits and pieces, "Child of the wandering sea, Cast from her lap, forlorn!"

Jeez-o-Pete's, out of the blue, it hits me, I gotta talk to Daddie. It just hits me full in the face, almost like someone got inside my brain and talked to me from the inside out. All the while I was thinking about Dibble's and Cecilea and her sisters, and Reverend Zollar and Father Perotta, and whether God shouts, something else was nagging at my soul.

There's no way I can ever make it right, but I gotta tell Daddie the fire on Vermillia Street was my fault.

I talk it over in my head the whole rest of the way home: what I'll say and what he might say, and what I'll say next. I know he's gonna be mad as all get out, and disappointed, and maybe even give me a whooping, like he always says he's gonna do, but never does.

Daddie's sitting in his chair, listening to the radio when I get home. I just stand there looking at him from behind. He's got his head bent back against Mama's doily covering the back of the chair, one hand resting on his bad leg, his King James in his lap. Daddie's got his eyes closed, like he's asleep, but I know he's not, on account of the foot under his bad leg is heel toeing. The words scramble around in my head.

"What?" Daddie says without opening his eyes.

I just stand there looking at the back of his head.

"What's on your mind?"

The words move so fast in my head, I can't get them get in line to come out my mouth.

Daddie turns in his chair and looks at me. There must be something in my face that scares him a little 'cause he springs up out of his chair and grabs me by both shoulders.

"What's wrong?" He gives me a shake. "What is it?"

"I got something to confess to you," I say. "But my words are stuck. I want to make sure I tell you right."

"Just tell me. Is someone hurt? Where's Itsy-Bets?"

"She's at the Tamaracks'. No it's about our house on Vermillia Street."

"No use talking about it. That house is gone." Daddie switches the radio off before he sits back down.

"There's something I gotta say to you, Daddie."

"Leave the past behind," he says. "There's no use crying over spilt milk."

"I'm sorry."

"Sorry changes nothing. It's behind us, son. We gotta keep our noses pointed to the future." Daddie picks up is King James and lays it open on his good knee.

The words start pouring out of my mouth like it's disconnected from my brain. Everything just spills right out; some stuff I forgot I had up there. How I shoved in all the wood the stove could hold. How I was mad about doing my chores. How it was my entire fault we lost our home and we got all split up. How I go over there sometimes and all that's left is the darned chimney, and it sits there like a judge and jury. And how I was sorry for everything.

Daddie slumps in his chair and buries his head in his hands. His bad leg jumps under his right elbow so his head shakes out 'no' over and over again. I stand there; just waiting for him to holler, recite a Bible verse, or something. Nothing happened until I hear the storm door groan on its hinges and Nate whistling as he comes in the house.

"What happened?" Nate says. He stops dead in the doorway.

"Nothing," comes Daddie's voice all muffled from his face still resting in his hands.

"Did somebody get hurt?" Nate says. "Where's Mama?"

"Nobody's hurt," I say. "Not in the usual way."

"What way, then?" says Nate.

"Don't you have some chores to do?" says Daddie.

"No."

"Well, go back outside and find yourself something to do."

Nate looks at me and gives me the two palms up shrug. I just stand there, looking at him. I want to go right out the door and maybe back over to the Moores' house to live, if they would take me. Maybe that's what Daddie wants, too.

"Sit down," Daddie says.

I sit in Mama's chair, which feels sorta strange. Daddie still has his face in his hand, and his head's still shaking back and forth. I just sit there, feeling like I swallowed a rock the size of my head.

"You been holding on to this for three years?" Daddie asks, washing his face with his hands and finally looking at me.

"I shoulda told you right away. I know I shoulda. It was all my fault."

"No." He gets silent again, looking me straight in the eyes. He combs his hand through his hair.

"I know there's nothing I can do to make it better."

"No," he says again. Daddie reaches over and puts his hand on my knee, then says, "Stop."

My heart sinks down below my belly button. None of the ways I practiced our talk worked out with these words. Daddie's got tears sitting in his bottom lid. He blinks and his cheeks are wet.

Just when I start wondering if I should just turn tail and get outta there, he says, "It was the new wood."

"What?"

"I didn't let the wood cure enough. There was too much sap and water left in the wood. All that sap built up and baked onto the edges of the chimney. After a while, it was like hard tar in there. The chimney caught fire, and spit balls of fire out on the roof."

"What?"

"It was a chimney fire. I should have cleaned the chimney. I should have let that wood sit another year and cure."

The two of us sat there quiet for who knows how long.

"I'm sorry you carried that burden around," Daddie said. "It was my fault, not yours. It would have happened that day, or the next. Even if I was right there, we couldn't have stopped it."

"What?"

I'm nothing but a Johnny-one-note, quacking out 'what' over and over. My head has cotton stuffed up in there. All the thoughts struggle to find each other and struggle even harder to find my mouth.

"Chimney fires are so hot they melt the bricks and mortar and then spill right onto the wood on the roof," Daddie says. "No one could have saved the house."

We just sit there together, both studying the floor. I feel Daddie look at me, but I keep my eyes to the floor. Thoughts are still bouncing around up there. We lost our house because of wet wood, the Kerschkes' barn burned on account of wet hay.

"Daddie?"

"Yes."

"It seems wrong that the very thing we use to put a fire out, makes it burn worse than the devil's own hell."

"Never thought of it that way," Daddie says. "Reverend Zollar could use some of your wisdom."

I take my eyes off the floorboards, and look straight at Daddie's face.

"No doubt about it," he says.

A smile spreads up one side of his face, and lights up his blue eyes like stars in a winter sky. I feel my chest lighten up from the insides out.

"How'd it go at the Tamaracks'?"

"I start Monday. Breakfast and lunch at their farm."

"Good."

Daddie sits back down in his chair and presses his hand deep into his bad leg before opening up his King James.

"Take your brother fishing for a while, why don't you?"

I scram out of there, give Nate the heads-up, and we head for the river. No way I plan to let the door hit me on the way out.

Chapter 24
Exodus

"Wanna play Robin Hood at Torrey Yard later?" Nate about pulls at my overalls, he's that anxious. "Maybe Dallas and Ephraim can play, too."

"Maybe," I say. "I, next to never, see Ephraim these days."

I wonder what he's up to, but I stay mum on that one. Summer's two-thirds of the way over, and I never had time to get bored or wonder when school would start again. Nate's over all his baptism holiness now, and got back to being a normal kid. Still, he can get kinda blabby about asking questions when he should keep quiet and just figure things out on his own.

"It might be late. Mr. Tamarack keeps me working 'til sundown," I say.

I give Prince a scratch behind the ears.

Prince is one smart dog. He already knows how to stay and fetch. He's tan and black, sorta like Butch was, like maybe they had a relative somewhere in their past. But Prince is taller and he's thicker in the chest and his muzzle is broader. Daddie said Butch was a purebred, and Prince was the Heinz-57 variety, which means he's like us, nobody can say for certain where we come from.

I head outside, telling Prince to stay, and giving Nate the go-ahead to teach Prince to sneeze on command. That's the trick I'm working on now, on account of Mama said no to teaching Prince to speak. She said that's the last thing our house needs, is a dog barking for attention.

I think I satisfied Nate's questions. For some reason or another, he follows me, just walking along beside me as I head over to the Tamaracks' to work. He's chattering on about Robin Hood and the Torrey Rail Yard. He's all red in the face, probably thinking about the fun he wants to have.

"Mama might not let us go after dark," I remind him.

"We could sneak out onto the roof and climb down the walnut tree."

"Now there's an idea," I say.

For Cripes sake, I'm dead tired at the end of the day. Farmers work hard in the summertime. Girls too. Now that's embarrassing as all get out. In July, Mr. Tamarack was just getting in the second cutting of hay. I never had so many blisters in my life, and there is Theresa and Cecilea picking those bales up by the wires and throwing them on the conveyor like nobody's business. I was up in the loft about dying from the heat. All that good green smell of fresh-cut hay filled up my hair and clothes and stuck inside my nostrils, so even after supper and home in my own bed, that's all I smelled. I sure am glad Cecilea and her sisters never saw me up there, sweating like no tomorrow, hands covered in blisters. Just when I felt like I got a system going, toting and stacking cross-wise like giant bricks on a tower, we finished. Whew.

"Maybe I can teach you mumblety-pegs," I say to Nate.

Nate starts skipping. Maybe he remembers he's in long pants now because he turns mid-skip into a long stride. Yep, he's hitching up one leg, just like Daddie. What the heck, I start examining how I walk, but I can't tell a thing. Maybe I'll ask Cecilea what she thinks of my walk. Funny how I work side-by-side with her most days, and I have less time to talk to her now than when we used to walk by the river.

"Where you going?" I say, 'cause Nate just keeps walking along beside me.

"I just like walking, that's all. Maybe I'll go down by that old willow, that got struck by lightning."

"Maybe you will, and maybe you'll just hightail it home."

My neck gets tight. That's Cecilea's and my place. Nate should stay away from there, which makes no sense at all, and I know it, but still I feel aggravated at Nate, like he's trespassing or something.

"You have some chores to tend. Take Prince with you. And keep him at the house so he learns his boundaries."

That's another thing I'm working on with Prince. I gotta remember even if he's the smartest dog in the world, maybe even smarter than Rin Tin Tin, he is still a pup. That's what Mama says to me all the time. Prince needs to be reminded of all his lessons, every day, same as Mrs. Bidrall does for us at school. Shoot, now I'm like an old school marm. I wish Mama came up with a better way to tell me what I need to do.

"I hate those chickens," Nate says.

I laugh out loud on account of how Cecilea said the same thing, especially when the hens are sitting.

"Wear gloves and pry the hens up with a big stick," I say. "Ask Itsy-Bets to help you; she'd probably love to get out of the house."

"'Liz'Beth, probably would."

Nate underlines Liz, like he's Mrs. Bidrall correcting me at school.

"Mama won't let her out of the house. Says she looks kinda pale, maybe she's coming down with something," says Nate. "'Liz'Beth's staying home with Daddie.

"Maybe you're sick, you seem sorta fevered."

"That's just from the running to keep up with you."

"Well, go on home then."

Prince nips at the dust floating around in the sunshine. He notices his tail and goes after that. Nate and I both laugh out loud and all that tightness in my neck just melts. Still, I'm in a hurry. All his long-striding, keeping up with me, is for the birds, which is probably why he heads home.

Walking alone makes me notice stuff I never see when I'm with somebody: like the way the chickadees light on the morning glories, and pick for bugs, and the way the Queen's Anne's Lace smell pinches at my nose, or the way the light filters soft through the branches of the choke cherries, just before the road opens up to meadow and fields on both sides. 'Course as soon as I see the Tamarack silo sticking up at the side of the barn, I start to think about the work day and maybe how I'm just like that chickadee, scratching away all day, getting plenty to eat and hoping it lasts. Soon as I get to the Tamarack drive, I smell breakfast: flapjacks, patty sausage, and maple syrup. Just smelling Mrs. Tamarack's food makes my stomach start begging me to send some down. I'm glad Nate went home and never got a chance to smell this. Mama's johnnycake tastes dry and lifeless next to a Tamarack breakfast.

I got a lull in the work today: checking and mending fences around the back pasture. The breeze blows the wheat field like waves; the heads are getting heavy and starting to turn yellow. As soon as they are golden, the hard work starts again, cutting and thrashing and getting the wheat into the Butler Bins. I never did it before, but Cecilea says it's not as hard as baling hay.

"Go home after you check the back pasture today," Mr. Tamarack says after lunch.

His breath comes out of his nose in grunt as his chair scrapes against the floor.

"I take Cecilea and Theresa to see Father Perotta." Mr. Tamarack stands there for what seems like minutes, studying his knuckles resting on the tabletop. It's probably just seconds.

Cecilea's chair scrapes against the floor and she starts clearing up the dishes, keeping her eyes turned down. The color's coming up her neck into her cheeks. Margaret wipes at the table with the dishcloth before she looks up at me and smiles. Maybe she never notices how her blouse lets loose a little in the front when she bends over like that. I feel the back of my neck start to heat up, so I glue my eyes down at my plate, which is empty, so I push back and head out the door. Lucy and Analie, for no reason at all, giggle behind their hands and look at each other. In a million years, I doubt I'll ever understand girls.

Anyways, I have lots of time to think about things when I'm out checking the fence. I come to see the cattle in a whole new way. Used to be they seemed so dumb, just chewing their cuds, throwing back their heads to scare away the flies. Nowadays, they seem smarter, and maybe even conniving. Cows seem to walk the fence themselves, checking for a chance to break out and chomp on the crops, 'specially the cornfields. Cows do love fresh corn; they eat the whole plant, and trample what they don't eat.

Maybe I can play mumblety-pegs with Nate, after all, and maybe even have time to check up on Dallas and Ephraim. I start wondering what Ephraim's been up to lately, 'cause with me working at the Tamarack farm, and Dallas working at Dibble's Five and Dime, we hardly see hide nor hair of Ephraim. If I get done before dark, maybe we can have a game of Robin Hood and his Merry Men out at Torrey Yard.

I work until I see Mrs. Tamarack's white dishtowel hanging down from the second story window; that's my signal lunch is ready.

The house is dark and cool under all those trees, something I come to think of as more than just pretty. Itsy-Bits, Analie and Lucy are playing on the tire swing. The little girls always eat first, before I come in.

Mrs. Tamarack has a plate of cold meat and sliced bread and pickled eggs and sliced tomatoes, first in from the garden. I eat it all, 'cept for the pickled eggs. Just looking at those gives my stomach a squeeze like it's telling me don't send that down here. Everything is quiet as a church in here with the girls and Mr. Tamarack gone to town. I could just doze off in all this quiet, with a full stomach to boot. Mrs. Tamarack brings me a giant piece of peach pie she's got hidden under a checked dishtowel on the sideboard. Man-oh-man, why I didn't smell all that goodness through that cloth, I'll never know.

I feel heavy in the legs as I head back out to the pastures. I already finished what Mr. Tamarack told me to do, so I start on the bull's pasture. I'm supposed to stay away from that pasture on account of bulls being unpredictable and all. I just walk around the outside of the fence, and only climb in if I see a break that needs mending. I push one line of barbed wire down and climb between. Nothing's in need of mending today, so I just sit awhile and watch the Tamarack bull get cozy with the one cow that's in there with him. It's like they're courting, rubbing their heads together, and touching noses. I got my back up against the hickory nut tree, swatting flies, just the same as the cattle with their tails. I'm gonna surprise Nate and take him on over to see what Ephraim's up to. Funny how he stays off my ninth nerve when I see him less often. I even miss him.

"Did you get the eggs in for Mama?" I ask Nate when I get home.

He's got his penknife out, with a circle drawn on the ground, playing mumblety-pegs all by himself. My shadow falls over him. He squints up at me, on account of my back being to the sun. I feel sorta low, leaving him in the lurch all the time. I sit down in the dirt, spread my legs wide and shimmy up so my heels are touching Nate's. A grin washes up over Nate's face.

"Grip the handle like this," I say. "And flip your wrist."

My knife sticks in the ground, dead center between Nate's knees. He does exactly what I show him, and sure enough, his knife lands almost on top of mine. We keep it up, right up through the top of the head flip, which sort of scares me with Nate sometimes landing his knife outside of our legs. I stay still until his knife nicks up against his pant leg.

"Mama's gonna be mad if she has to mend those pants of yours."

It's a good reason to stop, even if the real reason is I'm losing my nerve.

"Aw shucks, I'm just getting good," Nate complains. "You afraid to lose?"

"Let's get some wood in for Mama and go meet Dallas at Dibble's."

Mama gave us some money to get her LIFE Magazine.

"What's Life?" I start out.

"A magazine."

"How much does it cost?"

"A dime."

"I only got a nickel."

"That's life."

"What's life?"

We keep it up halfway to Dibble's.

When he hears the bell ring, Dallas looks up from dusting Mrs. Dibble's spools of Coats & Clark threads. Mr. Dibble trusts him so much, Dallas runs the till now, and so he keeps his eyes peeled for customers coming in.

"Did you see Ephraim?" Dallas hisses at me.

"No."

Dallas's freckles are standing stark against his white skin, like every bit of him's at attention.

"He didn't tell you?"

"Tell me what?" I ask.

"He's leaving next week."

"Where? Going to Pittsburgh?"

Ephraim always bends my ear about going to Chicago. I never believe that. Sure as shooting, he's gonna go live with his brother Thomas, in Pittsburgh. First, anyways. I never guessed he was really gonna set off for Chicago on his own. Especially now.

"No. Do you want me to tell you, or would you rather hear it from him?"

"Spit it out," I say.

Dallas is makin' my ninth nerve jump with all his fitzing around, looking pale and excited at the same time.

"He's going to Chicago."

"What?"

"He's going to Chicago."

"Where'd you hear that? Some wife's gossip going on at the Five and Dime?"

The Irish comes up in Dallas and washes all the pale right out of him, right up through the roots of his hair.

"Go ask him yourself," he says.

I turn to go, then remember Mama's LIFE. I give Mama's two-bits to Nate and remind him to get some Lemon Heads for 'Liz'Beth not to eat them all on the way home.

"Remember to give Mama the change," I say right before the bell rings as the door springs closed behind me.

Sure enough, Ephraim's going to Chicago, and is going to live with Thomas and his wife, who both got fed up with Pittsburgh.

"What? Thomas got married?"

"Yup. Married Bette."

"Wait. I thought Bette went home 'cause of all the trouble and her folks not liking Thomas. What about your Ma?"

"What about my Ma?"

"Well, did she go to the wedding? How come I never heard about it?"

"You never heard about it 'cause you're too busy for me anymore. Ma found out about it in one of Thomas's letters. Just dropped her a line like he does every so often, then at the end, 'P.S. Me and Bette got married.' Ma's reading the letter out loud like always, and then dead silence. I don't know whose jaw dropped down the furthest.

"Anyways, the two of them are coming here first, then on to Chicago. Thomas is taking me with them. Says we can break into the music scene together. Says he'll be less scared of the big city with blood along. Imagine that. Me helping Thomas be brave."

I can imagine it, on account of how brave Dallas got trying to keep up with all Ephraim's shenanigans. My insides jitter around just hearing Ephraim talk all excited and seeing his big grin just about split his face in two.

"What's your Ma say?"

"Not much."

"What about school? What's your Ma say about that?"

I'm sorta sorry I asked, 'cause my question melts the smile right off Ephraim's face. Even his eyes can't hold on to the happiness.

"I got a feeling that bothers her less than the both of us in Chicago. She hardly says a word. Popi's working on her though."

The light goes back on in Ephraim's eyes. "Ma can't stay mad at Popi long. He'll work things out for me."

I clap my hand down on Ephraim's shoulder. "Wanna go out to the Torrey Yard?"

"Naw. I got lots to do to get ready."

"Come on."

I shove him in the back, right between the shoulder blades. "Nate's been begging to play Robin Hood. You know how that is, the more the merrier."

"You mean the more the Merry Men," he says.

He throws back his head in a wide-open laugh and punches me in the shoulder.

That's the way the day ends: me and Ephraim and Dallas, like old times coming to an end, and Nate no longer a tag-along, but Nate as Robin Hood himself.

We're walking toward home, the shadows pulling long in front of us, Nate dusting off Mama's LIFE, when something comes into my head and straight out of my mouth without a thought in between.

"Leave your outgrown shell by life's unresting sea."

"That's from the poem you were supposed to memorize," says Nate.

"You turning into an egghead?" says Dallas.

"Last one home's a rotten egg," I shout out over my back. They'll never catch me.

Chapter 25
A New Beginning

"Stop by and tell Mrs. Taylor I'm staying home today," Mama says to Dallas.

"Why?" Dallas keeps his elbow going shoveling breakfast in as fast as he can, so's he can get to Dibble's on time.

"Itsy— 'Liz'Beth is feeling poorly. So am I."

Itsy-Bets lays her head on her arm, right on top of the kitchen table. Mama never says a word about elbows or hair, or any bit of Itsy-Bets sprawled on the table.

"Baby," Dallas mouths over at Itsy-Bets. He cradles an invisible baby and rocks it back and forth behind Mama's back. Itsy-Bets sticks her tongue out at Dallas.

"Mama, Itsy-Bets's being nasty," says Nate.

Mama gives Nate her tight-lip face and her lower lids halfway covers her eyes. Itsy-Bets looks up at Mama all pitiful and pale around the mouth.

"Look at her tongue, Mama," I say. "Looks like a strawberry."

Itsy-Bets sticks her tongue out for Mama. She's still lolling her head on her arms right there on the kitchen table.

"Better go by Doc's and ask him to stop by."

Mama's talking to Dallas, 'cause I'm on my way to the Tamaracks like usual and he's going to Dibble's, same as every morning. Mama puts her hand on Nate's forehead.

"You're all pasty, too," she says.

"That's the way he always looks," I say.

I wink at Nate, to let him know I'm kidding around, and to put the stops on him from getting up in a knot at me.

"Where's Daddie?" Dallas says.

"He's going to the Tabernacle. It's Thursday."

"Don't forget about stopping by the doctor's," she says. "Give the breakfast scraps to Prince on your way."

Mama never even asks why Dallas wants to know about Daddie; she's so distracted with Itsy-Bets. That question's burning at my Adam's apple, but I know enough to wait until Prince's fed and we're on our way down the driveway and more than out of earshot.

"Why'd you ask about Daddie?"

Prince pushes his nose up against my palm, begging to be pet. I comb my hand through the fur around his ears.

"Just wondering, is all."

"Are you going to the soup kitchen?"

Dallas gives me the one eyebrow up look. "I'm coming to get you, as soon as I'm done working at Dibble's. We're meeting up with Ephraim before he leaves tomorrow. You know the plan."

"Daddie expects us at the Tabernacle. Mr. Tamarack will be delivering milk, or maybe asking me to go."

"Make up some excuse and meet me by that fallen willow by the river."

"Why?" I ask.

"What's with all the whys? We can play a little hooky from work, work, and work. For Cripes sake. Summer this year is worse than school. Sometimes I wish I was going to Chicago with Ephraim."

"Next year we're going to a different school. The High School."

"Next year is two weeks away."

"That seems impossible," I say.

"We won't be at Cronk with Nate, and we won't see Itsy-Bets."

"Liz'Beth's starting up school."

"I'm never calling her 'Liz'Beth," Dallas says.

I tell Prince to get on home and he turns without looking back. He sure is the good dog I knew he would be. I kick a stone down the road, and Dallas runs to kick it before it stops. The two of us keep tagging the rock back and forth, getting a few words in as we go. Prince tag teams back and forth between the two of us.

"What about Nate and Ephraim?" I say.

"I told Nate to meet us at the willow."

"What about Daddie? He's gonna be on a slow boil."

"Better to ask for forgiveness than permission."

That's something Ephraim would say. He never said it right to me. Still, the words sound just like they're coming out through Ephraim's teeth. I look over at Dallas and see Ephraim's toothy grin pasted on Dallas's face. I kick the rock hard with the side of my shoe so Dallas has to sprint to keep it going. Prince chases after his heels. Shoot.

"Go home, Prince."

This time I say it low down and give Prince a scowl. He heads toward home again. Dallas slows down to a walk and holds his side.

"When Ephraim's gone, it'll be just us Craines," he says. "Like normal again."

I get about a half-mile on my own to think about that after we each go our separate ways. Seems like forever ago, I was trying to find ways to ditch Ephraim and Dallas, sticking to me like flies on flypaper; Me at Ephraim's house every single night. Summer comes, when we should be fishing and playing mumblety-peg, and each of us has our own thing going. 'Course Ephraim and Dallas are still working at Dibble's Five and Dime, but afterwards, seems those two have had enough of each other, they're same poles of two magnets. Pushing away from each other. Dallas's sort of sore at Ephraim for taking off to Chicago. As for me, I'm right there at the Tamaracks', sometimes working side-by-side with Cecilea and her big sisters, but I never seem to get a moment alone with her. Just a little over a month ago, the willow is where I kissed Cecilea. That's our place, even if we never did go back there again.

"Take it easy on Ephraim," I say. "He's gonna be gone."

Dallas combs his fingers through his hair, and turns his back on me. He sticks one arm over his head and shouts out a goodbye.

"Home, Prince."

He's such a good dog. Does everything I tell him.

"Stay out da back pasture," Mrs. Tamarack says, slapping potato pancakes and sausage down on a plate for me.

Margaret snickers behind her hand and red rises up her neck before she looks away from me and studies the table in front of her. I look over at Cecilea for a hint at what's got Margaret going, but she's staring at the table, too.

"The bull's with the cows," Margaret says, wiping her hands on her apron, before turning to the sink.

Cecilea mouths something to me and rolls her eyes toward the back door.

"So," I say to Margaret, still hoping for a clue about why that's something to blush about. "That's nothing new."

"They need privacy," says Margaret. "Everybody does."

She leans over to pick up the sausage plate, and looks straight in my eyes. Her dress front is all loose again. She's got green-blue eyes with dancing gold flecks; same as Cecilea and her Papa, only when Margaret's dance, they seem to have a secret they're laughing at me about. It's my turn to study the table. It takes all I have to keep from looking back to see if she noticed the gap in her dress neck.

"Sure," I say, like I know what she's talking about.

I feel heat creeping up my neck into my ears and cheeks. Never mind, I got work to do. Plus, I need to think about how to get away with Cecilea, 'cause sure as cows come to the barn at milking time, she's got something to talk to me about.

I keep looking all morning for a chance to talk to Cecilea. Her mother's got her and Analie under the clothesline all day: hanging, picking, and folding. Something I better stay clear of, since I'm in the barn, cleaning out the gutters and throwing down lime, getting the stanchions ready for milking time. That's all I need is Mrs. Tamarack barking about the laundry smelling like manure. I was down that path a few weeks ago.

Margaret gives me her glitter-grin after I wash up for lunch. "Looking for my little sister?" she says.

I keep my head down and my mouth shut.

"She went in with Theresa to see Father Perotta. Again."

I glance at Margaret, hoping I can figure out what's eating at her; at the same time, I'm afraid to find out.

"Those two love Father Perotta."

"I like him, too," I say. For no reason at all, I feel like defending Father Perotta.

"Sometimes people keep secrets," Margaret breathes at me, taking my empty lunch plate out from under me, and turning to go to the sink.

She looks back over her shoulder at me. Maybe she's looking to see how I react; maybe she's waiting for me to say something.

"When's Theresa leaving for the convent?"

Maybe that's the secret Margaret's getting on about. I wanna let her know I'm already wise to that one.

"Soon. What's it to you?"

"Just wondering, is all."

Margaret leans over the table and slides a plate of apple pie over at me.

"I make the best apple pie," she says. "I made this one just for you."

I never ate so much pie in my entire life, before I started working for the Tamaracks.

Margaret smiles her green-blue eyes at me. She looks way different than Cecilea. Almost as different as me and Ephraim. Sure they have the same chestnut-blond hair and the same gold-specked eyes, and the same parents. Still, Margaret acts so different, it's like the two of them are from different continents. It makes them even look different.

I pay attention to the pie, all the time Margaret's watching me eat, not saying a word, just licking her lips from time to time. Soon as I'm done, I high-tail in back to my work in the barn, getting hay ready in the manger for the cows. I keep trying to figure out what Cecilea mouthed at me earlier, before she left for town, wondering what she wants to talk about.

I get my chance right before supper. Cecilea's coming in from the chicken coop, with Lucy tagging behind, the same time I'm coming in from the barn. She's got a basket full of eggs.

"Let's take a walk," I say.

Cecilea gives the eggs to Lucy.

"Gently. You can do it all by yourself today."

Lucy keeps her eyes on the eggs and heads for the house.

We walk along the path to the willow tree, our hands brushing. I want to grab her hand, and hold it in mine, but I hold back. She never did tell me how she felt about me kissing her. Then again, she's here on her way to the willow, so if she ever was mad, she's over it. Anyways, that's the way I reason it.

"I've got something to tell you," Cecilea says.

She leans up against the willow and looks straight down the riverbank. It's always bad when a person has something to say and looks away. Good news comes with dead on looks and smiles. My stomach twists around. Ripe elderberries scatter purple like a halo around the bushes and down to the riverbank. A shame I think that some's gone to waste. I could get a bucket later and come back to get some.

"I'm going to the convent."

"What?"

"I'm going to the convent, same as Theresa."

"You mean to watch her be married to Jesus? To say goodbye?"

My stomach eases up. Neither of us ever traveled to Detroit before. 'Course she's nervous about that.

Cecilea looks straight in my eyes. Her bottom lids are filled with tears, and her bottom lip quivers.

"No, Eldie. I'm going, too. I'm going to stay. I'm going to become a nun, the same as Theresa."

"You're going to be married to Jesus, too?"

"Yes."

"How many wives does he need?"

Cecilea laughs at that and wipes her eyes with the tips of her little fingers. How she keeps delicate as fine china, with all the work she does, is something for the scientists.

"I'll be back at holidays. I'll miss you. I'll miss everyone at Cronk and Mother and Papa and Analie and Lucy. Maybe not Margaret so much."

That makes us both laugh.

My mind is going every which away. Some puzzle pieces are slipping into place, others I'm all confused about.

"What about me kissing you?"

The words slip away from me before my brain has a chance to put the clutch in. Cecilea puts her hand to her lips and looks at me. I gotta fill up the space.

"I mean, is that some sorta sin for a nun?"

"Maybe," she says.

Cecilea starts to giggle, with her hand still over her mouth.

"When I get to be a nun, I'll take another name. Maybe Sister Mary Therese, the Little Flower or maybe Sister Mary Sophia, the patron saint of wisdom. Wisdom is sure something I can use. Until then, I'm still Cecilea."

I wish I was better at figuring out girls and how they talk. Cecilea is looking straight at me, gold flecks in her eyes with their happy dance going, eyelashes glistening in the afternoon sun. She sounds like she explained everything clear as daylight, but my head just fills up with more questions. So many they run over each other and into each other and tangle all up inside my head. Not a single question comes out of my mouth.

"I'll miss you most of all," Cecilea says. She takes my hands in each of hers and kisses me square on the mouth. "This will be one of my most cherished memories." She buries her face in my shirt.

"I knew you would be here!" I jump at Dallas's voice and Cecilea pulls back.

"What's she doing here?"

"Her Papa's farm's right here."

I point up toward the road. Heat floods up my neck, till my hair roots tickle. I forgot all about my promise to Dallas.

"I guess a promise between brothers is not worth saying."

"I'm here."

Dallas looks at me hard, then at Cecilea.

"I should be getting back," says Cecilea.

She sweeps her hair behind her ear. I hold on to every move she makes, in my mind's eye. This is probably the last time I will see her here. I'm still watching her head up to the road when Dallas speaks up.

"Where's Ephraim?" I say, looking around in back of Dallas, like he's hiding him or something.

"Says he wants to be with Popi and Ma his last night here.'

"Where's Nate?"

"I guess he forgot, too." Dallas is sore. "Come on, let's go home."

"I thought you wanted to skip out," I remind him.

"I'm outta the mood."

I'm out of the mood to argue, so we both head down the river toward our house. I pick up a stick and hit at the Queen Anne's Lace as we climb the bank and cut across the meadow. Dallas just digs his fists deeper in his pockets and kicks at the wild wheat. His foot gets tangled up, on account of the meadow's about thigh high, and he almost falls, which is sorta comical 'cause his fists are so deep in his pockets he has a hard time keeping himself balanced.

"For Cripe's sake," Dallas says.

"Jeez-o-Pete's, stop your wooden swearing." Dallas tries to pull his face straight, but I see the grin creeping up over his face.

I get concentrating on Dallas, in between thinking about Cecilea, so I miss that something's out of sorts as we get into our yard. Everything is too quiet. 'cept for Prince running up to meet me, tongue lolling out one side of his mouth. My foot hits the bottom step of the porch before I see the golden sign tacked up beside the door:

SCARLET FEVER

I read the rest out loud:

NO PERSON OR ANIMAL OR ITEM
IS PERMITTED TO ENTER
OR LEAVE THE PREMISES
UNDER PENALTY OF LAW.

I look at Dallas who is already looking at me.

Mama pokes her head out the door before I lift my back foot to the next step.

"You can't come in," she says.

"Why?"

"'Liz'Beth's got scarlet fever."

"What about Nate?"

"He's here. Doc says he could have the beginnings. Nate and I have to stay here for at least the next six weeks. Maybe longer if Nate or I get sick."

Dallas and I look at Mama and back at each other.

"Where's Daddie?"

"Still at Reverend Zollar's. You better go find him."

Daddie and me and Dallas stay with Reverend Zollar for the night. The next day Daddie moves in with the Moores. Ephraim's Popi is happy as all get out to have a ride to work every day, instead of taking the bus. Besides that, he says it will be good for Ma to fill up the space

Ephraim's leaving. I know Daddie is never gonna fill up Ephraim's space. Anyone with half a brain can see that.

Mr. Tamarack tells me the very next day that me and Dallas can both earn our keep and stay with them, especially since his two best workers are going off to the convent. Dallas chews on that one a while on account of Mr. Dibble and the cash he earns there. He turns a corner when Mr. Dibble says that now Dallas is eating like a grown man and earning a paycheck, he's gonna take room and board out of his pay if Dallas stays there. Maybe me talking up Mrs. Tamarack's potato pancakes and sausage helps a little. Or a lot.

Cecilea and Theresa leave the very next day. That about shocks the living daylights outta me. How could she wait to the eleventh hour to tell me? Heck, more like five minutes before midnight.

"I planned to tell you so many times," Cecilea says, out behind the chicken coop the day she leaves.

"First I couldn't decide. Then I didn't want to spoil anything between us. I thought we'd have more time to talk about it. Maybe I could answer all the whys you always ask. I planned it all out in my head, and finally decided to tell you that day Dallas showed up. But not with him there."

Her leaving puts a hole in my heart I can never explain. Probably will never go away, that hole. Still, having Dallas to clown around with stuffs up the hole a little. Daddie is right: Brothers are forever.

It's sorta funny how things can go along as perfect as Middie's chocolate cake, no trouble in site, and a boom, like a *Flash Gordon* comic, life punches all the predictability out. That's the way it was with Daddie saving for a new house, putting all the money, plus his insurance money in the bank right before the bank closed down. That's the way it was with Mama keeping Itsy-Bets close as if she were still growing inside of her, and Itsy-Bets rambling off to Dibble's Five and Dime, while our house burned to nothing but ashes. I suppose that's the way it was for the Kerschkes, too. Making plans, and hoping and wishing for good things. Sometimes the good things we plan go right as rain; sometimes they wash away like a summer flood. Still, most times, when one set of plans disappears, something just as good pops up. Same as Mr. Tamarack's Timothy-grass hayfield all chopped down and dead looking, growing new sprouts, stretching up to the sun healthy and new and hopeful and never knowing a second cutting is coming along before the summer's over.

CHAPTER 26
LABOR DAY

Labor Day's got a whole new meaning from when I first remember it. It used to be an end of summer picnic and a chance to eat Mrs. Sterling's best ever chocolate cake. Used to be picnics marked the summer: beginning, middle, and end. Seems like a lifetime ago when we lived back in Pearl, and Mama took that picture of us sitting on our Kiddie Kar. That was before Vermillia Street, and before the fire. That was before Cecilea or Ephraim or Dibble's Five and Dime or Mrs. Bidrall and before I even heard about the Kerschkes or the Zybers. Heck, that was before Itsy-Bets was even born.

And now here's Mama expecting a new baby any day now and 'Liz'Beth is off to school with Nate, as soon as Quarantine is lifted. She can hardly wait. Ephraim and Cecilea are gone, and me and Dallas are picking up the slack at the Tamarack farm, eating like The Great Depression never left a plate empty.

The picture Mama snapped with her new Brownie of Nate and Dallas and me sits on the sideboard that the Taylors gave Mama when we all moved to the Kerschke farm.

I know that's the three of us, I remember that day like it was yesterday. 'Course I do. I'm nothing like that little boy, just like Middie Sterling is nothing like she was back in Pearl. Jeez-o-Pete's, she's a Reeve's now, all grown and married. She's nothing like the girl that held Dallas's hand on the way to school and calmed all his caterwauling or showed me tried to show me how to steer a wagon by moving the handle the opposite way I wanted it to go. Too bad I had to careen off into a tree before I learned that lesson.

Sometimes the Middie I knew in Pearl peeks out of the grown woman. She might smooth her dress a certain way, or blush at something Daddie says, or speak my name, and all of a sudden the Pearl-Middie is right there full-faced so anyone who knew her then can see plain as daylight streaming through the kitchen window. Maybe she's like me, feeling like the same person from the inside out, only different. I suppose we'll both keep getting layers on top of old, until none of the young in us shows anymore, like Mama and Daddie.

Tomorrow, I'll be back on the Tamarack farm with Dallas. And the day after that'll look the same, but it will be different. We decided to stay on at the Tamaracks', and work after school and summers. Mr. Tamarack's two best workers left him. Someday, me and Dallas will have our own farm. That's what we talk about every night when we climb into bed and all the lights are off. Darkness sorta clears up the airways for talking. Sorta like the way the clear night air brings in radio waves from far away. That's the same way laying in bed at night clears my head so ideas and dreams come out like they can really happen.

I guess me and Dallas will be sorta like Ephraim and Thomas, working together, keeping an eye out for each other, and daring each other to stay brave. Now that sorta makes me laugh, if I think too much about it. There's a whole lot more for Ephraim and Thomas to be brave about than me and Dallas ever hope to have. But then again, tomorrow's full of surprises.

I guess Reverend Zollar would say, "nothing is new under the sun." I suppose he's right in some ways. But in other ways, everything is new every moment. We're just like that old Chambered Nautilus, growing and changing because of learning new things. Dallas's wrong about my good memory being a curse. I'm gonna hold on to everything, even the stuff I wish I could forget 'cause for one thing I never know when a something that seems worthless is gonna come bubbling up in a useful sorta way. Like Mrs. Bidrall explained about pearls starting out as a little bit of grit getting under the skin of an oyster. Besides, why would I want to forget a bit of this year? I got about the best life a fella could hope to have.

Well, I'll be darned. I gotta admit, Mrs. Bidrall and that Oliver Wendall Holmes fella taught me something when I was looking the other way. That's what I mean about memories bubbling up, even when I'm not trying to remember a darned thing, stuff sticks up in my noggin and comes out when I need it most. I'll have to thank Mrs. Bidrall someday. I'll remember that for another day. Today I'm taking it easy.

ACKNOWLEDGEMENTS

This book took years to write with many starts and stops, some dawdling and discouragement, along with much patient persistence. Writing can be a lonesome endeavor. A novel may be written by one person, but without the consistent encouragement of many, and the off-hand, perhaps unrecognized, comments of a few, this novel might still be in a draft drawer. I borrowed the title of Anne Lamott's book *Bird by Bird* as my mantra; just put fingers to keyboard and attack the monumental task one word (bird) at a time.

For their many stories, smiles that wash up one side of their faces, brighten their eyes, and slowly illuminate their stories, I have my father and his six siblings to thank. Great story-tellers all, their humor and grace are a constant source of encouragement. By name and birth order: Merle, Dean, Glenn, Barbara. Ellis, Frank, and Gerald.

I owe a debt of gratitude to Lisa Romeo for her gentle yet firm editing. She made me laugh, she provided encouragement, and offered invaluable advice. Her eagle eye, her sense of story, and her love of the craft, highlighted improvements I was just too close to see.

I had the great pleasure of interviewing the real Mrs. Bidrall. Although a stern teacher, she loved her students and remembered them and their parents by name. Mrs. Bidrall often used a portion of her meager salary to anonymously pay for her students' books.

My most constant cheerleader, Love-One and best friend, George, believes in the story, the message, and me. I will ever be grateful for my mother, Rita who encourages me, questions me, and wonders about me, but never, ever doubts me.

The Crandells grew up near Flint, Michigan, as did I. Their relationship with the one black family in the school gave me pause. The black sculptor, Thaddeus Mosley from Pittsburgh, generously shared some of his history, which gave credence to the Crandells' story. "Sunday is the most segregated day of the week," is a phrase that I heard throughout my interviews with various people who grew up during the Great Depression.

Besides numerous interviews, I relied on visits to the Smithsonian Museums and resources such as *Since Yesterday* by Frederick Lewis Allen and *As the Twig is Bent* by Elinor C. Bemis. And, of course that ubiquitous source of information, the internet.

Because of Stephen King's *On Writing* advise, I joined The Resurrection Book Club and listened, listened, listened to what people like to read. They all contributed in ways too numerous to count. I owe my deep appreciation to Karen, who reminded me how important sound and smell is to the reader.

My sincerest thanks to my beta readers: Britt, Geri, George, and Christa who picked the nits and offered priceless words of encouragement.

About the Author

Adela Crandell Durkee comes from a family of storytellers. Being a little more introverted, Adela puts pen to paper. First published in the Flint Journal at the age of seven, the thrill of seeing her stories in print never fades. Adela lives near the exciting city of Chicago with her husband, George. Within driving distance are her four children, and her twelve grandchildren. Add two cats on the balcony and her vegetable and water gardens in the backyard and Adela has it all.

About the Cover:

Chad Green designed the cover. Chad grew up in Flushing, Michigan, and graduated from the Louis F. Garland Fire Academy in Texas before serving in the U.S.A.F. as an aircraft crash/rescue firefighter. Besides Michigan, Chad and his wife, Becky, lived in Delaware, Florida, Arizona, Puerto Rico, and now in Nashville, Tennessee. When he's not designing, Chad is a career firefighter E.M.T.

CPSIA information can be obtained
at www.ICGtesting.com
Printed in the USA
BVHW031132020619
549938BV00001B/126/P